Counterspell:

Age of Fools

Volume 3 of the Counterspell Chronicle

Robert C.A. Goff
and
Micah M.A. Goff

Dreamsplice
Christiansburg, Virginia

This book is a work of fiction.

Counterspell: Age of Fools
Volume 3 of the Counterspell Chronicle
by Robert C.A. Goff and Micah M.A. Goff

Arnold Toynbee's conjectures on the causation and consequences of the fall of civilizations throughout history, discussed in his many volumes of A *Study of History*, have provided some of the conceptual foundation for this fictional narrative.

Dreamsplice
3462 Dairy Road
Christiansburg, VA 24073

www.dreamsplice.com

Cover design by Robert C.A. Goff, Copyright © 2025 by Dreamsplice

ISBN-13: 978-0-9761559-9-7
Library of Congress Control Number: 2025903656
First Edition: April 2025

I dedicate this final volume of the Counterspell Chronicle to my talented son, co-author and bladesmith, Micah. Thank you.

RCAG

For Amberle, an inspiration, and the star in my eye.

MMAG

A special thank you to Diane Porter Goff, whose editing and suggestions contributed to the narrative of all the Counterspell books.

RCAG and MMAG

The Counterspell Chronicle:

also from the world of Counterspell:

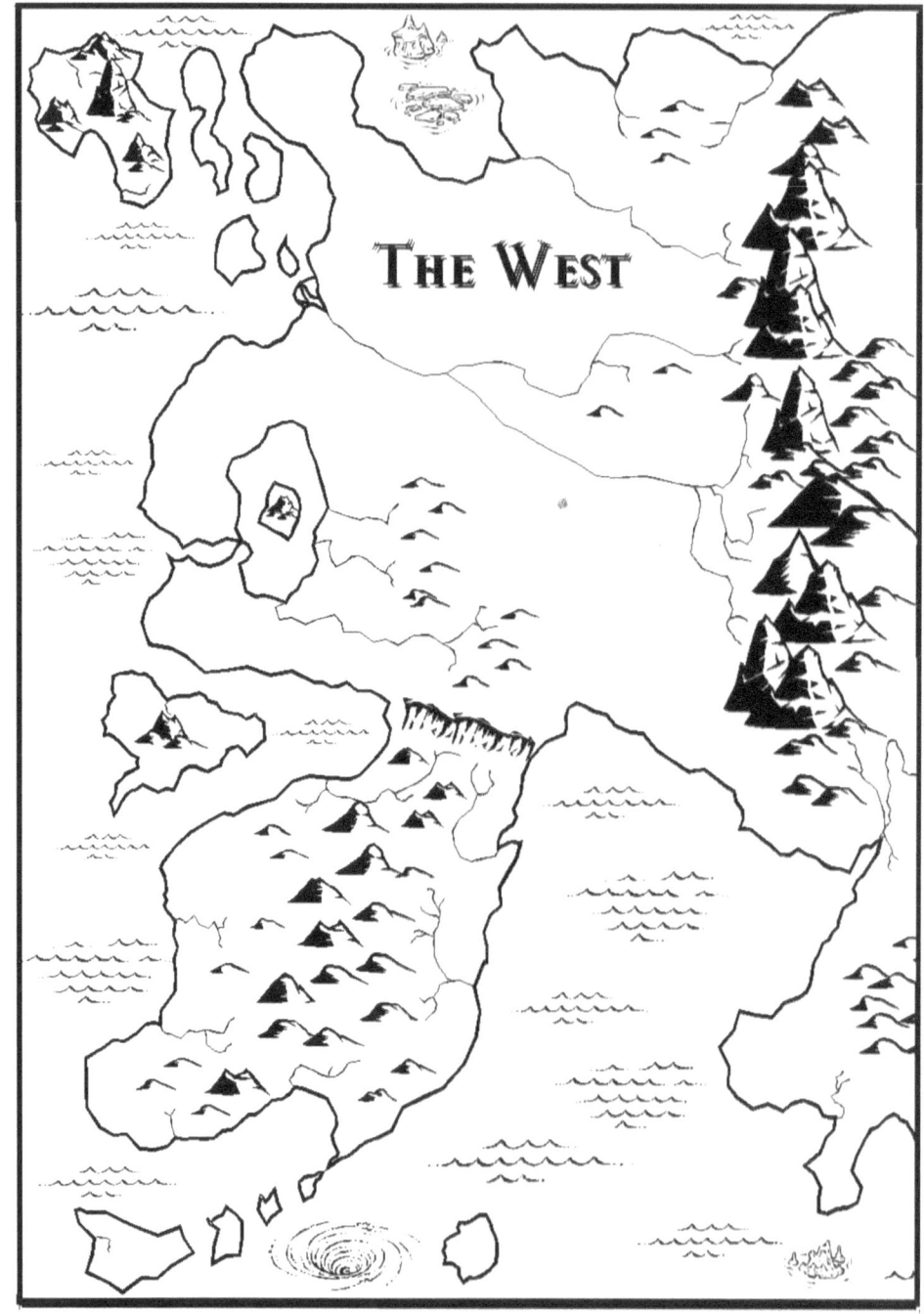

THE WEST

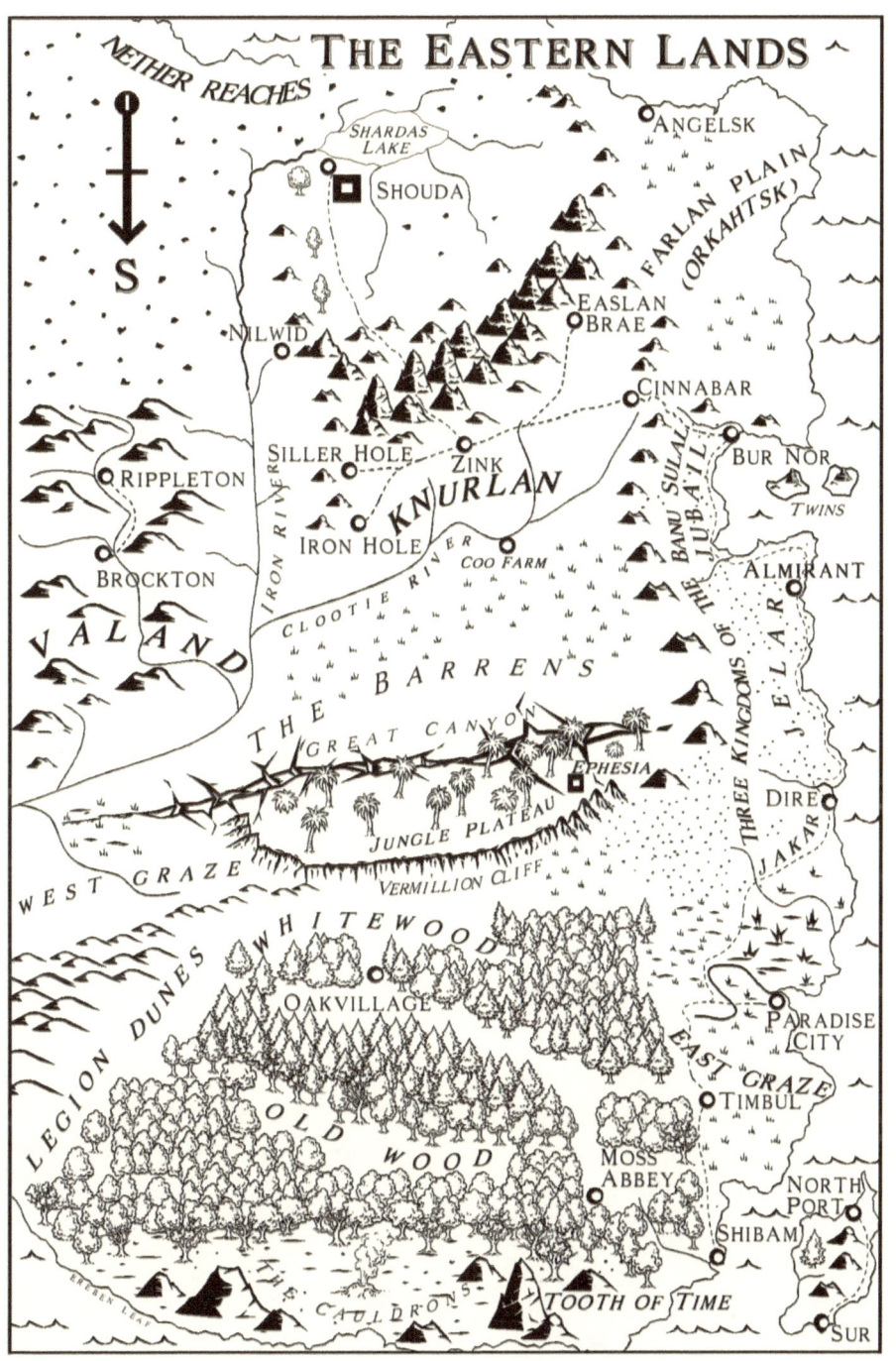

ঔৎ

In the years following the Battle of Four Armies, our hopes for a peaceful life gradually gave way to the bleak reality.
Ereben Leaf: Chronicle of the Counterspell

A sudden gust of wind tipped Ereben Leaf off the edge of his rain-soaked roof, and into Brindle's waiting arms below. They both tumbled into a muddy sprawl.

Brindle lay, immobile for a moment, then slowly turned her head, casting admonishing eyes at Ereben, only a half yard away. "I told you," her words as chill as the mud in which they lay. She inspected the mud slopped over her tunic and bare, muscular legs, then wiped some from her face with a muddy finger.

Ereben considered his observation that none of his bones seemed to have been broken in the three-yard fall. "Are you alright?"

Without answering him, Brindle rose to her feet, then extended a hand to Ereben. "You appear still to be in one piece." Her Nanish accent and contralto voice lent a sarcastic quality to her simple statement.

When Ereben cautiously took her hand, Brindle promptly hoisted him upright, and with her free hand, gently smeared mud into Ereben's beard, apparently taking care to be thorough about it. Then she released his hand.

"I told you that as well, if I had to catch you." She looked up at the low sky. "Looks like more rain now. I'll just walk home real slow, and be shiny clean by the time I get there. I'll be back in the morning."

"Thank you, Brindle. And I'm sorry about getting you all muddy. At least you weren't wearing your cloak." He felt foolish. And too old to be climbing on the roof. But it had been leaking in the rain all week, so he had taken advantage of a pause in the near-constant showers to replace a cedar split. It might stop the leak, he thought, but so many of the other cedar splits looked equally decayed.

Ereben watched, as Brindle Meadow walked the dirt path toward the Rippleton road. On her left arm, she had draped her white caribou cape. Her sturdy right hand held an iron-bladed mattock, which she carried with her everywhere—as a tool and as a weapon. He knew that the young woman, a widow now for several years, lived alone, beyond the road, up in the scant remaining forest of the eastern slope.

When he was a young man, the creek that separated his family's home from the eastern slope of the mountain always flowed, and only occasionally flooded for a day or two. Crossing that creek had been part of the long forest path he had trudged to his grandfather's house and smithy in the next valley. For the past few years, the creek had alternately flooded for a week or more, then run completely dry in between the flooding. He never walked there any more. The smithy had been destroyed decades before, and his grandfather, Chrysanthus, had gone to live with the ice leopards after the Battle of Four Armies. He had not seen him since.

A light rain, whipped by a chill breeze, swept over his house, and gradually rinsed away much of the mud that had spattered him. As he headed toward the door, he surveyed the widespread deterioration of the house—his family's old house. In the twenty years that he had lived here alone, since the great war, he had lapsed into a lazy habit of only repairing whatever had finally broken, rather than caring for it all. He shook his head at himself as well as his ramshackle house. *Ereben Leaf, the last Guardian of the Ruins.*

Ereben was awakened by a knocking on the door. Dull daylight streamed through his tattered window curtain.

"Ereben Leaf...are you here?" The resonant voice sounded familiar, but he could not attach a name or face to it. He seldom had visitors. Occasionally Yarnish Blen, who still lived in Rippleton, would drop by to relate news—usually bad news. But this was not Yarnish.

"I'm here," he shouted, rolling out of his bed, and tossing a blanket about his shoulders. Every part of his body ached. His foggy mind recalled the wind blowing him from his roof yesterday—Brindle breaking the fall. Stiff joints propelled him into the main room, and toward the door. "I'm coming."

When he unlatched the heavy door, and swung it toward him, he found three tall, dark-brown, Shouda men standing before him. Each carried a travel pack over a dark cape, and held a long, Shouda spear. They had obviously been on the road for many days. "Yes?" He seldom saw Shouda near Rippleton.

After all three bowed in the Shouda fashion, one of them said with a smile, "Will you invite old friends into your home, Ereben Leaf?"

Ereben finally recognized that one of the three was Minkar Jarad, who had helped him survive many adversities. He couldn't remember the last time he had spoken with Minkar. *Perhaps before the Great Battle?* Ereben clumsily returned the bow, his muscles protesting. "Minkar! Come in. Come in. Bring in your friends. Don't mind the mud on your boots. It's everywhere these days. Find somewhere to sit, while I put on some clothes." As he turned away, Minkar grasped his shoulder and turned him about.

"Ereben," Minkar said softly, "it has been far too long." Minkar wrapped his long arms about him. Ereben returned the embrace. "Make yourself decent, and then I will introduce my companions."

By the time Ereben had returned to the main room, his blanket now draped over his clothing, one of the two younger Shouda men had already started a fire in the hearth. He set his blanket aside, and sat alongside Minkar at the large table that occupied much of the room. "I have only water and some bread to offer you."

"Thank you, Ereben Leaf, but we need nothing more at the moment than to speak of important matters." He pointed to the older of his two companions, who appeared to Ereben to be in his mid-thirties. "This is Yassar Khayin, whom I have known well for many years now."

Ereben remained seated, but offered an amended version of the Shouda bow. His body ached too much to consider standing again so soon after sitting. Yassar returned the seated gesture.

"And this is someone *you* have known for many years. My son, Bahsa. He has become a remarkable man."

Ereben was speechless. Bahsa had been just a lanky, young boy the last time he had seen him. And he had never spoken, since witnessing the death of his mother.

Bahsa smiled, as he reached both hands across the table, and took hold of Ereben's. Tears beaded in Bahsa's eyes. "It gives me great joy to see you once again, Ereben Leaf."

Ereben looked from Bahsa to Minkar, then took Minkar's hand, while still holding on to Bahsa's hand. He smiled, and nodded his head. "A wonderful morning. So, what is this important matter that would bring you so far?"

The door thudded again, as though someone were kicking it. "Ereben." It was the voice of Brindle. "Open the door."

Minkar bounded to the door, nimbly snatching his spear from where he had leaned it against the wall. When he unlatched it, Brindle stood there, momentarily surprised, but upon seeing Ereben seated at the table, stepped into the room, carrying a limp and bloody man.

"It's Yarnish," she panted out. "He was attacked by robbers on the road." She laid him gently onto the heavy, wooden table about which the others sat. "It's pretty bad. I thought maybe you could do some magic or something to save him."

Ereben briefly inspected a scarcely bleeding, yet deep wound in his upper chest, then felt his neck and over his heart. "It's too late for munu to help him. Yarnish Blen is dead."

Minkar Jarad's eyes widened. "This is so sad." He reached to a small, leather purse tied to Blen's waist, and jingled it. "Perhaps they were not robbers."

"But why, if not to rob him, would they attack a man?" Brindle unlashed her mattock, which she had tied behind her back, and rested it on the floor. Slowly, she sat on the bench beside Bahsa, and sobbed for only a moment. She looked about her at the three Shouda men, then down at her blood smeared, white caribou cape. "I need some water to clean off the blood, before it sets."

Ereben introduced Brindle, then allowed Minkar to introduce himself and the others, while Ereben brought her a jug of water and a basin. "We will bury Yarnish after we've talked."

Minkar lowered his eyebrows. "We can wait until after the burial, so Brindle Meadow will not be burdened by our discussion."

"Brindle," Ereben stated, "is an honorable and trustworthy woman...even for these important matters, that I suspect may involve secret things of which she has no knowledge...yet."

"Secret things?" Brindle looked up from her scrubbing.

"Magic," Yassar whispered.

"Oh." Brindle stared at the dead man on the table as she spoke. "Everybody knows about that stuff. And all the magicians in Rippleton stay away from Ereben. They say he's a master wizard. So I share-crop here, and nobody steals my vegetables."

Ereben shrugged. "I've never heard anything about magicians in Rippleton, and I've lived here most of my life. Why would anybody think I'm a wizard? I make metal tools."

"They speak of it everywhere, Ereben Leaf" Bahsa acknowledged. "Even among the Weather Shouda, they tell how the legendary wizard, Ereben Leaf, defeated Holnick Firth, who was himself the greatest of wizards, and then went on to slay the Sarcite beast, the Sarcoptis, though you and I know that it occurred differently." He winked at Ereben. "Even my father is known as a wizard, for having ridden upon a dragon."

Minkar shook his head. "Some people would name a toad which easily catches a fly a wizard."

"But Father, a Shouda riding upon a dragon is hardly a toad."

This exchange seemed to draw Brindle's attention from Yarnish. "You really rode on a dragon, Minkar?"

"Graybeard was the kindest and most gentle of the dragons," Minkar said. "He invited me to ride his shoulders."

Brindle's eyes widened. "The dragon talked?"

"He did...until the Rock Gnomes killed him." Minkar placed his hand on the forehead of Yarnish Blen, whose body still lay on the table before them. "All of the dragons talk, if they chose to."

"How many dragons are there?" She regarded Ereben's guests with greater interest.

Bahsa quickly replied. "There are six remaining dragons, and they are neither kind nor gentle. They are filled with hate."

"You generalize," Minkar admonished him. "Only their brother who is hateful...One-eye, as you call him... has caused...

Ereben raised both hands. "Important matters? You said there were important matters to discuss."

"Perhaps we should bury our friend first," Minkar suggested. "Then we shall discuss these matters. You as well, Brindle Meadow. Ereben trusts you. We Shouda shall trust Ereben's judgment."

The grave was dug behind the house, near where Yarnish Blen, decades ago, had buried Ereben's parents after their murder, and alongside the grave of Ereben's older brother, Caris. Perhaps all three, and now Yarnish Blen, had been murdered because of their roles with regard to the Guardians of the Ruins. Both Ereben's father and grandfather, Chrysanthus, had been Guardians. Caris had been groomed by them to become a Guardian. Yarnish Blen had worked diligently all of his adult life as a Protector of the Guardians, and had saved Ereben's life more than once.

Each of those who knew Yarnish spoke a few words. The three Shouda men then solemnly bowed toward the grave. Dirt was returned to the deep hole, covering Blen's still bloody body. No marker was placed.

As the others returned to the house, Ereben paused briefly at each of the other graves. He had not visited the graves for years. He always felt the weight of having been unable to do anything to save them. He had known nothing about Guardians of the Ruins, until after their deaths. Reluctantly, he turned back to his house to join the others.

"...was a handsome and kind man." Brindle, seated at the table, again beside Bahsa Jarad, spoke to them of her family. "He was a Valander, so my parents did not approve of our marriage. But he convinced them to allow it, and insisted that they too come to live with us—to live in Rippleton. Because of the famine in Naneland, they agreed. It was four years ago that my two beautiful young boys died of the chest rattle. Then both my parents and my husband were afflicted with it as well, and soon died. I never even became ill." She fell silent, holding her head high. Her long, blond-white hair, which she always kept braided, rested as a tightly wound bun on the back of her head, adding a sense of dignity to her chronically sunburned face.

"Brindle has been growing vegetables here, for herself and to sell in the market." Ereben had heard the sad tale before, and knew that the telling of it left her melancholy. "She shares part of her harvest with me, so I don't have to grow so much."

Minkar sighed. "Rippleton now seems like a dangerous place for a young woman to be living alone."

"I'm never alone. I always have my mattock with me. It...discourages...those who might wish to do me harm."

"That is a sturdy tool, but ponderous weapon," Bahsa offered.

"The perfect weapon for a sturdy and ponderous woman." Brindle paused. Ereben could not argue with her solid build and determined attitude. She had prevented him from breaking his neck just yesterday. And smeared his beard with mud, as she had threatened.

"Ereben," Minkar interrupted. "Let us discuss the matters that have brought us here."

"Yes," he replied. The death of Yarnish Blen had pushed that to the back of his mind.

"You appear to be unaware of the wild and irresponsible use of magic here," Minkar continued. "Surely you have noticed that the weather has changed from when you were a boy here."

"I have."

"That is happening everywhere. There are unheard of floods and droughts in every land, in every kingdom. Crops are failing where that has never occurred. People are dying of starvation and diseases in the towns and all along the roads. Whole populations are migrating. But they do so in all directions. There is nowhere that is much safer than anywhere else."

"Worse than I had heard," Ereben mumbled. "But what can I do to help that? What can all of us do to help that?"

Yassar Khayin squared his shoulders. "It's the magic, the counterspell of all that magic, that is causing this. There are now thousands of magicians and wizards, carelessly casting spells for convenience or fear or amusement."

Minkar raised a finger, to interrupt. "Yassar was born among the Lamblari Shouda, who lived their entire lives beneath the great Shouda Shrine...for generations. When Yassar was a lad, it was I who taught him to speak Valish. The Lamblari Shouda speak and write what you know as ancient Shadae."

Ereben was stunned. He had never known that. Many of the massive tomes of magic that he had sequestered within the rock at the bottom of the Great Canyon—to prevent them from being exploited—had been undecipherable to him, because they were written entirely in ancient Shadae. "You can read the Shadae?"

Yassar nodded in affirmation. "It is my first language."

"But," Minkar continued, "Yassar discovered, over the years, many very ancient histories—some of magic—within the archives of Lamblar itself. He read all of them that he could, before their elders forbade him from doing so. They abjure all magic, and those who practice it, as unholy. When he disregarded their ban, and was caught reading them again, they cast him out of the city. He has been living with me and Bahsa ever since."

"What did you learn?" Ereben had learned only a few critical things about the counterspell from his own bumbling translation of some of the ancient Shadae manuscripts.

"I will begin by saying that the dragons—the seven dragons—were initially created by a Shouda wizard, many centuries ago. That same wizard, al Bryn Adin, designed and made a special suit of armor—what Minkar Jarad describes as the Chamberlain's golden armor from the ancient ruins of Ephesia, as well as two special axes designed to kill a dragon."

Ereben considered the placements of the small Jadeite stones on each separate piece of the Chamberlain's armor. And the sketch of an unusual ax that his grandfather had drawn. Individual components of the armor had been distributed to each of the various members of their group, when they explored the ruins. "So one person must wear *all* of the pieces of the armor at once?"

"That is correct. The ax with the hooked head will immobilize a dragon, if someone can approach close enough, while the golden ax of the Chamberlain's armor is used to behead it. The complete armor protects the wearer from dragon fire and most other forms of magic, though not from being dismembered."

"The words of the Pythia at Parnoth were, 'That which has been divided must be rejoined, or all shall be lost.' Perhaps she meant that one person must wear all of the pieces." He paused, and recalled how ambiguous the Pythia had been about everything she had said to Phaena. "This is interesting, and I want to hear more about it, but I still don't understand an urgent purpose that would cause the three of you journey here. Do you intend to kill the dragons?"

"The urgent problem," Bahsa interjected, apparently to prevent his father from straying again into the question of whether or not the dragons should be killed, "is that ignorant people everywhere are now acquiring a limited knowledge of magic, and using it haphazardly. We believe magic use has become so widespread that the counterspell of all that magic has disturbed the weather and the seasons."

"I believe," Minkar said, "that much of the library of magic held within the stone keep at Ironhole is being scoured for spells useful to petty rulers, and the rest offered to others for money. We need to remove all of it, or destroy it."

Yassar raised his hand. "And if we travel to the tomes that you have hidden within the rock of the Great Canyon, I can translate them for you. They may provide us with a means to remedy the upheavals of nature."

"If that is not urgent enough," Minkar added, "there has arisen an evil power in the distant East. We have not heard many details about it, but it has been constantly rumored among travelers and refugees passing through the Shouda lands."

"So, you are suggesting that I—that we—travel to Ironhole and to the Canyon?"

"Yes." Minkar replied.

"It would require weeks of travel, and in uncertain times." Ereben grimaced at the thought of yet another lengthy journey. Although he was of an age to take on such a journey and its risks, his brief climb of the Tooth of Time had aged his body by nearly another generation. He felt old. His graying beard and balding head reminded him that he was growing old. And his muscles and joints often balked at the simple tasks of living.

"I will go with you," Brindle said.

The Shouda turned to look at her, then at one another. "Why would you chose to do that?" Minkar asked.

"Five on the road would be much safer than four. And I could be helpful, if there is an unpleasant encounter."

Ereben shook his head. "If I do go, you could just live in this house while I'm gone."

"I could not. If you were gone, the fear of a great wizard would also be gone. Thieves would pillage the vegetables at every opportunity. You would be safer with me along, and I would be safer among you."

"Will you go, Ereben Leaf?" Minkar's question brought a long silence.

Ereben lowered his head, and thought for a moment. "It will take me some days to ready everything. Yes. I will go. But I'm not comfortable involving Brindle in this."

"I suggest she come along," Minkar stated, then pointed to each of his fellow Shouda."

"She should come," Bahsa answered.

"I agree," Yassar added. "She should come."

"I've been out maneuvered by clever Shouda warriors." He turned to Brindle. "If you are coming, I should forge you a steel sword to carry, in place of your mattock."

"I wouldn't know what to do with a sword. I know exactly what to do with my mattock."

Ereben held up both hands. Both shoulder joints ached. "I surrender! We will depart in five days."

Ereben squatted within a small, low shed, and harvested every munu mushroom but one. He would have to dry them near the hearth for several days, since there was seldom sunshine.

He entered his cold smithy. His orderly array of tongs and hammers and finished metals always filled his spirit with peace and satisfaction. On the wall to his left hung the blade of his completed Dragon Ax, its long, bizarre prong recurving from the back of the blade toward the absent haft. Multiple, contrasting layers of steel scalloped the entire surface. He decided to pack the blade among his travel gear, and again use its intended haft—the staff of blood locust that he had acquired on the slopes of the Tooth of Time—as a walking staff.

He had asked Brindle for her iron-bladed mattock, in order to clean and sharpen its head. That was what he had told her. She agreed to temporarily part with it, so long as she remained in the company of the Shouda warriors. Ereben rested it, head up, on a plank of flooring, then knocked the iron head from its wooden haft. He made careful measurements of the head—its weight, its dimensions, and the precise internal slope of its opening, and recorded them on a scrap of vellum. Ereben decided to modify the finished blade of a layered steel double-ax head to replace her iron mattock head. It would be difficult, and require annealing it, and yet more folding of the layered steel, before re-tempering it. He set about firing up the forge.

In addition, he would finish two layered steel blade ingots into spear points. Minkar's spear still bore the layered steel blade that he had forged for him decades ago. Those of Bahsa and Yassar were of a more ordinary steel.

Since he would need to return Brindle's mattock to her now, he cleaned the head, and dressed its two relatively blunt cutting edges. After tapping the head back into place on its haft, and applying a thin coating of oil paste to the metal and wood, he headed back through the drizzle to his house.

On opening the door, his senses were treated to the unexpected aroma of a stew, slowly simmering at the hearth. Brindle busied herself with spackling a drafty crack in the wall, while the three Shouda men sorted through the contents of their large backpacks.

Ereben spread his crop of munu across the narrow, stone mantle above the hearth.

"It's never been so handsome!" Brindle had noticed her refurbished mattock. "The haft looks slippery."

"All the wood that you grip is actually a little tacky now. Once it gathers some dirt and some oil from your hands, it should feel the same as before."

"Thank you, Ereben." She stroked each cutting edge with the back of her thumbnail, smiled, then propped the mattock against the wall near the door.

"Ereben," Bahsa said, "here is what we have assembled from the Dragon Armor." Spread onto the floor were some of the golden pieces of the Chamberlain's armor: a plate girdle, a shield, two epaulets, a pair of gauntlets and a chain hood. "Before his death, Otah Kadeef passed us his epaulets, the gauntlets of Amal Hidad, and Menash's shield. He came to understand that they needed to be assembled together."

"The breastplate." Ereben then retrieved his deceptively light-weight golden breastplate from a storage box, and presented it to Bahsa. "The collection is still incomplete."

"Yes," Yassar replied. "We lack the helmet and the golden ax. And so far as I know, the special dragon ax has never been made."

"The helmet is with Jasper of Nilwid," Bahsa added, "and the golden ax with Barrow."

"And you want to travel to Zink and Almirant as well?"

"Emerald," Bahsa said. "Almirant is now called Emerald." He nodded. "Yes. It seems like a long journey, but I believe we need to assemble the entire set of armor."

"It seems like a long journey, because it *is* a long journey— a very long one." Ereben lowered his head, stared at the floor planking, then nodded in acceptance. "Rippleton will lose its only remaining metal smith. And I will return to a pillaged home and smithy."

"Many years ago, I saw what Rippleton once was," Minkar said sadly. "Now I have seen what it has become. Perhaps the difference has crept upon you too slowly for you to see that it no longer is the place of your childhood and youth. The croplands are wasted, the forests nearly gone, and there seem to be too many people who prefer to take what belongs to others, rather than provide for their own needs."

The morning of their planned departure, Ereben dragged himself from his bed. He had slept poorly, and felt exhausted even before their journey had begun. He dressed himself for travel, fastening his dagger to his waist, and cast his ice leopard cape over his shoulders. The one item he would wear about his neck, in a velvet bag, rather than storing in his pack, was the bauxium filigree, pentalphic sphere—the Gnomish sphere—crafted for him by Brother Richit Mor, engineer of the Rock Gnomes.

With his blood locust staff, he walked into the main room, where the three Shouda warriors were preparing their gear.

"I see Brindle hasn't arrived yet."

"Look outside," Bahsa said.

When Ereben opened the door, he was surprised to see ankle-deep snow, topped by a crust of ice. Snow was now falling again, whipped into swirls by the wind. He retreated into the house, and latched the door.

Inside was warmer than outdoors, and free of the wind and blowing snow, but no one had bothered to build a fire. Ereben returned to his room, and retrieved Brindle's new, layered steel mattock head. The new spear points had been mounted on their shafts by Bahsa and Yassar the previous evening.

"I've never seen this kind of weather in Rippleton this time of year." He was not sure if his prematurely aging body could manage travel in such horrid weather.

"Nature has been altered, Ereben Leaf," Minkar said. "Everywhere that I have been has changed from the way I remember it. This may already be beyond hope."

"If there is no hope," Ereben replied, "then there is no urgency to depart in this weather."

"The choice is yours, Ereben Leaf."

The door swung open. Accompanied by a gust of snow, Brindle stomped in, then turned to latch the door. "Only in Naneland would we see such weather in late spring." She looked over the silent group of men. "I worried you would not hear me knocking."

"How difficult is travel?" Bahsa asked.

"Tiring." She dusted snow off her shoulders, then lowered her pack to the floor. "The ice on top gives way with every step."

"We were discussing if we should wait for better weather, before setting out," Ereben explained.

"Wait until when?" Brindle Meadow seated herself at the table. "If it clears by tomorrow, it may start again when we are days along on our journey."

Ereben placed the new, laminated steel mattock head on the table in front of her. "See how you like it."

Brindle knocked off the iron head, and fitted the steel one to her haft. "It is very pretty. It feels about as heavy, and the size looks the same." She stood, walked a distance from the others, then swung it is various ways. "I do like it, Ereben. But I hate to leave my old iron friend to be pilfered."

Ereben carried the iron mattock head to the hearth, and placed it on a small stone shelf a short way up the chimney. "Let's get ready, and start this *perhaps* hopeless endeavor."

Stomping laboriously through the crusted snow, they headed east along the cart path leading to the rebuilt bridge over the Iron River, on their way toward the mining town of Siller Hole. Stinging snow and occasional ice pellets forced everyone to keep their heads lowered beneath the cowls of their capes. No one else was heading east along the path, but a few individuals and families with children passed them from time to time, heading toward Rippleton.

Bahsa walked in the front, and Minkar at the rear, as the group moved as quickly as their tenuous footing would allow. Bahsa, immediately ahead of Ereben, tripped over an object hidden by the snow and ice. The young Shouda warrior tumbled forward into the snow. Ereben looked down to see in the snow between them a still face. It was a dead body. It appeared to be a man, covered in snow, frozen with his arms wrapped about his knees.

"Should we stop to bury him?" Ereben asked the others.

"No," Minkar replied. "We will surely see many more today. People leave their homes out of desperation, and have no notion of where they might find refuge. They walk on, until they stumble into an unlikely haven, or simply drop by the roadside, from cold or starvation or assault by robbers. A foraging patrol of vermin known as *cleaners* will relieve the corpses of anything valuable they might still have—coins, food, shoes—whatever items that can be sold or traded."

"I'm surprised that Valand has become such a merciless place," Ereben said.

"I have seen such things around Rippleton, Ereben," Brindle added.

Throughout the day, the number of individuals and small groups heading past them toward Rippleton increased, all of them trudging along in silence, with expressions of exhaustion on their lowered faces. Ereben could only sigh when he passed an elderly couple, apparently Dwarfs, lying dead along the path. Their frozen hands still grasped one anothers'. *Dwarfs too.* Already, their belongings had been taken. *Cleaners.*

By mid-afternoon, the day had warmed enough to rain, soon melting the snow on the ground. Walking became easier for a brief time, until the mud of the road softened. Travelers in the opposite direction slowly tapered.

A line of six thoroughly drenched, ragged looking men, mounted on horses slowly approached from the East. The horses and their riders seemed drained of energy and motivation. As they passed alongside Ereben and his companions, each horse suddenly cut sideways, intruding between each member of Ereben's party. A large, rude sword appeared at Ereben's throat.

"Take the woman," one of them shouted.

As Ereben cautiously looked about, he could see that each Shouda spear was now in the hands of a mounted bandit. Two men hoisted Brindle between two horses, where she struggled silently to free herself.

While the other bandits held their swords to four throats, the two with Brindle—still struggling, rode back toward the East. The remaining bandits slowly backed their horses away, then turned to join their companions.

In a flash of motion, Bahsa swept Hobart's rod from beneath his cape, and touched it to the knee of the nearest rider. Bahsa immediately grasped that horse's reins, and shoved the now solidly frozen bandit off the saddle, and into the mud, where the rogue shattered into three large pieces.

"Wizards!" one of the remaining three riders shouted. They galloped eastward. The closest of the riders arched his back, a dagger protruding from between his shoulders, then fell off. The riderless horse followed the two mounted riders as they fled.

Ereben slowly noticed the red handle of the thrown dagger—Bahsa's Bat Slayer. "How can we rescue Brindle?"

Bahsa retrieved the two Shouda spears that had been dropped by the dead bandits, and reclaimed Bat Slayer, wiping its blade on the dead man's clothing.

"We have only a single horse," Minkar observed. "They still have my spear, but I will use Bahsa's, since he has a dagger. I believe, Ereben Leaf, that we will have to run through the mud to find them, before they reach the bridge. You will ride the horse, and stay with us."

Ereben mounted the horse—a gelding, turned it about, to get a feel for its response, then trotted to catch up with the sprinting Shouda men. They continued at a grueling pace for a quarter hour, before they were brought to a sudden halt by the vision of what approached them from the East.

A single rider atop one horse, led four riderless horses toward Ereben by their reins. That one rider was Brindle. She drew up beside Ereben's horse, and handed him the four sets of reins, then dismounted.

"Have you been harmed?" Bahsa asked.

"I got some mud and some blood on my caribou cape," she replied. "I have to rinse it, before it sets. Ereben, your fancy mattock blade works well."

The Shouda men looked at one another, then at Ereben. He shrugged.

"I couldn't manage that long spear, so I hid it back there. We should get it, before somebody discovers it."

Ereben awakened within his small tent. He ached all over. It sounded like the rain had stopped. Dawn light softly filtered through the waxed canvas. Maneuvering as best he could within his cramped quarters, he worked his feet into cold, wet boots, threw his cape about his shoulders, and climbed out.

The others were already up, and packing their gear silently. The three Shouda men had shared a tent, and Brindle's small tent had been situated between the other two tents. One Shouda had remained awake and outside their tent during the night, to watch the horses as well as their tents. The three of them had taken turns.

A clear sky overhead and to the West looked promising of an easier day of travel. On the eastern horizon, the high mountains across the river appeared to be cloaked in dense clouds or fog. They would not be traveling that far east, but turning south at Siller Hole.

"Fires," Minkar said. "Fire is burning in the forests above Shouda."

"How can there be fires in the forest, after all this rain?" Brindle asked.

"The rains sweep in from the West, but often never cross over the mountains," Yassar explained. "There have been droughts in Shouda for the past several years."

"You remember Shardas Lake, Ereben Leaf." Minkar drew his hands close together. "Its shores have shrunk. The waterfall is only occasional now. And the snows of the high mountains are diminished."

"Parts of the forest above Shouda have been blackened with fires." Bahsa shook his head. "No one has ever seen such a thing before."

Ereben looked about at the others who had slept in the small encampment. Some used tents of various sorts, while others slept in the open, huddled beneath scraps of cloth. He assumed they clustered for safety, though he doubted that there was any safety to be found on the road. Only sharp blades, and the skill to use them, provided a modicum of safety.

At least, Ereben thought, he and his companions would not be on foot. And the extra horse could carry much of their packed gear. The previous owners of the horses, according to Brindle's reluctant recounting, would not be coming to claim them.

They finished their packing, and rode eastward along the drying mud of the cart path, heading for the bridge over the Iron River. By mid-day, the cut of the river became discernible in the distance, with the high mountains rising beyond.

The nearer they approached the river, the more apparent was the spread of the fires toward them, moving down the western ridges. In addition to the dense, black smoke swirling in the mountain winds, bright orange flames occasionally flared high, then diminished.

Minkar pointed in the direction of Jasper's childhood home village of Nilwid. "There are so many dead trees, the hot fire can move over even the damp ground."

Ereben watched the fire's progression. "Do you think it can reach the bridge?"

"It will be a close thing," Bahsa said. "It may suddenly swoop down the valley, or jump ridges, and reach the river before we have crossed."

Ereben urged his gelding to a faster pace.

❦

The continual striving toward orderliness is unique to life. It is the very core of this balance between order and disorder which the ancient practitioners of magic failed to regard. They ruptured bonds that can not be restored.

Maha Neruti: as recorded by Ereben Leaf

Brindle raced her horse away from the bridge, back toward where Ereben and the Shouda men had halted. Although the Iron river was much diminished from the last time Ereben had seen it, there was still no way to cross, other than over the wooden bridge. The eastern bank of the river to the north of the bridge was now engulfed in flames.

"The bridge is yet unburned," Brindle shouted, "but the heat of the flames is too much for the horses to pass its end."

Ereben hurriedly extracted the filigreed, Gnomish Sphere from its velvet pouch at his neck. "I will try to drive away the heat." He inserted an entire, dried munu mushroom into his mouth, then swung the small lever that latched the sphere's final Sarcite stone into position. When his fingers of both hands were carefully positioned on a specific pattern of apex stones, his vision shifted to reveal the flows and patterns of force and substance. With a small adjustment of its balance, he deflected the heat of the flames nearest the bridge, curving the flames' radiance upward and away from their path. Through his clenched teeth, he shouted, "Go!"

The others struggled with their horses, but eventually gained their cooperation, as they trotted over the bridge. Ereben realized that he could not, with his legs alone, force his horse toward the appearance of flame, even without its searing heat.

The horse's reins were twisted over his wrists, but offered too little control while his hands were occupied. If he released the Sphere, in order to control the horse, then he would be unable to cross.

Brindle pivoted her horse, and drew alongside Ereben. She grasped the cheek piece of his bridle, and forced Ereben's horse forward, and across the bridge. Once they had turned southward along the bank, away from the flames, and had reached a safe distance, Ereben disengaged the single latch of the Gnomish Sphere, moving only a single apex stone out of its required location. His normal vision returned. His mouth was empty. This brief thwarting of nature had consumed the power of an entire mushroom. He returned the delicate sphere to its neck pouch.

The flames instantly surged over the entire length of the bridge, engulfing a pair of sprinting travelers at mid-span. Nature was recouping its distortion. Ereben had failed to look back at the bridge, before releasing the heat of the flames. Now, he felt sick at what he had caused by his carelessness. *I am no better than the bandits and murderers.*

There was no road here, south of the bridge. The westward road up the mountain slope to Siller Hole was nothing but flames and ash. There were no other travelers in sight. He wondered how many more travelers had perished in the fire.

"Minkar," Ereben asked, as they continued southward along the bank and away from the fire, "do you think it would be easier to just follow the river bank to reach Iron Hole, or to risk climbing up through the hills to find the road at Siller Hole?"

"At Siller Hole," Bahsa said, "we might at least find lodging. The river bank below appears badly cut by the rains."

"There may be fire at Siller Hole," Minkar observed. "And the way through the hills, without a road, may be as difficult as following the bank."

Bahsa continued, "Siller Hole is within today's ride, and then there is a broad road. Iron Hole would mean over two days, without even a path."

"Siller Hole," Brindle stated.

"Siller Hole," Yassar added.

Ereben ached all over, and was too fatigued, as well as heart broken at his most recent use of magic to care about either choice. "That's three for Siller Hole."

Minkar rolled his eyes. "Young people," he mumbled. "Bahsa, you will choose the route up the hills, and we will follow. Watch for fire."

"Yes, father."

Off to their left, the smoke and flames seemed to fade, as the horses wound their way generally eastward, up the gullies and slopes. Ereben sensed that Bahsa was veering them slightly northward, toward Siller Hole. After half a day of slowly ascending the steep foothills, they reached a road, crowded with travelers. Most were going about setting up camps alongside the road.

Ereben noticed a solitary Beddu woman—a Giant from West Graze—setting up an uncommonly large tent farther from the road than most of the travelers. She wore a full-length, beige robe, her head covered in a darker beige, draping head scarf. A massive cudgel rested on the ground beside her.

Ereben had seen no Beddu since the Battle of Four Armies, and had heard nothing more of them. He guided his horse toward the woman. When she looked up, after first grasping her cudgel, Ereben raised his right hand to his face, his thumb almost touching his nose, and tipped his head downward. She hesitated, then returned the Beddu gesture of greeting.

"I am Ereben Leaf. I once knew many Beddu. I am surprised to see a Beddu woman so far from home."

The woman shook her head. "I have no home. The Beddu are no more. The Western Graze is nothing but wasteland." She returned her cudgel to the ground. "And I know you, Ereben Leaf. You surprised me once while I washed clothes—when the Little Ones visited Thom Na, who then followed you to the big war. I am Ja No, and the only living Beddu."

Ereben felt stunned. He had never imagined the Beddu giants being vulnerable to anything. And he now remembered Ja No, the Beddu child who had alone driven off the Sarcoptis with her cudgel.

"I remember you, Ja No. You were much younger then."

"You were not so old a man then, Ereben Leaf."

"Where are you headed?"

"I am not headed. I simply walk, hoping to find food. I was moving toward the river below Siller Hole, when the fires drove everyone back."

Minkar brought his horse alongside Ereben. He offered the Beddu greeting. "I am Minkar Jarad. If you have no destination, then perhaps you would join us in a difficult journey."

Ereben turned to Minkar. The thought had not occurred to him. Turning back to Ja No, Ereben said, "We would be honored by your companionship. But it will be a difficult journey of many months."

"It would not be seemly for a woman to travel with five men."

"Four men," Brindle said from behind Ereben. "It would be four men and now two women." Brindle pushed back the hood of her caribou cape to reveal the braided bun of hair atop her head. "Please consider coming with us. I'm Brindle Meadow."

Ereben introduced Bahsa and Yassar. "Perhaps you could join us as we seek lodging in Siller Hole." He sensed something precious about a link to what was good and noble in his distant experiences.

"Siller Hole is nothing. The water there was poisoned by the mines. No one lives there. All the buildings have decayed, and have no roof. There are places where the road itself has dropped into the mine tunnels. Siller Hole is nothing but a name and a turn in the road."

Minkar knowingly looked back at his son and Yassar. "Then may we join you here for the night?"

"Yes. There is sufficient room for more tents. There is clear water in the creek." She pointed over her shoulder. "I will decide about accompanying you by morning. This evening, I would much enjoy speaking with Brindle Meadow."

Ereben had slept better, knowing a Beddu was in the next tent. The lowered voices of Ja No and Brindle could be overheard for a short while after dark, then Brindle had insisted to the Shouda men that she be included in their watch rotation during the night. Now, actual sunlight seemed to be bathing their campsite, and filtering into his tent. His shoulders and neck ached, as he slipped his feet into his boots, and crawled out of his tent.

"They all were exhausted," Brindle whispered. No one else had stirred yet.

"How long has it been since we've seen the sun?" He asked her, in a subdued voice.

"Three weeks...maybe longer. It makes the morning chill feel warmer than it is." Brindle was seated against a small maple tree, her white, caribou cloak dappled with brilliant light that shifted as the gentle breeze moved thin, leafless branches above her.

To the North, small, scattered puffs of smoke still rose above the mountains, but the sky was otherwise clear. Toward the South, the direction in which they would be heading today, an occasional white cloud drifted slowly westward. With his mood elevated by the change in the weather, and with the mud of the campsite now mostly dried, he set about quietly striking his tent, and packing his gear.

"These poor creatures need names," Brindle said, as she untied the six horses, and led them away to a nearby area with taller grass and a creek. "All of them are shod, but not very well," she said softly, over her shoulder.

"We'll plan to visit a blacksmith in Zink when we get there," Ereben answered. "Call mine Starfire."

Ja No stepped out of her tall, Beddu tent, carrying her gear in one hand, and her yard-long cudgel in the other. She set them on the ground, then dragged the center pole from the tent, allowing it to deflate onto the ground.

Ereben watched as she silently and efficiently folded, rolled and packed the tent. "Have you made a decision about coming with us, Ja No?"

She squatted beside Ereben, and helped him finish his packing. "Brindle explained to me enough about your journey for me to decide that I will join you, with a hope of improving your chance of success. I can think of no better way to honor the memory of Thom Na, than for a Beddu to join hands, once again, with Ereben Leaf and his companions."

Four bedraggled men approached them as the two completed packing. Each carried a simple farm implement. As Ereben looked up at them, one said softly, "Give us your gear, or we will kill you and your woman."

Ja No slowly rose from a squat to her full height, half again taller than the men. Her right hand held her massive cudgel.

"Holy gods!" They turned and fled, without further comment.

Ja No appeared to comfortably walk at a brisk enough pace to match that of Starfire, and the other five horses, still nameless. Of her gear, only the Beddu tent was added to the burden of their pack horse. No amount of encouragement or cajoling could persuade the giant to attempt mounting, much less riding a horse. "The Beddu walk upon the ground," she had stated flatly. Her yard-long cudgel seemed a natural part of her body, usually rested on her shoulder, occasionally carried like an improbable sword, and sometimes used as a cane, for support over rough spots—but always in her right hand.

As they moved along, Bahsa spoke of the huge, powerful stallions ridden by the Trolls of Timbul. He had been just a boy then. Ja No seemed to remain unimpressed by possible equestrian advantages.

With drier, warmer weather, the occasional dead along the roadside rotted and stank. Bickering clusters of vultures ignored passing travelers, and feasted on the increasing bounty of reeking flesh.

At the road junction to Zink, they turned southwest, and continued on to Ironhole, approaching its eastern gate—its only gate—by early evening. To Ereben's surprise, the wooden picket wall that he remembered had been entirely replaced by a mortared stone wall surrounding the town, and reaching a height of over four yards. Small stone towers stood to either side of the town's massive wooden gate. Even though the sun was just beginning to set in the West, the gate had been firmly closed for the night.

Scattered camps of refugees were already assembling alongside the road, and in the vicinity of the town gate. Among them, a Kasazi, wearing the traditional tunic of the ancient cliff people, complained loudly to a similarly garbed companion, "...only Dwarfs and Valanders. No Kasazi." He angrily threw his backpack onto the ground. "Lord of the Keep says. Lord of the Keep..." He spat onto the barren ground.

A nearby Orkahti woman turned to the Kasazi man, and offered with caution in her voice, "They say he is a mage, and can see and hear beyond the walls."

Bahsa approached her. "Do they also forbid the Orkahti and the Shouda?"

"Only Valanders and Dwarfs are allowed into the town, and only during daylight. No other races." She led a lean horse toward a stand of grass some distance away.

Ereben looked at Bahsa, then at each of the others, and shrugged his shoulders. He pointed to an area southwest of the town's stone wall, and well away from the road, the gate and other travelers. "There is grass down there for the horses."

They set up camp, and gathered around a small fire to prepare dinner—a broth of two wild onions and some greens, while Ja No and Brindle took the horses down to a creek. The Shouda men and Ereben discussed the issue of magical items and manuscripts within the tower of Ironhole Keep.

"If the Lord of the Keep is a magician," Minkar said, "then he surely must be aware of their value, and the need to guard them."

"All the greater reason to remove them or destroy them," Bahsa pointed out.

"But it sounds like only I will be allowed into the walls," Ereben replied. "Maybe Brindle as well."

"That would be a great risk to you, Ereben Leaf," Yassar said. "to venture in alone to confront the Lord of the Keep and his guards."

"I have seen no other Nanish travelers today." Minkar pointed out, a pained expression on his face. "The guards may not distinguish between Valanders and Nanes."

Ereben slapped his knees. "Brindle and I will attempt to pass into the town tomorrow morning, if only to observe the situation. We can talk more about this tomorrow night. I don't like this place. I don't like this journey."

"Can you use your Gnomish Sphere to look into the town and into the keep?" Yassar asked.

"If the Lord of the Keep has a sphere of his own, which might explain how he might see and hear beyond the walls," Ereben explained, "then he could identify me easily, if I activate the Gnomish Sphere. Holnick Firth was able to do it."

The two women and the horses returned to the campsite. "I have named my horse Turnip," Brindle said in passing, "since he performs well in the snow and sleet."

Ereben, mounted on Starfire, and Brindle Meadow, riding Turnip, slowly approached the front gate of Ironhole, after the gate was opened, and the initial rush of Dwarf and Valish travelers had entered. Not one of those who preceded them had been stopped and searched by the guards, and some of them had openly carried swords, daggers and other weapons. As he and Brindle passed through the gate, the two Dwarf guards seemed more concerned with keeping everyone moving into the town, to prevent a slowing of the traffic. They paid no particular attention to Brindle.

Ereben noted that the interior of the town, its streets, and even its aging wooden buildings, had changed little since the last time he had seen it, though the crowds of people were not as large, nor as exuberant. With a splinter of hope, he led Brindle toward the Goat's Teat Inn. There, hanging above the door of a broken down, though still apparently active business hung the weathered symbol of the Goat's Teat. They dismounted, hitched their horses, then strolled inside.

The dining area, dingier than he recalled it, was nearly empty of customers. A thin Dwarf woman limped from behind the bar, and out to the table that Ereben and Brindle had chosen.

"Wha' will ye huv?" She balanced herself with one hand on the splintery edge of the table.

"A small sip of barley-brei," Ereben said. He knew better than to request water in Ironhole.

"Do you have pickled fish?" Brindle asked.

The Dwarf woman looked up at Brindle with her right eye. The left one seemed to stare in a different direction. "Yer a courageous one, ye are," she whispered. "Nae too many Nanes slip past thae guards a' the gate. Hmm. We huv a wee cask o' fish pickle, bu' huv nae looked upon it fer a lang while. I'll huv the boy check it fer ye, sweetie." She turned her good, right eye at Ereben. "I know ye frae somewhere, bu' kinna quite recall." She turned, and limped back behind the bar, and vanished through the kitchen door.

As Ereben imbibed a token sip of his barley-brei, a small, boyish face peered from the side of the bar, apparently surveying the customers present at the few occupied tables. Then, as clear as day, the adult Rock Gnome, dressed as a Dwarf boy, came out to Ereben's table, and served a small dish of pickled fish and baked bread slices to Brindle. Only by standing on his tiptoes, could his arms reach over the table edge. He headed back toward the bar, then turned about, and walked directly to Ereben.

In a subdued, high-pitched voice, he stated, "You are Ereben Leaf!"

After a moment of stunned silence, Ereben replied, "Have we met before?"

"Have we met? You carried me on your shoulders. I rode on your back when I was little. How could I ever forget that! I rode on your back! And then you won that war, and got famous."

Ereben looked about at the clientele of the Goat's Teat. Nobody paid the slightest attention to them. "I am. And this is Brindle Meadow. But I don't remember your name."

"I'm Brother Palmer, but they know me here as just Palmer. Just Palmer. So you can call me Palmer." He turned to Brindle. "If you want more fish pickle, there's plenty more in the cask. Plenty more."

"The guards allow you to pass the gate?" Brindle asked quietly.

Palmer leaned toward her. "I don't have to pass through the gate. I go through the stone wall."

"Is there somewhere that we could talk to you privately?" Ereben asked."

Palmer's eyebrows lifted. "Where are you staying? Tell me where you are staying, and I can meet you there."

"Well...we are camped with some companions outside the walls south of the town."

"Then I will meet you there this evening." He walked back into the kitchen.

The sun was setting, when the tiny figure of the Rock Gnome, Palmer, approached Ereben's campfire. Ereben waved to him. He had earlier explained to Brindle and Ja No that the Gnomes were capable of merging and passing through solid rock.

He himself had done so within the rock of the Great Canyon, but had found the inviting tranquility of rock to be both difficult to resist and frightening. Only by forcing himself to bite the bitter Nagel radish that he had placed into his mouth before the journey, had he been able to emerge. But he had indelibly learned what it is like to be a rock. He had determined to never again experience that profound seduction.

Palmer seated himself on a small, flat rock beside the fire. After introductions had been made, Ereben inquired about the Gnomes that he had met decades before.

"The weather," Palmer explained. "It is the weather. The weather has changed, and ruined everything. Now, the Legion Dunes are sometimes sand, but sometimes swamp. When it is dry, the water within the pots fails, and the crops die. When it is too wet, the water tops over the rims of the pots and floods them. When we raised the rims, the water flooded from beneath. I left two years ago. Many Gnomes had already died, and all but two pots had vanished beneath the sand or muck."

"Did the others leave as well?" Ereben asked.

"Most of them stayed. Some of them may still be alive somewhere. But in two years, I have seen none. Living in the Goat's Teat, taking meals there for my work, and wandering outside the walls from time to time is my life now."

"It saddens me to hear about the others," Ereben said. He reflected on the fact that the men of the Rock Gnome pots had always performed whatever tasks they were instructed to do by the women. Now, Palmer does the same under the direction of the Laird of the Goat's Teat, and seems content with that.

"What is the story about the Lord of the Keep?" Brindle asked.

"Oh, I overhear a lot about him from the customers. All the farmers in this part of Dwarfland have to bring him a third of their crop each year, or he uses magic or something to damage their farms. That's what he's like. And everybody in the town has to pay him a tax. Every now and then he stands on the top of that stone tower, and holds up a big ball of sticks, and does magic on it to bring rain or sun or sometimes a globe of fire that just floats up there."

Ereben knew that the "ball of sticks" was a pentalphic sphere—perhaps the very one he had seen a monk constructing in the basement of the Keep years ago. His own Gnomish Sphere was a miniaturized pentalphic sphere. He considered what he might do to render the sphere of the Lord of the Keep inoperable, without its alteration being easily detected.

"This might be dangerous, but would you be willing to pass into the basement of the Keep, and just look and see how many books and scrolls are there?" Ereben imagined that if Palmer were discovered doing that, he could simply vanish into the stone to escape, but would then be left without a home or livelihood.

"Sure. I'll do that tonight. It shouldn't take too long."

Minkar Jarad frowned. "How would you see in the darkness?"

"That's easy. Really easy. I can just make some of the stone glow."

Yassar Khayin appeared stunned. "How do you do that?"

"I don't know. I just do it. It just happens when I want it to happen."

Palmer returned not long after he had headed up to the stone wall of Ironhole. Ereben and his companions were waiting by the fire for his report, but Ereben assumed that something had gone wrong.

Palmer walked to the campfire, and seated himself, cross-legged. "Nothing but stuff like a storage room. No books. No scrolls. I even peeked into most of the chests. Just regular stuff."

"Perhaps it was all removed long ago," Bahsa suggested.

"Or the Lord of the Keep has sold or traded it all for gain," Minkar added.

"Thank you, Palmer," Ereben said. "Is there anything that we can do to repay you or assist you?"

"No. It was easy. And it was kind of fun to look around. The iron mine is boring. I don't explore very much any more."

"If we come across any other Gnomes in our journey," Brindle said, "we'll be sure to tell them that you are here in Ironhole."

"Oh. Don't do that. Some of them were angry when I decided to leave the pot."

"But that was over two years ago," Brindle continued. "Maybe they understand better now."

"Okay. It probably doesn't matter anyway. There probably aren't any more Gnomes for you to come across."

After more conversation of less consequence, during which it became clear to Ereben that Palmer had little interest in leaving the comfort and security of his position at the Goat's Teat, the cheery Gnome bid them good night, and walked into the darkness, toward the wall of Ironhole. "My understanding," Ereben stated to the Shouda men, "is that our remaining interest in Ironhole is the sphere used by the Lord of the Keep."

"Can anything be done about it?" Minkar asked.

"We can't take it by force." Ereben pondered the situation. "Later tonight, after I feel that the Lord of the Keep is not likely to be handling the sphere, I will see what I can learn about it, and if anything can usefully be done."

Warm, dry winds swept gently across the grassy hill on which Ereben had seated himself. The solitude and unexpectedly pleasant weather raised his mood from the dreariness of the past week. He had decided that he would use his Gnomish Sphere in an attempt to locate the "ball of sticks" used by the Lord of the Keep, and, if possible, to subtly alter the lengths of its rods, so that it no longer formed a pentalphic sphere. The change would have to go unnoticed by its owner, who had handled it for likely months or even years.

As Ereben carefully removed the Gnomish Sphere from the bag at his neck, a soft crunching sound nearby caught his attention. He turned his head to see Ja No seating herself nearby. "I had hoped to be alone," he said.

"We know," she replied. "But the times are unpredictable." She rested her cudgel across her legs.

"We?" Ereben looked over his other shoulder. Brindle Meadow had silently seated herself close by as well."

"You always underestimate the hazards, Ereben," Brindle added.

After a long sigh, he explained, as simply as possible, what he was about to do. He showed them the latch on the Gnomish Sphere that would disable it instantly. "Using the sphere carelessly is dangerous. It nearly took my life. It is far more dangerous than the device used by the Lord of the Keep."

He placed a slice of munu mushroom into his mouth, then promptly removed it. "Thank you," he said, turning to each of them.

His task of locating the sphere within the Keep was surprisingly easy. He saw it resting on a large pillow within the same upper chamber in which he had awakened after the Battle of the Four Armies. Nearby, an obese Dwarf snored obliviously upon an absurdly overstuffed, round, feather bed, draped with darkly colored velvet and satin. Beside him, an entirely naked dwarf woman also lay sleeping, uncovered. She seemed to be at least a generation younger than the Lord of the Keep—perhaps in her mid-teens.

Ereben focused on the "ball of sticks". Its apices bore no Sarcite stones. Only its precise construction into a perfect pentalphic sphere enabled it to amplify power. He made a subtle deformation of its shape, spread over all the rod segments. Then flipped the lever on his own sphere to disengage.

Ereben returned the Gnomish Sphere to its velvet pouch around his neck, and placed the lightly consumed slice of munu into a separate pouch to dry. Standing up, he offered a hand to

Brindle, who politely accepted it, as she raised herself to her feet. When he similarly offered a hand to Ja No, the Beddu woman laughed softly, and stood.

"Do we move along to Zink tomorrow?" Ja No asked in the darkness.

"To Zink."

Hot, southerly winds swept across the pasture lands and hills of Dwarfland, carrying a fine, gritty dust into the foothills. It stung Ereben's eyes, and forced him to squint most of the time. Their horses seemed equally annoyed, as they plodded eastward along the road to the Dwarf city of Zink. Ja No, who remained the sole pedestrian of their group, seemed to pay no attention to the blowing dust.

The land showed no memory of the recent rains. Everything appeared parched. The road surface felt solid and worn smooth, for which Ereben was grateful. The dead, scattered randomly along either side of the road, reeked their foulness in the sunlight. But with the brisk, prevailing wind cutting directly across the path of the road, the stench was noticeable only briefly with each body they passed to the leeward side. As he had previously noticed, none of the dead attracted the slightest attention from passers by. Some appeared to have recently succumbed, some had already been stripped naked by the *cleaners*, and still others stripped to bare bones by carrion birds and assorted wild animals. Ereben found it difficult to muster either pity or outrage. They were simply refugees who had failed in their quest for something better. The dead were just nameless, and absent of recognizable humanity. For Ereben, the grimmest aspect was that the living who marched without emotion, past the dead of all ages and races, had also apparently lost their sense of membership in humanity. He was beginning to include himself among the guilty.

Travelers passing Ereben's party gave them a wide birth. The three conspicuous Shouda spears, and the massive cudgel in the grip of a Beddu Giant created an intimidating enough spectacle that no armed parties that passed them seemed inclined to test their skills against them.

The fields and gardens surrounding the moated, walled city of Zink were as desolate as everywhere they had passed, since leaving Ironhole. Shortly before reaching the rise leading up to the moat and gate of Zink, they encountered a sizable stable alongside a busy blacksmith's sheltered forge. Nearly a dozen Dwarfs were occupied with various tasks. Nearby each of them rested an ax.

Ereben guided his party to the blacksmith. All of the Dwarfs looked up simultaneously, then went back to their work. When Ereben rode directly up to the blacksmith at his forge, the Dwarf ignored them, while he completed his final hammering on a glowing horseshoe, then used his tongs to plunge it into a bath.

He now looked up. "Wha' kin we offer ye?"

"We will be going into Zink," Ereben replied. "Would you be able to shoe these six horses while we are there?"

"We tak only siller. Nae coppers. Oop front."

When Ereben nodded, the blacksmith quickly inspected each hoof of each horse. "Ye should ha' got them replaced sooner. Thir hoofs continue tae grow aneath a shoe. They come oop lame, should ye neglect tha'. Thae shoes need replacin' e'ery six or eight week. Better a' six week."

"How long will it take to replace them?" Ereben asked.

"They'll be ready the time ye walk intae Zink an' back. One siller fer the lot. Wha' be thir names?"

"Mine is Starfire. That one is Turnip. The others have no names."

"Wha' sort o' person fails tae give a horse a name?"

Ja No spoke up. "I've named our pack horse Fart. I walked behind him for days."

"Will our things be safe here, so near the road?" Bahsa asked.

"Ye see my friends here? They're also my guards. An' we huv a gong tae sound..." The blacksmith pointed out a heavy sheet of metal suspended by two ropes. "...should we wish guards frae the city tae assist us."

Ereben and his companions dismounted. Ereben paid the blacksmith one silver, then the group moved back out to the road on foot, to ascend into Zink.

After crossing the swinging bridge across the moat, at the northern perimeter of Zink, a cluster of six ax-wielding, and smartly uniformed guards stopped them, and questioned their purpose in coming to Zink.

Ereben explained that he was a personal friend of the current mayor of Zink, Whittig Trench, and needed to consult him on important matters privately. He introduced each of his companions to the guard in command.

"Ye shall need tae leave yer weapons ahind."

"In these times, we would not dare to do that," Ereben replied. "Just send a message to Barrow that we are here."

"Tha' be the magic word." The guard commander smiled. "There be few nowaday who knew him by tha' name." He signaled to one of the guards, who turned about, and headed into the city. Then he waved Ereben and his companions, weapons and all, into the tunnel beneath the broad, earthen wall.

Although Ereben and Brindle could walk through the low, Dwarf-height tunnel by slightly lowering their heads, Minkar, Bahsa and Yassar were forced to stoop considerably in order to fit. Ja No could pass through only on her hands and knees, which she did without complaint.

While the multistory buildings of Zink appeared to Ereben to be in a better state of repair than he recalled, the great market was a mere shadow of what he remembered. There were plenty of stalls offering crafts and goods, but vendors of fruits and vegetables and grains and meats were few. And the Dwarfs themselves appeared leaner than in previous times.

Ja No offered to spend time in the market, replenishing their food supplies. Ereben and his four other companions stopped at a tent maker, to request that he sew them a heavy, waxed cape, with a hood, for Ja No. When Ereben pointed to the Beddu woman, wandering through the market, the tent maker's eyes widened.

"Tha' shall require one entire tent." He glanced over his inventory, pulled out a brown tent, and tipped his head to one side, then the other, while unfolding and inspecting the fabric. "I kin huv it fer ye later the day."

They paid him, and proceeded to the three-story city hall. An elderly Dwarf in a dignified, though oversized robe, supporting himself with a walking cane, stood in the doorway, between two Dwarf guards.

"Ereben Leaf and Minkar Jarad!" the old Dwarf called out.

Ereben only then recognized him as Barrow—Whittig Trench. "Barrow! They told you we were coming." He clasped Barrow's forearm. "It's been far too long."

The three Shouda men offered a bow, which he acknowledged with a slow nod.

"You do not recognize my son, Bahsa," Minkar said, slapping Bahsa on the shoulder.

"Aye, thae years pass," Barrow mumbled. "Come inside, so's I can sit." He led them to his mayoral parlor.

Barrow lowered himself with a grunt, into a well-stuffed chair at the center of the far wall. The Shouda men, Brindle and Ereben seated themselves on various wooden benches.

"How is Liddie Burn?" Ereben asked.

"Aye. Ye huvna heard. Liddie, poor soul, suffered o' several maladies o'er the past year, growing weaker as time passed. We placed her in her grave two month ago." He said this with little visible emotion.

Minkar lifted both of his arms toward the sky. "May her noble soul rest in the arms of Elloh."

Bahsa and Yassar then lifted their arms in a similar fashion, and lowered them without speaking.

To Brindle's puzzled expression, Ereben said softly, "They married some years ago." Ereben stood, and stepped over to Barrow, and placed his arms about him. With tears in his eyes, he whispered, "I am so sorry. My memories of her will always remain."

Barrow patted Ereben's hand. "Enough sadness," he grumbled, wiping tears from his own eyes. "I huvna many years, afore I rejoin her. Now, what brings ye tae travel aa' the way tae talk wi' Barrow again?"

Ereben seated himself on the bench near Brindle. He introduced her to Barrow, with apologies for having not done so sooner. After polite exchanges, he went directly to the issue. "I'm sure you have noticed the change in weather here over the last few years."

"Aye. Drought an' flood huv made difficulty fer aa' thae farmers o' Knurlan...excuse me, aa' thae farmers o' Dwarfland tae grow thir food. Many moved away tae ither lands, hoping tae find better. An' tha' one-eye dragon visits and kills Dwarfs whene're he chooses."

"That is happening everywhere," Ereben continued. Every race in every land has met with crop failures, famines, fires and floods...and dragon attacks. The people wander the roads in every direction, looking for a better place. But there is none."

"Wha' cause brings this tae be?"

"As you and the other Watchers long feared, knowledge of magic has spread to both the ignorant and the power hungry. There is too much careless magic. It corrupts nature."

"An' Yarnish Blen? I huv nae word from him."

Ereben lowered his head. "He was killed shortly before we started this journey. We buried him behind my house."

Barrow slumped in his chair and wept openly. "So much dying. Is this how it aa' ends? Starvation and death?"

"Maybe," Ereben replied. "But we hope to find a remedy among the ancient books and scrolls that I locked within the stone of the Canyon."

"Thae book an' scroll wha' ye kinna read?"

"Yes. I still cannot read them. But I have someone with me who can read them. Yassar Khayin was raised beneath the Shouda Shrine, in the city of Lamblar. His first language is the ancient Shadae."

Yassar sat up straight. "I can read them. And I have also read much from the ancient archives within Lamblar. It was an ancient Shouda wizard who created the dragons. He also created the golden armor that Hobart found within the ruins of Ephesia. It is Dragon Armor, and is designed specifically for killing a dragon. All of the components must be worn by a single man. Chrysanthus' unusual ax drawing, that Ereben now possesses, is the design for one of two axes required to be successful. The second ax is the golden ax which you have carried and used for these decades."

"We have assembled all of the pieces of the armor," Ereben continued, "and carry them in our baggage—except for your ax and the helmet in the possession of Jasper."

"Auld Barrow kin hardly lift his golden ax the day." Barrow rang a small bell beside his chair. "Ye may tak it with my blessing. I wouldna' care tae fight a dragon, armor or nae."

When an assistant entered the parlor, Barrow instructed him to fetch the golden ax, and put it in the keeping of Ereben.

"We will be traveling into the Great Canyon," Ereben explained. "Has anyone cared for Liddie Burn's coo farm all this time? It's just about the only sheltered place to stop along that route."

"Aye. Sawney Burn. He is Liddie's son frae her first marriage. Sawney's father first built tha' coo farm. Efterin his death, and Liddie decidin' tae accept my attention... Sawney couldna abide it, an' departed. Once Liddie moved tae Zink, she asked Sawney to tak the coo farm intae his own hand. He lives there the day, with his wife an' thir boy of fifteen. When Liddie died, the three o' them visited for a couple day. Sawney is a good man."

Moving in the downpour, along the flooded path south of Zink, Ja No gratefully covered her robes and head with the waxed cloth cape that Ereben had presented to her. As usual, she brought up the rear of their group, walking immediately behind the pack horse, whom she had authoritatively named Fart.

By pressing their pace, they were able to reach the northern bank of the Clootie River just after sunset. Since it was in flood, Minkar suggested that they make camp, then scout a possible crossing in the morning. In the darkness, Ereben could see a faint light from the hearth of Liddie's old mound house— now Sawney Burn's mound house.

With soaking wet clothes and gear, they didn't bother to attempt a campfire for dinner. Instead, each one consumed whatever ready food they carried—biscuit or dried fruit.

❦

Despite their three learned academies having explored and debated the impacts of removing the threat of the Banu Sulal to their way of life, they were unable to prevent the rapid collapse of both their democracy and their culture.

Jasper of Nilwid: The Fall of Timbul

Jasper steadied himself against the gusts of wind that buffeted him, threatening to tip him out of his saddle. Since the last of his great horses of Timbul had grown too feeble to serve as a mount, he had contented himself with riding into battle atop one of his sturdy, white Sulalian stallions. As always, he rode at the head of a triple column of Free Sulalian cavalry, alongside his trusted friend, Atan.

"Bad weather again, sahib Mahweud", Atan shouted. The older man shuddered in his padded leather armor, his lance held vertical in its stirrup pocket. "That Corban filth has no bounds!"

"We are its bounds." The gusts quieted momentarily.

"I continue to suffer frightful dreams of the kelpie spawn. It lingers in my thoughts through each day."

Jasper lowered his head. "We fight, again and again, and kill so many of its demon spawn, but we never seem to make any progress against Kehl."

A large fireball descended from the sky, but exploded into the sea, well beyond their location near the Sulalian coast north of Almirant.

To his north, Jasper identified a widely spread body of Orkahti horsemen approaching. It had been several months since they had agreed to coordinate their fight against the Evil in the East with Jasper's efforts. As they drew nearer, Jasper could identify his own son, Ethnan, riding near their center. He was easy to spot, since, unlike the individually unique, colored tunics of the Orkahti horsemen, Ethnan wore the standard garb of a high-ranking Sulalian officer. Alongside Ethnan, their leader waved a greeting to Jasper.

"What have you found?" Jasper shouted.

The Orkahti leader, Khumartakin, called back, "The same." We kill many little demons, and the tree demon flies away. I worried that this last fireball had struck near you."

"It landed in the water." Jasper looked out at the sea, and noticed that the water had risen enough to submerge the sandy area of the coast, and was now receding."

"Ethnan has spoken to me of the shortages of food in Almirant."

"Yes. The fertile areas have become desert, and swampy areas have become dry clay. Our fishing boats return with smaller and smaller catches. And the vagabonds and thieves from Timbul range the roads in between."

Ethnan pulled his horse alongside his father's, opposite Atan's horse. "Khumartakin's horsemen are running short of supplies," he said, leaning close to Jasper. "He would never mention it, but could you invite them to Almirant—and resupply them?"

Jasper paused, then said to Atan, "Plan a feast for the Orkahti horsemen, and arrange for their resupply." He turned to Khumartakin, and shouted through the noise of the wind, "You must return to Almirant with us, for a celebration."

ৡৡ

Brief intervals of balance lull our senses into believing that it is the way things are. Yet flood and drought, fire and famine, pain and death are just as much a part.

Yassar Khayin: A Place of Peace

When Ereben awakened, and crawled out of his tent—every joint and muscle protested. Seated on a low stone in the center of their encampment, Ja No turned her head toward him, then silently gestured with one finger toward the southern bank of the flooding Clootie River. Ereben looked past his tent.

Every scrap of grassland, as far as he could see south of the river, was blackened and deeply eroded. The mound house, 60 yards beyond the river bank, was likewise blackened. Yet everything was soaked by yesterday's rain.

"It's all burned," he mumbled. "The cows are gone."

Ereben's other companions had yet to stir. He scanned the flooded, Clootie River. On the far bank, a small barge floated restlessly beside a sloping, wooden pier. The barge appeared to be securely tied to the single post that stood above the pier. A thick rope, also tied to that post, spanned the river to the near bank, where it was tied to a single post attached to a similar, sloping pier. *A ferry!*

He stomped through the mud to the near pier, and stared at the mound house, for any sign of activity. He recalled seeing what appeared to be light coming from its hearth the previous evening. This morning, no smoke rose from the hearth.

"Hallo Sawney Burn!" he called. Ereben was certain that it could be heard within the damaged mound house.

A round face, below a bald scalp, and framed with a full, dark brown beard peeked from the doorway. "Who comes?" These two words appeared to trigger a bout of coughing.

"An old friend of Barrow. I'm Ereben Leaf and I have five companions with me."

"What do..." He coughed again. "What do ye want?" The raspy voice revealed a deep exhaustion and impatience. "I huv nary a thing remainin' tae steal."

"We are traveling south, and need to cross the river with our horses. Can you help us with the ferry?"

By now, all the others had emerged from their tents, and were gathering beside Ereben. A Dwarf emerged from the entryway of the mound house. In his right hand he held a substantial war hammer, bouncing its handle, and rotating its iron head. He walked only a short distance from the entry, then stopped.

He coughed some more. "Who might ye be again?"

"Ereben Leaf."

The Dwarf stood more upright, then lowered his hammer to the muddy, blackened sod. "The Ereben Leaf what fought in the Great War?"

"Yes. And this is Minkar Jarad and his son, Bahsa, who fought beside me." He motioned for the two of them to stand with him along the flooded river bank.

Without further discussion, the Dwarf abandoned his hammer standing in the mud, and slowly walked out to the crossing barge, episodically coughing as he approached.

Sawney Burn spoke through a mouthful of biscuit that Ja No had offered him—his first food in two days. "They wer both oot carryin' hay tae the coos tha' sun shiny morn, on account o' the drought o're the pasture what kilt the grass." A spell of coughing interrupted him. "I wes aside the house, feedin' Moap...."

"Moap?" Brindle interrupted. They were all seated about the stone hearth in Sawney's mound house.

He cleared his throat. "Aye. Moap is the mule. I wes feedin' Moap, an' a fiery star dropped oot o' the sky. Looked tae be comin' direct at me. Afore strikin' the ground, it burst apart, louder than anything in my forty-five year. Fire scattered e'erywhere, and set on the pasture. My wife...my boy..." He swallowed, cleared his throat again, and paused a bit. "They both burned. The coos burned. I couldna' reach them. Only me an' Moap could escape the flame. Tha' wes three week ago, right afore the rain finally come." He sipped a cup of water.

"I am sorry," Ereben mumbled. "I've know Barrow and your mother for so long, that I feel like I know you as well. So many deaths."

Minkar raised his hands. "May they rest in the arms of Elloh."

Yassar and Bahsa both briefly raised their hands as well. "Your mother," Bahsa said to Sawney, "became my mother. I regard you as my older step-brother. I have lost the chance to meet your wife and my nephew."

"Will you continue here?" Brindle asked.

"I huv nae family, nae coos, nae food. Only a bit o' grain fer Moap...an' that'll be soon spent. All my barley-brei I guzzled in a week, else I wouldna' be sober the day." He coughed again, then thumped his chest with a thick finger. "The chest gets better day by day, though Moap still has the wheeze. My thought is o' headin' southwart, tae look fer fodder an' food. Perhaps I could ride alang with you folk, 'til I locate a suitable spot."

Ja No, bending low beneath the stone roof, despite being seated, said, "We have enough supplies for you, but you may not find a more suitable place, no matter which direction you go."

"I kinna remain amongst all tha' I huv lost."

For two days, they moved south toward the Great Canyon. Midway through the first day beyond Sawney's destroyed coo farm, the wet, blackened prairie, scattered with burned carcasses of rabbits, foxes, deer and rodents of various kinds, abruptly transitioned to parched, brown grass beneath a scorching sun. Ereben sighted no other people, as far as the horizon in every direction, other than his now six companions. The hooves of six horses and one mule, together with the footfalls of a Giant, aside from Sawney's occasional coughing, maintained a ceaseless rasp of crunching grass, droning sometimes for hours, between conversations.

"Ereben," Bahsa asked, as they approached the northern rim of the Great Canyon, where they would camp for the night, "have you noticed those dark clouds to the South?"

"More rain?" Brindle added.

Bahsa continued, as their party walked their horses in that direction, "They seem to rise up from the plateau of the far rim. I believe that is smoke."

"That would be along our course to the ruins of Ephesia," Minkar pointed out. "We will be unable to see its risk until we have gained the south rim, and judge the wind."

"The plateau is mostly jungle," Ereben stated. He considered how prolonged a drought would be needed to render it dry enough to burn. "We don't know what has happened to the grasslands and forests to the South. So many years since I passed through there." He thought of tiny, vulnerable Ternaria, home of the Fairies and Thistlepix, and protected by the monks of Moss Abbey.

"We won't get up to the south rim until another three or four days." Bahsa dismounted, and began to unpack his gear. "By then, the fire may be gone...or be much worse."

While Brindle led Starfire, Turnip, Fart, and the three still-unnamed horses, together with Moap, to a more grassy spot for the night, the others erected their tents in a wide circle, leaving a spot for Brindle's tent. At the center, Ereben cleared the ground down to bare earth, then collected stones, to build a small fire ring for cooking. He had come to appreciate how rarely they would be able to eat a cooked meal on their journey.

Sawney Burn returned with an armful of small twigs. "Tell me now, Ereben Leaf, what destination draws ye through such blighted times?" He coughed.

Ereben looked at the others, none of whom appeared to object to his discussing their objectives. Minkar was the only one to actually nod his consent to Ereben. "It's *because* of the blighted times. We believe that the wide and careless use of magic is bringing about all of these unexpected changes."

"I huv heard o' wizards in e'ery town an' village."

"That is true. They have enough knowledge to cast many spells of magic, but not enough knowledge to understand the unintended consequences of those spells."

"Like what? Bad weather?"

"The counterspell. Every magic spell that is cast creates an imbalance in nature. Unless the counterspell is taken into account, the counterspell is unpredictable. It can be nearby or far away, but a counterspell always causes changes in the way things are. I can use magic to move this stone, but in order to maintain the balance of nature, I must also plan a source from which the force of that movement will be drawn."

Ereben removed his dagger from its sheath at his hip, and pointed its tip toward one of the stones in his fire circle. He focused on two tasks. In addition to moving the stone a hand's width from its present location, he directed the force for that movement to come from the substance of the rock itself. The dagger's milky green, Jadeite handle glowed slightly, as the stone seemed to move itself.

"It shrank!" Sawney said, his eyes wide. He cleared his throat. "Yer sayin' the shrinkin' o' the stone is the counterspell ye intended."

Yassar Khayin's eyes were also wide. "I have known of the counterspell, but never witnessed it."

"I would just move that little rock," Ja No said, "with my fingertip."

The others chuckled.

"Of course," Ereben replied. "But if I chose to bring down a rain shower onto the fire we see burning on the south rim, the counterspell would be equally impressive as such an alteration in the weather, and far more dangerous to ignore."

Brindle, who had heard only the tail end of the discussion, reached down to the fire circle, and returned the displaced rock to its place in the fire circle, then set about erecting her own tent. "So many foolish people all across the lands, are casting magic spells, and messing up the weather. We're hoping to find some answers about how to fix it from a bunch of ancient books that are hidden at the bottom of the Canyon. They're written in Shadae, and Yassar here can read Shadae."

Ereben was about to add further comment, but instead just pointed to Brindle, and nodded with a smile.

The morning sun had barely risen above the horizon, when they approached the trail that descends from the north rim of the Canyon. Ereben dismounted.

"We will have to go down on foot," he stated, "and lead our horses."

Sawney Burn rode to the edge of the precipice, looked down into the abyss, and at the frightening trail, then proceeded to ride Moap slowly down the steep treadway.

"I believe that is unwise," Minkar advised him.

"Horses kin spook, an' stumble o'er the edge," he replied, as he continued downward on the softly wheezing Moap. "There be nae sort o' cajolin' or spookin' or e'en commandin' what would convince a mule to commit sich a foolish act. Mules are stubborn that way. Moap'll do fine."

Ereben had never given that aspect of a mule much thought. He followed on foot behind Moap, while leading Starfire down the treacherous trail. One by one, each of the others led their horses downward, while Ja No, for the first time, walked in front of Fart, and led him by his halter rope.

As the sun rose higher in the sky, hot wind began to sweep up the canyon wall and over the trail on which they descended. The group seldom spoke, as they moved downward. Ereben kept his eyes on the treadway ledge, which was usually broader than it felt. But he found the view disconcerting in that a vertical cliff rose to one side, while the other dropped nearly vertically into the abyss.

When they reached a seep spring that Ereben had recalled, Ereben suggested that they all refill their water skins.

As Minkar parted the verdant vegetation that surrounded the spring, he lamented, "There is no longer standing water here. Only wet mud."

Ja No sat beside the spring, and used her hand to scoop mud into a spread portion of the hem of her long gown. Beneath it, she held her open water skin to collect the water that dripped through the fabric. When she was done, she waved to the others to bring her their water skins. Again and again, she dumped out the mud from the fabric, then scooped up fresh mud from the bed of the spring, until everyone's water had been refilled.

She then scooped out a deeper trough from the damp soil and gravel at the base of the seep, to allow water to slowly create a puddle. One by one, they led the livestock to it for a drink.

It was only after that, when Ereben resumed the downward trek, on foot, that he noticed a distant glimpse of Death River, mostly hidden by rocky outcrops. It was dry. "The river has no water flowing, so far as I can see from here."

Sawney Burn, the only member mounted, confirmed that the bottom, at least a thousands yards below them, appeared to be dry.

"Is there a spring anywhere down there?" Brindle asked.

Ereben searched his recollection of the Gnomes, Sister Zaratha and Brother Eretz Mor, who had watched the bridge across Death River. They had maintained a small cabin nearby. "Maybe. The Gnomes at the bridge may have used spring water, instead of the muddy water from the river. Neither of them was very young the last time I visited them, but they may still be there. Or other Gnomes may still watch the bridge."

"Palmer told us in Ironhole," Minkar said, "that the Gnomes may no longer exist in the Legion Dunes. If that is so, would they yet maintain a watch over the bridge?"

They pushed downward, with the hope of locating another spring after crossing the bridge. Ereben stood where he believed the trail should cross the now dry Death River. His knees felt swollen, and his thighs ached from the constant, downhill walk. He wanted nothing more than to cross the bridge, and sit down for a long rest. But there was no bridge, or even a trace of a bridge as far as he could see up and down the canyon. A jumble of boulders and small stones stretched along the river bed in both directions. He searched for the Gnomes' cabin somewhere on the far side, but did not see it. "I wonder if we missed the path somewhere."

Sawney Burn pointed to the shrubs in a side canyon. "E'ery bush an' shrub hes been scraped away aneath that line.

Harsh flood huv swept doon the river. If the Gnome cabin wes close by the water, as ye've said, that may be gone as well."

Judging from the elevation of the scarcely visible trail on which Ereben stood, the canyon had violently flooded at least ten yards higher than the previous water level. "It's all gone."

Sawney dismounted from Moap, and cautiously led the mule across the dry bed, through a maze of rocks. Though Sawney stumbled several times, Moap did not. One at a time, each of the others followed him across the river bed.

Bringing up the rear, Ja No simply stepped from one boulder to the next, like handy stepping stones, and waited patiently on each one for Fart to thread his way between the jutting stones. "There is no moving these big rocks," she observed. "What you see of them is only their tips."

Sawney led his mule to the first grassy spot upslope from the river, within the relatively small side canyon. He pointed to its western verge. "One post is all that remains o' yer Gnome cabin there."

Ereben led Starfire to the grass beside Moap, then walked across the thirty yards of the side canyon's width. There he saw a single, weathered wood post, partially shielded by the surrounding cliff wall. "I don't even see a foundation stone." His eyes followed a darker streak of sandy soil from near the remaining post up the steeply climbing drainage, to where it seemed to stop at a terminal cliff. "The spring must be up there. We can refill our water skins there, then climb the horses up to it for the night." His fatigue was too great to even consider locating the huge boulder in which he had stashed the ancient magic texts.

"Where are the texts hidden?" Yassar Khayin asked.

"Tomorrow!"

"There seem to be few choices for pitching our tents," Minkar said.

"How about right where the cabin was?" Brindle suggested.

Bahsa shook his head. "What if the river should flood during the night?"

"With no rain," Minkar replied, "and a dry river, how does it flood?"

Sawney Burn gestured upslope with his arm. "The rain o'er Knurlan an' the eastern mountain range feed Death River. Ye kinna know afore it flood."

Reluctantly, each of them unloaded their gear from the animals, and hefted it up to a modest slope near the spring. There, they set up camp, then laboriously filled their water skins from the small, shallow pool at the base of the spring.

Sawney walked down to the horses, bringing only one at a time up to the spring to drink their fill. Moap was the last to be retrieved, so Sawney stomped back down for his last trip. As the other members of the party were re-settling the horses for the night, Sawney, out of Ereben's sight, shouted, "Flood! Water's commin' fast."

By the time that Ereben had stood, and moved to a position where he could see the river bed directly, he saw Moap galloping uphill toward him. A wall of raging water, well above the level of the Gnomes' cabin foundation, cascaded past his view. Ereben and the others jogged downward, as far as seemed safe. Sawney was nowhere that they could see.

"Sawney Burn," Ja No called out.

Ereben doubted that even her Giant's voice could be heard above the rush of the water over and between the boulders. They all called his name, but there was no audible reply. Ereben looked at the others. All eyes were wide with fear, as darkness engulfed first their side canyon, then completely shrouded the wild, Death River. Sawney Burn was gone.

At dawn, they all went down to the river, now lower than on the previous evening, but still a raging torrent. The Shouda men searched a short distance upstream, in case he might have climbed to safety there. Ereben, with Brindle and Ja No, began the difficult scramble along the southern bank downstream. There was no foot path there, but a series of short ledges that paralleled the river, until abruptly cliffing out, preventing any further exploration.

Ereben stood with them on a large, pillow-shaped boulder by the water's edge. The three of them shouted his name in unison. There was no reply. He lowered his head in sadness. There, at his feet, was a deep imprint in the surface of the boulder. The imprint appeared to be what one might imagine remaining after a man had lain onto a feather bed—clearly identifiable depressions for legs, arms and a head.

Ereben realized that it was, indeed the "pillow rock" that he had landed upon, after being dropped from above the south rim by a giant vulture so many years ago. Sister Zaratha had told him that he had been willing to accept that the rock would behave like a pillow, and so the rock had complied. He knew that it was not from an inherent, magical ability on his part, but rather an openness to what is possible. Perhaps Sawney Burn had managed to save himself by being open to what is possible, even in the grip of a flash flood.

"I fear he has been dashed to pieces, and perished," Ja No said.

"That is likely," Ereben responded, "though not certain. He may have climbed out of the river miles downstream."

"That is a happier thought," Brindle added. "I'll think of him awaiting us on some distant day, should we ever cross the mouth of Death River."

Yassar Khayin paged gleefully through one ancient book after another, mumbling to himself. Ereben had located the huge boulder in which the books had remained hidden for two decades now. The boulder had opened itself at Ereben's silent desire for it to do so.

"I am separating the books into those that may be useful to you," Yassar said, as he closed another manuscript, and placed it into one of his two piles. "The others are of wonderful, historical interest to me, but would require months of quiet study."

"And the Glaive?" Ereben asked.

"What is the Glaive?"

Ereben reached past Yassar, and lifted a flat wooden box. When he recognized the claw marks in the wood as those made by his grandfather, Chrysanthus, tears immediately came to his eyes. He had not seen him since the great battle, decades ago, and had come to understand that Chrysanthus had died.

He lifted the lid of the box, revealing a gleaming, steel disk, shaped from what appeared to be four ax heads joined at their bases. Each "blade" was engraved in ancient Shadae, four words to each blade. "The Glaive of Brenden".

Yassar gasped. "The stories are true!" He gently stroked the steel with his fingertips, while shaking his head.

"What can you tell me about it?" Ereben asked.

"First, Glaive of Brenden is a misunderstanding of its true name. From its sharpened edges, one can easily see how the name of a bladed weapon was associated with it. The greatest ancient wizard of Lamblar went by the name of al Bryn Adin. The name of this legendary artifact is the Ghelaif al Bryn Adin, which can be translated as 'The cycles of al Bryn Adin.'"

Bahsa touched his finger to the outer edge of it. "If it is not a weapon, then why is it sharpened?"

"That I cannot answer," Yassar replied. He moved one book from his pile of interesting history to his pile of important books. "This book discusses the Ghelaif al Bryn Adin, which for many generations has been considered to be only a fanciful legend. Allow me to finish sorting the rest, so we can continue our journey. Along the way, I can talk about what I know of it, then spend some time reading more about it."

Ereben closed the wooden box. "So should we carry this with us?"

"Definitely."

Moap, loaded with all of Sawney Burn's gear, as well as the newly added bundle of manuscripts, passively followed the train of people and horses up the narrow trail, as unrelenting switchbacks ascended the south wall of the Canyon. If Moap missed Sawney, he had no way to show it. But Ereben felt the burden of having brought along the son of Liddie Burn, only to have him swept away. So many people and things were changing and vanishing. But Ereben was unable to focus on his regrets, or even his thoughts, since Yassar Khayin was speaking loudly enough for everyone to hear his voice, down the line of travelers.

"...his most trusted apprentice murdered him by slitting his throat from ear to ear, then vanished from Lamblar with the Ghelaif al Bryn Adin in his possession. Though al Bryn Adin had spoken of the Ghelaif to some of his colleagues, none of them had ever laid eyes upon it. And al Bryn Adin apparently never wrote about it or drew a picture of it, prior to his death.

"So the legend that al Bryn Adin had solved the puzzle of negating any magic spell, as well as a method of eliminating the counterspell, became the subject of discussions and...well...at least this one book that we just found among the trove. I had always thought it's secretive creation, followed by its suspicious disappearance was an overly convenient explanation for why there was simply no trace of so important a discovery. I am still shocked that it truly exists...and that we actually carry it in our baggage!"

Ereben gazed down at the river, farther below him at every switchback. He did not think that he would be able see or hear Sawney, even if he were standing at the water's edge waving his arms and shouting, but he had seldom seen a beach or a ledge on which a person might sit or stand or walk.

They climbed throughout the day, without a pause. He knew there would be no grazing or water for the livestock until the rim. And the trail to the south rim offered no clearings broad enough for safely pitching a tent. The jungle plateau, if any of its vegetation had survived the droughts and fires, would be more hospitable to man and beast. Perhaps Hobart's cabin still stood in its lush meadow.

Arriving at the rim, late in the day, came as a shock. Ereben had not remembered the upper trail well. But the appearance of the jungle plateau startled him the most. A nearby rivulet, tinged with green slime, trickled along the bottom of a shallow cut, where it nourished a small patch of stunted grasses and shrubs, then sank into the porous rock. But everything else within his view was blackened and thoroughly charred. He knew that he should be able to see Hobart's house in the distance to the West, yet there was no trace of it from here.

What he had previously seen only as a plateau of dense jungle was now a flat, black tableland, nearly free of living vegetation. Jagged stumps of absent trees were everywhere. When he squinted his eyes, and gazed off to the Southeast, where he knew the ruins of ancient Ephesia had been hidden by the jungle, he saw a rough distortion to an otherwise flat horizon.

"The fires are out," Ja No stated.

A slight haziness in the late day sky was all that remained of the fires they had last seen from the Canyon's northern rim, before heading down. But Ereben flared his nostrils at the intense odor of burned vegetation. Not the smoky aroma of hard woods burned within a hearth, but a somewhat acrid stink of burned wild grasses. "That's good," he replied. "I guess we should camp nearby this spring. It's water that we can see. And the animals can graze."

Brindle Meadow turned to Ereben, then looked out across the desolate landscape. "We have to cross this?"

"Yes," Ereben answered. "I've never traveled to Ephesia on foot, but I think it's about two days away."

"And water? Grazing?" Brindle scanned the horizon. "How can we do that?"

Ereben pointed to the adjacent spring. "If we can locate more of these..."

"None of us has walked across this plateau," Minkar said. "We have no detailed map—only Ereben's rough map from decades ago, and we have no notion of where the creeks and small side canyons cut through the land. All we know is that the eastern edge offers the only footpath down the cliffs, if we can find that path."

"Do we need to spend time going through the ruins of Ephesia again?" Bahsa began to unpack his gear.

"Knights of the Redeemer," Ereben replied, "and other pillagers have been through there, looking for magical items and texts. I doubt there would be anything left."

"Ephesia is so close to the eastern cliffs of this table," Minkar added, "we may as well spend a little effort there. Perhaps there may still be a water source for the old city. The one, deep side canyon shown on Ereben's map must be passed to the South. That path takes us directly to Ephesia."

As all the others began the nightly chore of unpacking their gear, and erecting their tents, Ereben stood beside Starfire, gazing over the bleak horizon to the South. He slowly turned toward the West, and to the North. Everything he recalled had changed. He expected the things of men—homes and farms and towns—to change.   But the land itself had become unrecognizable.

A sense of dread came over him. He had not felt that way since... He looked straight overhead. A bright speck in the dusk sky brightly reflected the sun that had already begun to set for Ereben. The speck circled slowly, as it increased in size, until he could recognize the silhouette of a dragon. "Hold onto the horses!" he shouted. "Dragon!"

Each of them held a restive horse. Moap was beyond anyone's reach. The mule brayed frantically, and bolted off to the East, still carrying his packs.

As the glistening beast soared lower, Ereben sensed a familiarity. He knew this dragon. The dragon knew him. Along with that wave of certainty, Ereben watched the dragon pull up, and sail off to the South. He had experienced the same feeling years ago, on this same plateau, while with his grandfather, Chrysanthus.

"Their brother who hates," Minkar mumbled. "It was the one-eye dragon. I felt his mind. He approached with hatred, then fled with fear."

"Fear?" Ja No patted Fart's flank, calming him.

"What would he fear?" Brindle asked.

Ereben scanned the sky once more. "I don't know."

"I can try to catch Moap," Ja No offered.

Minkar placed a hand on her elbow. "He has nowhere to go. We will find him tomorrow."

"Sawney was right about Moap," Brindle said. "*All* of us should have run away. Moap was smarter than the rest of us." Brindle joined Bahsa in unpacking gear. "We were just lucky."

Keeping the south rim of the Canyon in view to his left, Ereben rode Starfire in the lead. He allowed the horses to move at a slow walk, since they had just completed the arduous climb to the rim the previous evening. The sun shone hot and bright on the plateau, and a gentle northerly breeze kept the residual smoke and drifting ash away from them most of the time.

Immediately behind him, Yassar Khayin sat slumped in the saddle of his unnamed horse, allowing the animal to follow Ereben as it wished. In Yassar's lap, a large, open book held his attention. From time to time, he would softly exclaim his apparent surprise at reading something unexpected, but never looked up from the book to explain. From what little Ereben could determine from the color of the book's dark leather binding, it was the material Yassar had identified as being about the Glaive of Brenden.

All the others straggled behind, occasionally gazing out at the horizons or directly overhead. With Brindle next to last in the line, riding Turnip, and, leading Fart by its rope, Ja No was free to bring up the rear at her own pace.

Vultures had circled about, early in the morning, as soon as the updrafts from the Canyon could lift their plump bodies high into the air. But soon, all of them had located a carcass on which to feed. Dead animals lay scattered about the blackened landscape. Most of them were small or tiny—voles and rats, squirrels and rabbits. Fewer of them were common predators, like foxes and various cats. With so many animals dead from the fires, most of them were left unmolested by the carrion feeders.

Ereben veered Starfire toward what appeared to be a wild boar, killed by the fire. "We should probably check if this is edible." As soon as he said the words, he wondered if the Shouda were permitted to eat swine. "Or we could look for a deer." He looked back down the line to judge their responses.

Both Yassar and Bahsa turned to see Minkar's response. Minkar Jarad shrugged, nodded, and gestured toward the boar. Yassar and Bahsa then turned their horses toward it.

They butchered the animal, taking only as much meat as they agreed could be dried as thin strips at their next two campfires. When they were done packing the meat, everyone's hands were bloody and sticky. Ja No patted her huge hands into a nearby pile of wood ash, then dusted them off. Each of the others followed her example.

It was nearing mid-day. After once again mounting Starfire, Ereben glanced at the ruins of Ephesia, still just distant irregularities on the southeastern horizon, then scanned the areas closer to the Canyon's south rim, hoping to locate a cut or spring. About two miles distant, he saw what appeared to be a grazing horse. "Moap!" he called. The animal did not respond. Ereben headed Starfire directly toward it.

When they reached Moap, still carrying his packs, the mule paid them little attention, instead grazing on a patch of dense grass that surrounded a small spring. Ja No walked up to Moap, and praised him, lavishly scratching his neck and between his long ears.

Everyone dismounted, and led the horses to what they now called Moap's Spring. One by one, first Brindle, then each of the men thanked Moap, and patted his shoulders or flanks. Their mood of sadness and hardship faded.

"Can we just rest a bit?" Minkar asked no one in particular.

"You have my permission," Brindle replied, smiling.

Everyone found a spot of grass, and sat. Yassar seated himself beside Ereben.

"I believe I understand what I have read about the Ghelaif al Bryn Adin." Once Ereben turned his attention to Yassar, the Shouda man continued. "The Ghelaif contain the names of sixteen categories of magical spells, engraved in four rings of text. If a spell of one category is cast by someone, that spell can be negated by someone else casting a spell from the next category to its left, looking at the top of the Ghelaif. This is true on either of the two faces of the Ghelaif. With regard to the counterspell, if you cast a spell from one of the categories on face one—it says 'one" right in the center of that face—then simultaneously casting a spell from the category shown directly behind it on face two, will consume the counterspell of both."

"That's confusing," Ereben said, "but I think I understand what you've said. Unfortunately, I was never taught magic. I learned it on my own. So I generally have no notion of categories of spells. I just sense the forces and connections, then adjust them."

"I suppose it might take some time for you to clarify the nature of your magic into its respective categories." Yassar scratched his head. "Forcing the fire away from the bridge over the Iron River would be 'abjuration'."

"Or 'elemental'," Ereben argued. "I didn't really banish it. I just adjusted it."

"It may take time."

"Does the book speak of a sequence of learning magic? And what is the significance of one cycle of category names being inside another cycle? And why is it forged of steel, and sharpened as a weapon?"

"The book does not discuss those things." Yassar sighed. "The only other writings that I found about the Ghelaif concerned the rumors of its existence, and its mysterious disappearance. But it seems to me that knowing about a negating spell, and how to eliminate a counterspell is quite a lot."

"It is, indeed, a lot." Ereben searched for words. "I am grateful for what you have learned. My reservations are about myself, and my inability to utilize such a treasure effectively."

"The book was written by two authors," Yassar said. "I have read everything from the first author, but I have not read the second half of the book, by the second author. I may find more detail there, but a glance of it seems to be mostly about geometry."

Ereben smiled at him. "I have so much to learn. If my grandfather had been able to speak, that would have made a big difference. I could have learned so much from him. And from Hobart. And from Ailantha. I missed all those opportunities. Now there is nobody left, other than hordes of amateur magicians."

॰॰

The mineral Sarcite exhibits amplified interactions when grouped as five equally distant specimens on a flat surface. By contrast, the mineral Jadeite does so with three equally distant specimens on a flat surface, and this with a more profound effect.

Gedzik the Blighted: Observations of Interacting Bodies

"I cannot locate the trail down the eastern cliff." Bahsa Jarad spoke to Ereben and Ja No, who had just completed the searching of two of the five pyramid structures of Ephesia. Both had found only cowering wildlife and debris. Minkar, Yassar and Brindle had not yet come out of the pyramids that they were searching. Bahsa's task had been to scout the eastern rim of the escarpment, and find a route that the horses could navigate.

Ereben ached everywhere. The interiors of the pyramids were each comprised of numerous chambers, each with numerous alcoves, and interconnected within each pyramid by dozens of staircases. His knees throbbed. "I guess Ja No and I will help you look again. It's got to be there, somewhere."

Bahsa drooped his head, then nodded, as he turned to repeat his day-long inspection. Bahsa chose to begin again at the northernmost extent, Ereben the southernmost, and Ja No headed for the center of the escarpment edge.

Ereben had carefully inspected every notch and slope along his stretch for about an hour, when Ja No shouted out, "Come here, Ereben. Come here Bahsa."

On approaching Ja No, Ereben saw a long train of people emerging onto the plateau from below. They all wore sleeveless tunics of a coarse, beige fabric, sparsely decorated with tiny, silver beads. Each carried a large basket on his or her back. The men sported a twine headband which dangled a few silver beads at the back of their heads. The women wore no headbands. Two of the women carried infants, while several others led children by the hand. *Kasazi!*

"I have found your trail," Ja No quipped. She smiled broadly at the Kasazi, and had even dropped her massive cudgel to the ground. They looked back at her with expressions of wonder, and not of fear.

Once the Kasazi had all reached the plateau, Ereben counted about thirty of them. They seemed to be carrying all their possessions in their baskets. A middle-aged man cautiously approached Ereben, then pointed a finger at him.

"You grandson of Chrysanthus spirit man."

It had been two decades since he had been among the Kasazi with his grandfather. The Kasazi man looked vaguely familiar. "Yes. I am Ereben Leaf."

"I Pimaqua," he replied with a broad smile. Only then did Ereben notice the single, milky-red Sarcite bead in the center of his headband—the distinctive mark of their head man.

Ereben pointed to his own forehead. Pimaqua had been a young man back then.

"I now only Kasazi elder. This all of Kasazi people." He swept his bronze, bare arm toward the others. "Food not grow in Kasazi land. No rain. No water. People hungry."

"Where will you go?" Ja No asked.

"We plan to go to here. I see smoke in sky. Smoke go away. We go here."

"Do you plan to settle here?" Ereben asked.

"Yes. I see it is burned. It will grow again when rain comes. Water is here?"

Ja No answered. "There is a water well here among the ancient buildings. It has water."

"Then we live in buildings. We have maize seed and squash seed."

Ereben adjusted the twigs holding strips of boar meat well above their campfire. He and his companions were finishing a meal of meat and wheat cakes. Although the Kasazi graciously accepted some of their supplies, Pimaqua chose to move his people inside one of the pyramids. for the night, and remained there to prepare their food.

"You were talking about geometry?" Ereben reminded Yassar.

"Yes," Yassar continued. "It discusses the different geometries of various minerals. What captured my interest is a comparison of Sarcite and Jadeite. It says that Sarcite resonates with power when placed in an arrangement of five stones. Your bauxium sphere is built of nothing but many identical arrangements of five Sarcite stones, in the shape of a ball. This, it says is ideal, and the most powerful configuration possible with Sarcite, yet is the simplest method of making it into a solid structure."

"I was aware of that, but not that it was the simplest. It is how the monks of Moss Abbey had arranged their sphere of Sarcite stones to protect Ternaria." Ereben replied.

"But...with Jadeite—the stone of your dagger's handle, the geometry is different. Jadeite resonates with power in an arrangement of only three."

"I am also aware of that."

"Were you aware that the simplest and most powerful arrangement of Jadeite into a solid object is only four stones—a tetrahedron? It is made of four identical triangles, each of which shares three of the four stones. It makes a three-sided pyramid."

Ereben was stunned that he had never considered that. "Is there more?"

"Like Sarcite, the power of the solid Jadeite object increases with its size, but unlike Sarcite, the greater the distance between the stones, the heavier the Jadeite stones must be."

"How much heavier?"

"It does not say."

"It would be helpful to talk to the monks about this," Ereben mused. "But visiting Moss Abbey would take us far to the South."

"Perhaps we could travel there," Minkar proposed, "then go by sea to Almirant."

"Emerald," Brindle corrected him. "The city is called Emerald now."

"Are you hoping to make this long journey longer?" Ja No asked.

A brilliant white light flared across the night sky, brightly illuminating their surroundings, then vanished before reaching the horizon.

"Yes." The dazzle in Ereben's eyes persisted for a moment.

Grasses on the expansive, flat land south of the plateau appeared shorter than Ereben recalled, though he couldn't be certain that it was just his own, faulty memory. Their color was a dull green, though their seed heads seemed to be maturing normally. Precipitous cliffs towered to his right, and the distant forest of Whitewood could just barely be seen to the South—the direction in which they must head, in order to reach Moss Abbey.

He hoped to avoid the forest-dwelling Mohani, who had attempted to kill him and his grandfather. Perhaps forest-burning might be a better term, he thought, since they had seemed to specialize in making charcoal from the trees they felled. He would stay toward the eastern extent of Whitewood, close to where it met the deserts and swamps of Sulalia and East Graze.

The temperature was rapidly rising in the mid-morning sun. This seemed to wordlessly encourage all the members of his party to waste no time in moving toward the forest, which was still several hours away.

"What is that?" Brindle asked with some degree of alarm in her voice. She pointed to the West.

A broad, gray cloud seemed to be rising from the ground far to their west. It expanded, contracted and streamed into the sky, vaguely resembling a large flock of starlings. With a westerly breeze, the cloud appeared to be drifting toward them.

Ereben tapped his heels into Starfire, to pick up their pace. But with impressive speed, the cloud neared them, and engulfed them.

"Locusts!" Ja No shouted, as she swatted the swarms of hand-size insects from around her head.

They landed by the tens of thousands—on the grasses, on the occasional shrubs, and on the animals and their riders alike. Although they did not bite either man or beast, their size and number caused Starfire to shake his neck and head, and to accelerate even faster.

As soon as they emerged from the cloud of locusts, Ereben brought Starfire to a halt, as did the other riders. Ja No, though on foot, and carrying her massive cudgel as well as a pack, had easily kept up with the horses. Ereben turned to look back at the land of the Kasazi.

Locusts had settled out of the sky, and now blanketed every living plant in a coat of glistening wings and frenzied, yellow bodies. As Ereben watched, the green of early summer seemed to fade from the landscape, in a swath many miles across.

While Moap and the horses grazed among the tall, green grasses just north of Whitewood Forest, Ereben looked beyond them at the odd pattern of damage among the pine trees. A quarter-mile wide path had been created by trees snapped off at the ground, and apparently flung about randomly. The damage receded into the forest in a curving course, vanishing in the distance. "What kind of storm does that?"

"Maybe a whirlwind," Ja No replied.

Bahsa grimaced. "I've never seen trees tossed in all directions like that. Does a whirlwind do that?"

"There are few trees in West Graze," Ja No replied. "But what else could it be?"

"If we travel beneath the trees, but close to the damage," Minkar suggested, "then we can easily step into the open to get our bearings along the way to Moss Abbey."

"Look at the standing trees," Brindle said. "Look at how many of them are brown or partly brown, like they are sick. They just don't look like healthy trees."

That evening, camped in the grassy plain north of the forest, Ereben studied the Glaive of Brenden, with Yassar assisting with translation of the ancient Shadae. He tried to make sense of the implications of Yassar's revelations about the relationships between the spells. It still did not make a lot of sense to him. And likewise, Ereben's attempt to explain why the Glaive itself was created as a sharp-edged, steel weapon, was futile.

At dawn, they packed up, and headed into Whitewood Forest, following a southward path a hundred yards west of the swath of damaged trees. Up close, many of the standing trees revealed countless holes through the bark, each the width of his little finger. Ereben saw no unusual movements of insects about the trees, but he assumed that they were infested in some way that was killing them. Along the way, they crossed a number of small creeks that still flowed.

Just before dusk, the swath of damaged trees abruptly ended. Minkar guessed that they had traveled twenty or twenty-five miles since entering the forest. There they made camp near a clear creek that flowed among the standing trees. Over their fire, Minkar prepared a stew of boar and potatoes for everyone to share.

Before the stew was done cooking, a group of seven people, dressed in Mohani garb of leather trousers on two men and boy—all three shirtless, and leather tunics on three women and an adolescent girl, paused at a short distance beyond Minkar's fire.

One of the Mohani men motioned for the others to remain, as he walked toward those sitting about the fire. He held up two empty hands. "Peace."

Ereben allowed a hand against the dagger at his hip to relax. "Welcome to the Mohani."

"We bring a gift," the Mohani man said. He lifted an empty hand to his side, which appeared to signal for the boy to walk forward holding what appeared to be a freshly skinned and gutted rabbit, suspended by twine about its hind legs. The boy looked up to the Mohani man, who then pointed toward Minkar. The lad carried it to Minkar, who had been stirring the boar and potato stew, and held the rabbit forward."

Minkar looked over to Ereben for guidance. "Thank you," Ereben said, pointing toward the small stew pot. "Will you and your people join with us for a meal?"

The Mohani man smiled broadly. To Ereben, all of them appeared somewhat gaunt, with wide eyes. He suspected that the rabbit might have been the only food they had, to share among the seven of them.

"We could just cut up the rabbit and mix it into the stew," Ereben hinted to Minkar.

"Of course," the Shouda man replied.

"Come and sit with us." Ereben swept his arms to indicate the circle around the fire.

The Mohani leader again smiled, and gestured for his people to come and seat themselves among their hosts. "I am called Little Moniku."

"I'm Ereben, this is Brindle Meadow, Ja No, Minkar Jarad, Bahsa Jarad and Yassar Khayin." He intentionally avoided his own full name, and buried it among the other introductions, hoping that Little Moniku, whom he had met as a boy, would not connect him with their previous encounter.

"Are you a Giant?" the Mohani boy asked of Ja No.

"I am," she replied. "Come sit beside me."

"Can I sit beside you too?" the teen girl asked.

Ja No patted the ground to either side of her crossed legs. They both seated themselves, and stared up at her in amazement. Ja No spoke to them in a most motherly manner, and softly told stories of where she had grown up, and entertaining experiences in her past. Brindle Meadow shuffled over to join them, and added some of her own stories of growing up in Naneland.

After another day of travel, they reached the path that separated the pines of Whitewood Forest from the ancient trees of Oldwood. To the West lay Oakvillage of the Mohani, which Little Moniku had said was now mostly abandoned. To the East lay the great Troll city of Timbul, at the eastern verge of the grassy hills of East Graze. Directly south of the main trail, another led to Moss Abbey, which Ereben hoped to reach by tomorrow afternoon.

The Mohani had been friendly. Talking with them by the campfire, Little Moniku provided a discouraging picture of the state of the trees of Whitewood, and the recent disruptions of the seasons, making it difficult for them to raise enough food. Likewise, the abundance of wild game in Whitewood had diminished, frustrating their hunting and trapping. The Mohani head man felt confident that if his small group continued their wanderings through Whitewood, rather than attempting to settle in one spot, they would be alright. They had said their farewells late that evening, and had not been seen since.

They made camp just beneath the tree canopy to the north of the trail, pitching their tents in a circle about their fire. Moap and the horses were tied at the trail edge, where grass seemed to grow in greater abundance than he expected for a well-traveled footpath. Apparently, he guessed, trade between the Mohani and the Trolls of Timbul had greatly diminished, if not ceased entirely.

"I shrunk both of us to the size of a Fairy," Ereben explained, for those who had not heard the story before. "That was the easy part. Life among the Fairies and Thistlepix was subject to dangers that we never consider, often from tiny creatures that we seldom notice. And they were engaged in constant war with one another. They had mastered the use of bees and wasps and even tortoises for transport. While they had longbows and crossbows, the most common weapons were raspberry pikes—those sharp bristles that prick our fingertips."

"How big is Ternaria?" Yassar asked.

"I don't really know. I was too little to make sense of such dimensions. But probably very small, by our concept of a territory." He recalled how close he had come to being killed by the queen wasp, before his grandfather had roused him from his enchantment. "When we reached the southern boundary of Ternaria, and I returned us to our original size, the magic sucked the life out of both plants and creatures within a wide circle about us. That experience of causing so much death, in order to replenish my life force remains with me as a reminder to always consider the counterspell."

While the fire grew dim, they chatted about the Abbey, and the dedication of the monks to maintaining magical wards surrounding Ternaria, in order to shield it from the outside world. Ereben had supplied them with an abundance of Sarcite, to replenish the stones on their huge, pentalphic sphere. But that had been decades ago. And the volcanic eruption that had followed the release of the Sarcoptis, had also destroyed the Sarcite mine to which the Fairies had regularly journeyed, to collect and transport the magical stones to the monks.

Ereben knew well that his identification of the warding stone at the mine entrance, and Chrysanthus' subsequent removal of it—in order for Ereben to enter the mine, unleashed the tremendous stresses that had been held in check within the mountain. He was responsible for the release the imprisoned Sarcoptis beast. He was responsible for the loss of the Monks' only known source of Sarcite, when the mountain erupted. He shuddered to think of all the less obvious catastrophes that his use of magic had brought about. He spoke about it all for the first time. By the time he finally climbed into his tent to sleep, his usual body aches, together with his seething sense of guilt over having caused so much grief, kept him awake until well into the night.

The afternoon of the following day, they approached the gardens and compound of Moss Abbey. To Ereben's dismay, the gardens appeared mostly barren, and the building itself seemed to be in a state of disrepair. The shallow cupola beneath which the monks tended their pentalphic sphere showed missing rain slats on one side.

"I'll go in and speak with the Abbot." Ereben dismounted from Starfire, and walked up to the building. He found the heavy door closed, but unlatched. It creaked as he gently pushed it inward.

"Is anyone here?" he called. Some debris littered the hallway. A crash of falling furniture sounded from the Abbot's study, its door wide open.

When he approached the open doorway, he saw two ringtails struggling in opposite directions, to free themselves from what appeared to be rope harnesses attached to a wooden contraption that lay on the floor.

"It's okay," a tiny voice said. The ringtails relaxed.

Ereben watched, as a group of what appeared to be Fairies ran over to the ringtails, and spoke with them as one might speak with a pet dog. They patted their legs, and scratched their chins, talking all the while. The Fairies, no taller than the length of Ereben's little finger, were dwarfed by the cat-sized ringtails. As soon as both of the ringtails were released from their harnesses, the pair scampered past Ereben, and disappeared down the hallway stairs.

"Your voice frightened them," a white-haired Faerie said.

Ereben squatted. The Faerie who had spoken, unlike his dozen Faerie companions, seemed to have no wings. "I'm Ereben Leaf. I had hoped to speak with the Abbot. Can I stand this back up for you?" He pointed at the lashed, wooden thing that the ringtails had apparently toppled in their panic.

"That would be nice." The white-haired Faerie pointed toward a point on the floor beside the towering book shelves, which held numerous books bound in assorted colors of leather.

Ereben stood the contraption on its wider base. Upright, it appeared to be a lever arm derrick. He followed the Faerie's hand motions, until it was placed where he wanted it. In one corner of the study, the floor was covered in a single, tidy layer of closed books, arranged like paving tiles.

"My name is Wisfel. Are you the famous Ereben Leaf who visited Ternaria many years ago?"

"Yes."

"I've heard many stories about that. Did you come here alone?"

"I have five companions with me. They are waiting in the north garden, with the horses...and a mule."

"We have to lower a book to the floor, in order to read it. We take turns walking along the pages, reading aloud to the others."

While Ereben and his companions were preparing a meal in the fireplace of the study, Wisfel explained to them that the monks no longer lived at the Abbey, because of the drought that prevented them from producing enough food for them to eat, or enough water to drink. He agreed to guide Ereben and his companions to the monks in the morning.

"It doesn't matter if the vegetables we can grow here are runted, since every pea or bean goes a long way." Wisfel spoke from atop a stair-step stack of four books that Yassar had place for him. Two other Fairies, both with dark hair and Fairy wings, sat alongside him. "And the little water we collect from the roof drain is enough for us."

"Why don't you just live in Ternaria?" Brindle Meadow asked.

"Ternaria no longer exists. When the monks could no longer protect it with their magic—that's been...four or five years now, humans and large animals destroyed all the Faerie villages. Humans built a single house in the lands of the Thistlepix, and cut down all the thistles. Every one. And they burned out the wasps. There are no more Thistlepix anywhere."

"What has happened to all the Faeries?" Ja No stirred the large cast iron pot in which their dinner cooked, though her attention was fixed on Wisfel.

"Most of us perished. Those who survived now live in the basement here—twenty of us altogether. We have heard about an isolated island, to the Northwest, that is uninhabited, but it is very far away from here. The Abbot, Maha Jalaj, has promised to make us a map small enough for us to carry."

"How large is the island?" Ereben asked.

"Huge. Maybe bigger than Malagaro—that big island east of Shibam. We would need to find only a tiny bit of it that would be safe for Faeries. But the seas that separate the island from the mainland are said to be always stormy. That's why it is still uninhabited. We would have to devise a way to get across."

"I've lived in Valand much of my life," Ereben mused, "but I've never heard anything at all about what is beyond the great Western Mountains. No stories. No people. Nothing about it. I always assumed there was just a coast at a vast ocean."

"Oh no," Wisfel replied. "There is a large expanse of land, with many people. At least, that is according to Maha Jalaj's map. He spread it out on the floor, and I walked across it. The western land is as broad as the eastern lands."

"That would seem a long distance for Faeries to travel," Bahsa said. "It would take you years."

"I am thinking it would be about a month, riding our ringtails."

"Ringtails?" Bahsa asked.

"Oh," Ereben interjected. "I didn't mention to you that they have ringtails that follow their instructions."

"I don't know what that means." Bahsa shrugged.

"They're kind of long and thin raccoons, I think." Ereben said. "I thought they just lived in deserts."

"But raccoons are vicious, and bite people." Bahsa seemed skeptical.

"We raised the two of them since they were tiny kits," one of Wisfel's companions said. "An eagle carried off their mother, and we found the two kits. They are as tame as a tortoise."

Wisfel continued. "One liked its head scratched, and the other one liked its rump scratched, so we named them Headie and Tailer." He smiled broadly, apparently proud of their clever naming.

As the sun rose, Ereben and his group followed Wisfel, who rode alone on Headie, easily guiding the ringtail with dusted, braided spider silk reins attached to a halter. They moved generally eastward along a scarcely worn trail that wound beneath the massive oaks of Oldwood. Moap and the horses stepped with care and precision between the hefty roots that intruded into their path. Headie scampered along in front of them, frequently stopping on the crest of an oak root to turn and wait for them. Ja No seemed to exert the most effort, orienting and reorienting her giant feet to the continually changing angles between splayed roots.

After about half a day of travel, they approached a cluster of nearly identical, small, red-roofed cottages, built in a circle, with flagstone paved spokes connecting them. Vegetables had been neatly planted in the wedges of soil between them. A small creek trickled nearby, vanishing from view among the trees to the South. Ereben identified the early growth of carrots, peas, beans, squash and cabbages in the garden plots. Several fruit tree saplings were beginning to leaf out, in the clearing beyond the ring of cottages.

"That is the head water of the Nettle River," Wisfel said, pointing, "but the Monks call it Nettle Creek."

Ereben recalled how the Nettle River seemed so substantial a waterway, cutting mostly north to south through

Ternaria. In retrospect, it was always no more than a minor creek.

They rode a short distance south of the cottages, and left Moap and the horses there to graze, and drink from the creek.

"I was just a novice when Ereben Leaf visited Moss Abbey," Maha Jalaj explained to the group of visitors. Five other monks had joined him in the sparse parlor of his cottage, all interested to meet Ereben and his companions, and to hear of the events in distant parts. On one wall hung a huge map that depicted, as Wisfel had said, a continuation of the land mass to the west of the Great Western Mountains of Valand. One of the monks had unrolled a miniature copy of the map for Wisfel. Its width was about twice that of Ereben's thumbnail.

"This was a challenge to create," Maha Jalaj said. "We all took turns with a drawing brush made from a single rat whisker dipped in ink. The work had to be done beneath a drop of water resting in a pinhole. Even then, we had to leave out much of the detail."

Wisfel repeatedly looked from the small map to the map on the wall, until he appeared to be satisfied with the copy. "Thank you all for your labor on this. I will carry it back to Moss Abbey, so we can make a decision." He rolled up his new map, waived to everyone in the room, then departed.

Ereben pondered the value of having such a map for himself. "Maha Jalaj, would you have a spare sheet of vellum that I could use to make a copy of your map?"

"I am afraid we have very little vellum remaining, and only in small squares. But I have a simpler solution." He rose from the wooden stool on which he had been seated, and rummaged through a collection of rolled documents that leaned in a corner of his parlor. "If you don't mind its being scribbled with notes and corrections, I still have my original map here somewhere. Ah...this one." He partially unrolled it, then shook his head. "It is indeed messy." He handed the scroll to Ereben. "You may take this if you like." As Ereben spread it out on the floor, Maha Jalaj continued. "I started with a map drawn by a Sulalian jeweler in Shibam. Though distorted, it was generally correct, but it simply stopped beyond Valand and West Graze. While we still had use of the sphere, we expended some effort exploring what we could see of what lay west of that. So our map is based on no actual journey on foot. It has only what we could surmise from visualizing it with the sphere."

"Thank you." Ereben passed the scroll to Minkar, for his examination. "Why was Wisfel so interested in the Northwest island? It seems an unreachable destination for the Faeries."

"Because we ourselves are interested in establishing an enclave there, against the rapidly increasing corruption of Nature that is gripping everywhere."

"Wouldn't that effect the island as well?" Brindle asked.

"The advantage," Maha Jalaj replied, "is a rather technical one that is best not to discuss."

"Each of my companions is well aware of the issues of magic and of the counterspell," Ereben said. "The entire purpose of our journey is to understand how to remedy the magical corruption of Nature."

Maha Jalaj looked to each of his fellow monks. When none appeared to object, he took a deep breath, then began to explain the five-sided geometry of positioning Sarcite stones, and their formation into a sphere. "But with Jadeite, of which we have none, a solid can be formed with only four stones. The challenge is that to create a large zone of protection, those four Jadeite stones must be positioned equidistantly around and above the zone, and be impossibly massive."

"The geometry!" Ereben shouted. He turned to Yassar. "I had hoped they would know about it. And they do!" Again speaking to Maha Jalaj, he asked, "How does that island relate to the Jadeite?"

"The Northwest island is nearly triangular, with a mountain peak close to each corner. That in itself is quite odd. But even more significantly, there is a high, central peak that has an elevation that is equal to the distances between the other three peaks. The four mountain peaks form a massive tetrahedron—the geometry required by Jadeite. If a sufficiently large Jadeite pillar could be placed on each of those four peaks, then Nature within in—that is nearly over the entire island—can be permanently shielded from what is exterior to it."

"Does such Jadeite exist?" Yassar asked.

"The only known source of Jadeite is mined on the island of Malagaro, off the southeast coast from Shibam. We do know that the Malagarans have mined solid pieces of adequate size in the past, for their religious shrine."

"How large?"

"The computation is murky...but columns a yard across, and five yards high is our consensus. Four of them, one for each mountain peak."

"How could you move even one such large stone?" Ereben asked in disbelief. "And how could four of them ever be transported to such a distant location?"

"And Wisfel understood that the seas were constantly violent around the island," Ja No pointed out.

Maha Jalaj raised both hands. "We are monks of Moss Abbey. We understand certain things. Transport of large objects over land and sea are not among those things. We have not addressed how one might raise such stones to the peaks of mountains, nor how one might appropriately install them there."

After discussing the Jadeite and the island and the transport a bit more, Ereben asked Yassar to fetch the wooden box containing the Glaive of Brenden. Ereben explained all that he had learned about it to Maha Jalaj, and his hope for further understanding of its meaning and its use, and why it might have been created of sharpened steel, and in the form of an apparent weapon.

The abbot read its engraving carefully, flipping it from one surface to the other repeatedly. The Glaive was then carefully passed to each of the other monks for a similar inspection, until it returned to the hands of Maha Jalaj. "I have difficulty conceiving of magic in the manner categorized on the Glaive. The arrangement seems clever, and with some logic, but I fear that I am unable to deny or endorse what you attribute to the positioning of the terms. And I know of no reason for the choice of materials or its weapon-like shape." As he looked to each of the other monks, one by one they shrugged and shook their heads.

"I'm not sure that we learned anything useful," Ereben lamented to his companions, as each of them pitched their tents in darkness, beneath the trees south of the monks' enclave. Ereben had insisted on not intruding on the their limited cottage space for the night. The livestock had been repositioned a bit further downstream, beside fresh grass.

"We did learn about the geometry," Yassar observed.

Ereben felt a sudden malaise. "A dragon!"

Ja No covered the ground between her tent and Moap in five giant steps, and held him by his face strap. A loud swooshing sound approached from the South, low over the treetops. A dazzling flash of fire filled the air above the ring of cottages, setting them all ablaze. The dragon rapidly circled back. Maha Jalaj appeared to be the only monk to exit a burning cottage, but the abbot was immediately engulfed in a second gout of flame from the dragon's mouth. As the dragon passed above the trees over Ereben's head, it seemed to look down on him with recognition.   And then it was gone into the night,   heading northward.

Minkar rose to his feet in the flickering light of the fires. "We must kill One-Eye."

⤳⤶

We were forced by circumstances to choose risking the
lives of some of us, in order to avoid the likely death of
all of us, and the destruction of all that we cared about.
                    Nebridio of Lilac: History of the War
                    Against the Faerie Lord of Kizikum

"At least humans seldom come to the Abbey," Timo pointed out. The Faerie sat cross-legged on the floor of the Abbey's Longhaulers' room, below the basement of the Abbey. "And Margarida wants to stay." He paused for the laughter from some of the other Faeries seated in the circle to stop. "Well...mates have as much say as anyone." Margarida patted him on the hand.

Wisfel felt a momentary pang of the reality that he would never have a mate. As a blighted Faerie, exposed to toxic silver while still in his mother's womb, he could never father a viable child, and as the only blighted Faerie to have survived the slow demise of Ternaria, knew that he was unlikely to meet another Faerie with a Faerie child's stature, white hair, red eyes, pale skin and no wings. He had been blessed with three gifts. It was apparent to all the Faeries that he was the most intelligent among them. What he kept to himself was his unique ability, due to some quirk within his eyes, to see the radiant strands of the flows of magic.

The final gift had been given to him by the dying Tribune of Lilac, during the final days of Ternaria's existence. They were treasures that had belonged to the famous Faerie, Gedzik the Blighted, created personally for him by the jewelers of Shibam. They included an ankle-length, lavender, hooded cape, with sleeves that reached partway down his hands. This would serve him well during portions of the journey where his fragile, blighted skin and eyes required shielding from full sunlight. At his hip, suspended by a jewel-encrusted belt, hung a steel saber within an equally bejeweled, gold scabbard. And covering the front of his chest, he wore Gedzik's elaborately engraved, steel cuirass.

Wisfel had practiced using the saber a few times, but without a competent instructor, felt he could not make much use of it. It might or might not be useful to him in a difficult situation. But his skills with a raspberry pike were so poor, compared to the other Faeries, he decided to bring the saber along, rather than abandon it forever in the deserted Abbey.

Quiri stood. "Once, we depended entirely on the magical powers of the monks to keep us safe. Then they failed. And Ternaria was destroyed." He looked down at Laia, his mate, and smiled. "We need a place where there is hope; where there is a future. Yes, we get by on the scant food and water that we find here at the Abbey, but both steadily decrease from one year to the next. There is no hope of a future here. We can depend only on ourselves." He seated himself again.

Of the twenty Faeries, eighteen were mated pairs, while the youngest of them, Albric—just barely an adult, had yet to find a mate, and would surely never find one near his own age. There simply were no other Faeries, beyond those seated in the circle. He slowly rose to his feet, looked into the eyes of each Faerie in the circle, then spoke in a crackling voice. "Look at all that's left. There were thousands of Faeries. There were farms and vineyards and towns. Now there are only twenty Faeries, huddled together in this space beneath the basement of a humans' abandoned building. Is this where we have decided to blink out of existence?" He sat without waiting for a reply.

When no one else spoke, Wisfel stood, and walked to the map he had tacked to the wall. "There is no longer any place that is protected by the monks. There is no place that is more dangerous, because of our size, than any other place. So the core question is this." He pointed at Moss Abbey on the map, then swept his hand toward the Northwest Island. "Is staying here worse than the journey to find a new home, or is the journey worse than staying here? We could surely remain here for at least another year, but then our time to undertake a long journey may have run out."

"But none of us," Timo protested, "not even the monks, know what is there. Who is there? What dangers would we face in such an unheard of journey? What would we find if we actually reach that island? How many of us would still be alive by then? I just can't see taking that risk."

"One choice we don't have the luxury of making is for part of us to go," Wisfel said, "while the rest remain. You know my preference, which is to go, and soon. You must all agree on one answer. I will be up in the Abbot's study."

Wisfel was startled from a troubled sleep by a hand on his arm, jostling him. He had fallen asleep part way through the long paragraph on which he now sprawled. It took a moment for him to realize where he was.

"We go!" Quiri was saying. Laia stood by him on the floor of the study. The wings of both of them were held higher than usual.

"What does that mean?" Wisfel asked.

Laia smiled broadly. "We've persuaded everybody. Everyone has decided to go."

"How late is it?"

"It's nearly morning," Quiri answered.

"Did you decide on how soon?"

"It got so late that we agreed to decide that within a day or two," Laia answered.

Wisfel sat on the nape of Headie's neck. Looking back over his shoulder, he counted the nine other Faeries who rode with him, Albric seated immediately behind him. Two large pack harnesses, one just behind Headie's front legs, and the other in front of his hind legs, each filled to bursting with all their belongings and food supplies, separated the Faerie passengers in to three groups. All of them faced forward, except for the very last rider—at the tail, who held a crossbow, and faced toward the rear, watching for predators, while leaning back-to-back against his mate. Each of the forward facing males kept at least one raspberry pike ready to hand, though Wisfel carried no weapon other than the saber beneath his robe.

By this, the afternoon of the third day since departure from Moss Abbey, everyone's fascination with Oldwood, through which Headie carried them at a rapid pace, continued to keep their eyes looking up to the impossibly high, ever changing canopy, or deep into the forest to either side. Within clear view from Wisfel's perch, when Headie's long, black-ringed tail was not blocking it, he could see the other ten Faeries, similarly divided, riding Tailer, not far behind. Quiri held Tailer's reins.

So far, the weather had held. By taking refuge at night in shallow caves formed by some roots of the massive oaks, and traveling only during daylight, Wisfel felt the risk from a predator who might enjoy a ringtail for a meal would remain low. Since Headie and Tailer truly preferred to be out and about at night, he kept them tethered within their impromptu shelters.

He had posted an armed rider at the rear of each of them during the day, and relied on all the other eyes to watch the sides and front. Not that he believed that a bolt from one or even both of their crossbows would injure an owl or wolf or wild cat. He understood it as a minimal, unexpected distraction, that might enable the ringtails to flee with their riders—up a tree or cliff face, or beneath a root. But Oldwood seemed to be home to very few animals and birds.

The forest, in every direction, was free of undergrowth, small shrubs and flowers. Only the colossal, ancient oaks appeared to thrive, though he recognized many varieties of oaks among them.

Fortunately, Headie and Tailer were happy to eat anything that would fit in their mouths—insects, snakes, voles, berries, bird eggs, and did not require the Faeries to carry a food supply for them. By their nature, they should also readily eat Faeries, but they had bonded to Faeries from the time their eyes had first opened. Maybe a Faerie was simply too small a morsel for them to bother with. Either way, Wisfel could not have considered this journey without their assistance.

Margarida, seated back-to-back with Timo, who held a crossbow at the rear of Headie, called out. "Wisfel. Look at that cave on the left."

Wisfel brought Headie to a stop. In the distance to his left, he saw a substantial cave created beneath a kink in an oak root. "I thought we might go a bit further, before stopping for the night."

"But it looks so spacious, and well sheltered," Margarida added.

"That is a nice one," Timo said.

After several other passengers voiced their agreement, Wisfel conceded. He guided Headie to the cave entrance. "It does look like a good spot." He turned to Quiri, who had halted Tailer behind them. "Stop here for the night," he called out. "Unload. Then we'll walk Headie and Tailer to find their dinner."

Since all the Faeries could hear Wisfel's instructions to Quiri, both ringtails were free of passengers, and nearly free of their packs, before Wisfel had made it down to the forest floor. After carrying his own gear into the cave, which was spacious enough for all the Faeries to spread out their sleeping spots, yet still have room for both the ringtails to be tethered at the rear, he and Quiri again mounted Headie and Tailer, in search of something for the animals to eat. They leisurely wandered about.

"Lizard!" Quiri shouted.

With whiplash acceleration, Wisfel held Headie's reins in one hand, and grasped a fistful of neck hair with his other. Somehow, he remained on the neck of the prey-focused animal. The attack of the lizard by the two ringtails ended in a blur, with part of the lizard in Headie's mouth, and the remainder going to Tailer. Wisfel relaxed.

One more fit of feeding on yet another small reptile completed the evening's husbandry duties. They headed back to the cave.

As they neared, the entrance seemed different. Timo stood inside the entrance, pointing at a lifting in the soil just outside the cave. "Mole!" he mouthed silently.

All the Faeries inside the cave withdrew into its farthest recesses. The soil parted as a pile of crumbled earth. Wisfel was immediately tossed into the air, somersaulting off Headie's neck. He thudded onto the forest duff. When he regained his orientation, and looked up, Headie and Tailer were tearing apart a still living and combative mole—a creature twice the height of a Faerie, and one that would promptly eat a Faerie, if given the chance. This mole was not.

Most of the non-edible parts were left scattered about the cave entrance by the ringtails, who rested nearby, licking their paws and faces, and were surely satiated now. Wisfel considered the bloody mess.

"Sorry," he announced to the others. "If we stay here tonight, we'll be awake the whole time, driving off the ants. Load up!"

Midway through the following day, they emerged from the western edge of Oldwood Forest. The sunlight was blinding. Many of the Faeries suggested that they stop at the boundary of the trees until morning, to give their eyes time to adjust. Wisfel encouraged them to continue westward. He knew, from the map of Maha Jalaj, that they could reach the southern coastline by evening. That would take them south of the Legion Dunes, which, in the best of times, was said to be impassable by Faeries, and surely by the ringtails.

Wisfel now wrapped his fragile body in Gedzik's lavender cape, unrolled the cuffs of its sleeves to cover most of his hands, and pulled the cowled hood over his head. The remarkable, Sulalian fabric blocked the sun, while allowing a breeze to easily pass through.

The ringtails carried them westward, over parched prairie, under a hot sun. Views from the ringtails' backs were nearly the same in every direction other than straight up, into a cloudless sky. Wisfel felt more vulnerable to aerial predators and large reptiles here. Perhaps there were also wolves and other hungry animals. He saw no motion, as he scanned the horizon.

The shadows grew longer. One of the Faeries shouted, "The sea. I think I can see it."

All eyes turned to the left of their path. In the distance to the South, a flat expanse of blue extended to a misty margin with the sky. To Wisfel's eyes, the sea seemed to shimmer.

"Should we head toward it?" Quiri asked from his seat at the reins of Tailer.

"I don't know," Wisfel replied. "It seems too soon to have reached the bay shown on the map. Unless the map distance is not correct."

As they discussed the decision, the sea vanished. Nothing but dry prairie extended to the South. Wisfel could not explain what they had witnessed. What was certain to him was that the transient image of the sea was not magical. Wisfel, through a quirk in his misbegotten eyes, could see diaphanous filaments of magical force—the intentional adjustment of Nature. There was no magic here.

"Bird!" Margarida shouted, pointing westward.

With the sun in his face, Wisfel looked up, but could not see the bird clearly. He leaned back. Suddenly a hovering kestrel seemed to brighten its sun-shadowed breast. The bird of prey abruptly veered away, and vanished.

"What just happened?" Quiri asked.

Wisfel thought for a moment, then realized that his steel cuirass had been exposed from under his lavender cloak, as he leaned back. He leaned back again, almost into Albric's lap, then held his hand up to the direction of where the hovering bird had been. The reflected sunlight shone on his palm. "I think my breast plate flashed sunlight in its eyes."

They continued on at a faster pace. The kestrel had not returned. As the sun was about to set, they reached an area of tall grasses above a short, barely flowing creek that fed into an expansive bay to the South. Locating a suitable spot windward of a fat hummock of grass, they set about establishing their camp for the night, with a full view of the dark blue bay. Wisfel had been told in Lilac that only the crew of the Faerie ship, Luli Shibami, which sailed the lower Nettle River, had ever looked upon the sea, decades earlier.

The landscape along the top of the bay dropped from a verdant, gradual slope of green grasses and low shrubs to a steeper, rockier plunge of about 10 yards, down to a narrow beach of coarse, brown gravel at the water's edge.

Laia struggled in a brisk breeze to keep from being tossed into the stand of grass by it. "Maybe we should set up on the other side of this, Wisfel."

"According to Maha Jalaj, winds coming from the sea change to winds coming from the land, after sunset, then change back after sunrise. We'll all get to see if that is true."

Timo stepped beside Wisfel, and spoke softly. "So what do we do if that Kestrel comes back tomorrow? I don't think our crossbows will do much, and there really is nowhere for Headie and Tailer to hide out there."

"I don't know."

"Maybe we could tie flags or long banners from the tips of their tails." Quiri had joined them.

The three Faeries looked at one another, then began to laugh.

"What's so funny?" Margarida asked.

Wisfel dropped his head on his chin, then turned and smiled at her. "Just three lost Faeries trying to think of ways to scare away that kestrel tomorrow."

Margarida shrugged. "Everybody just flaps their wings, when it shows up. That's got to look pretty strange to a kestrel."

"And fire our crossbows at the same time," Timo added.

"I'll try to flash my breastplate as well," Wisfel said, self-conscious of his freakish lack of wings.

The attack came at mid-morning. Timo, riding crossbow on Headie noticed the kestrel first. They had practiced the ruse three times this morning, before departing from their grassy campsite. "Kestrel!" he shouted.

"One...two...three...four...*five!*" Timo called out.

As the kestrel began to drop toward them from its hover, all the Faeries began wildly flapping their diminutive wings, while bolts from both crossbows were launched. Again, the kestrel broke off its attack, and flew northward.

A cheer arose from the twenty Faeries. Many of them congratulated Margarida on her ingenuity.

They saw no more of the kestrel throughout the rest of the day. But when the sun was just a fist above the western horizon, and with the southern extent of the Legion Dunes appearing in the distance to the North, Timo once again announced the kestrel's return, and began calling out the count.

Wisfel immediately realized that there was no effective way to reflect the sun from his cuirass toward a kestrel in the opposite direction, without removing it from his chest. The kestrel seemed to ignore the frantic wing flapping of the Faeries, and the distraction of two crossbow bolts launched at it. The bird continued its rapid descent toward them.

A small, moving shadow partially blocked the sun in Wisfel's eyes during the instant before the kestrel snatched Tailer. But with the predator within the reach of a raspberry pike above Tailer's back, a massive bird plucked the kestrel from its flight in mid-air, and flew away with its thrashing prey toward the East. As their salvation gained more altitude and distance, Wisfel recognized it to be a goshawk, easily triple the size of the kestrel held in the lethal grip of its talons.

Neither Headie nor Tailer had been aware of the kestrel during any of its three attempts, but they both reacted sharply to the passage of the goshawk, Headie darting abruptly to the South, Tailer to the North. Several Faeries tumbled from each of them. By the time Wisfel had brought Headie under control, the fallen Faeries were dusting off their clothes.

The two ringtails appeared relieved to rejoin one another, snuggling a bit, while all the Faeries climbed down to the surface of the prairie, and just sat down. No one spoke. They turned blank stares to Wisfel.

He looked over the area surrounding them. Nowhere nearby seemed more secure than any other for a campsite. "I guess we'll have to set up here for the night." His voice trembled.

Still no one moved. Wisfel stood and began to unlash the forward gear harness of Headie. When the gear slid off from below the ringtail's shoulders, and plopped onto the dusty ground, he moved on to undo the rear gear harness. As the second bundle of gear landed, Quiri slowly stood, and began to deal with the two bundles of gear lashed to Tailer. Gradually, the other Faeries silently joined in the labor of unpacking and arranging things for their evening meal of seed and water.

Some located individual shrub leaves that might serve as a shelter for one or two. Others just laid out their belongings in the area between Headie and Tailer, in preparation for sleeping in the open for the night.

Eventually, the Faeries began to discuss the recent events and the reality of the risks to them in undertaking this journey. Wisfel was generally not included in those conversations. Since he had grown up aware of his exclusion from many Faerie activities, from both his extreme sensitivity to sun exposure, and his abnormal appearance and short stature, he did not regard this evening's exclusion as a condemnation of his leadership.

"If you think about it," Wisfel overheard Quiri softly saying to Laia, "the kestrel saved our lives."

"It tried to capture Tailer three times," Laia replied.

"But if the kestrel wasn't up there," Quiri explained, "then that huge goshawk might have grabbed both of the ringtails—one in each claw."

"So what about the rest of the time we have to ride out in the..." Laia's voice faded to inaudible.

Wisfel had been pondering that very issue, ever since their narrow escape from the kestrel. They still had about five days of travel around the tip of the Legion Dunes, entirely along the coastal plain, and northward to where they might cross the mouth of the Iron River. He had no idea how they might protect themselves during that five days in the open. And beyond that, he had not been able to imagine how they might cross the powerful river—and with two ringtails.

"But you're the one who talked me into this!" Timo had raised his voice at his mate, Margarida.

"I can't help it if it's not the way Laia described it," she retorted.

When the bickering couple noticed that everyone else was looking at them, they fell silent.

As the sun rose, Wisfel stood, and spoke to the group. "Before we start out today, I would like for everyone who has an obsidian to search all these plants..." He swept his arms about. "...and cut the largest, branched sprigs that you can carry. Then bring them back here. The rest will load all our gear on Headie and Tailer, and figure out a way to tie the sprigs onto the packs. I want each pack to look like as big a bush as possible, sticking out above and to the sides of them."

"Maybe some really long pikes, too," Quiri added.

"And we could tie a little banner on the end of each one," Laia suggested. "So we can make Headie and Tailer look wider if we need to."

As everyone set about these tasks, Wisfel rigged the straps of his elaborately engraved cuirass so that he could carry it on his arm, like a shield. Then, he thought, it would be easier to reflect sunlight wherever he might need to.

Headie and Tailer seemed annoyed by the odd appendages to their backs, though they eventually turned to look at them less frequently. When they finally resumed their journey along the coastal plain, the appearance of the traveling party hardly resembled that of the previous days.

Several times during the mornings and afternoons of the following days, they spotted various predatory birds soaring or circling. With a shout from the tail riders, or any of the other passengers, the banner-tipped pikes, which were carried vertically, would be tipped to the sides. On each of these occasions, the predator would seem to lose interest, and glide away.

When Wisfel could see distant, high mountains to the North one morning, he felt that the mouth of the Iron River was within that day's ride. He increased Headie's pace, and pushed northward, having decided not to stop for the day, until he could see the opposite bank of the river.

"The Iron River!" Wisfel announced. Shielding his eyes from the setting sun, he saw a dark green line appear across the far edge of the water to the West. Although he had still not solved the question of getting them and their ringtails across, they had all discussed the possibilities the two previous evenings. Their arrival here felt like a victory to Wisfel, despite the new challenges.

"I hope that means we're stopping here," Quiri shouted from Tailer's neck. "These poor animals are starving."

"Yes." Wisfel pointed to a nearby clump of shrubs a short distance from the gently lapping water. "There's a creek here too, just ahead." A gentle slope rose to a knob just above them, obscuring a clear view of the prairie to their east.

All the Faeries dismounted, and those with long pikes stood them against a branch. The instant that the fancifully decorated packs were removed from Headie and Tailer, a fat lizard sprinted past them, and up the knob. The two ringtails bolted eastward.

Wisfel knew from experience. He shook his head. "When they're really hungry, there is no calling them back, until they've filled their bellies.

In the darkening shadows beneath a leafy shrub, the twenty Faeries arranged their belongings, prepared their dinners, and gradually gathered into several groups for conversation.

"Maha Jalaj told me that a ringtail can swim," Wisfel explained, "but only when forced to, and only to the nearest land. So they're not going to swim across, and certainly won't tow a raft across."

Timo shook his head. "You're saying that we have to build a raft huge enough to fit two ringtails. We don't even have the right tools to make a small raft. We have rope. We have our obsidian blades."

Laia stood. "If we leave the ringtails here, then we have to walk so far that we'll never get there. We have to bring them."

"Maybe we could locate a log or something," Quiri said, "that they could ride on. Then we just tow it."

Timo rolled his eyes. "Twenty Faeries on a tiny raft are going to paddle hard enough to tow a log? Across this?" He pointed toward the water. "I think we should have figured this out before we started."

"It was not a decision about whether we had resolved every possible difficulty of this journey." Wisfel never liked for these discussions to descend into a question about the choice to find a new home. "The decision was about whether or not we could survive at the Abbey for more than one more season. I think we made the only decision possible."

Loud hissing sounded from the darkness somewhere east of their shrub. Then high-pitched screeches and growls of unmistakable, animal combat ended in total silence.

Every Faerie stood, looking into the black landscape upslope from the water's edge.

"Tailer?" Quiri shouted. "Tailer!"

"Headie!" Wisfel called. When he began to walk into the darkness, toward the source of the commotion, Albric held him back.

"It's not safe, Wisfel." Albric turned Wisfel to face him. "We need you. If they're not back in the morning, then we'll look for them. But not now."

"Headie and Tailer are pretty resourceful," Quiri added. "They have either escaped and hidden somewhere, or they didn't make it. Either way, we won't find them tonight."

Wisfel endured a fitful sleep that night. He frequently sat up and squinted into the darkness, hoping to see the ringtails. Albric had positioned his sleeping spot between Wisfel and the upward slope leading toward the missing ringtails. Twice when he had awaken, he noticed Albric also awake, and facing him, with concern on his young face.

When morning came, he felt exhausted and fearful. Headie and Tailer, littermates, had been an important part of his life since they were first discovered, and brought to Moss Abbey. And they had an important role yet to play in their effort to reach the Northwest Island.

As a group, and carrying their long pikes, all the Faeries walked slowly up to the top of the knob. Wisfel wore his steel cuirass, and carried his steel saber in his right hand. From the crest of the hill, Wisfel looked down at the motionless body of one ringtail, its neck clearly broken. Nearby, a scant trail of blood paralleled footprints of what appeared to be a fox. The dark drips and the prints vanished eastward. Tears blurred his vision.

♦

Our deeply held desires to relive our treasured recollections of people, places and events, that seemed to be among the best moments of our past—even though such recollections may overlook our trials and pain during those halcyon days, may motivate us to attempt a reversal of the intervening events that seem to have destroyed that past. Or it may cause us, instead, to construct from nothing a fantasy of how it should have been.

Gumushtigin: Philosophical Meanderings

"The sooner we reach Emerald," Minkar said to no one in particular, "the sooner One-Eye dies." He finished packing his still unnamed horse.

Ereben had never seen Minkar Jarad so agitated. His Shouda companion had been the first to rise this morning, and had wandered alone through the ashes of the Monks' cottages. Minkar had always argued that if they killed One-Eye, then the remaining five dragons would become implacable enemies of all mankind.

Minkar mounted his horse, and rode eastward, alone on the trail that would eventually lead to the magnificent, Troll city of Timbul. Nobody else had yet to complete their packing.

"Do you think your father is alright?" Ereben asked Bahsa.

"He has argued since the Great War that we should not injure the dragons," Bahsa replied, as he assisted Yassar in folding the tent they shared with Minkar. "He refused to talk last night. He just seemed to be boiling inside."

"Is it safe for him to ride out alone?" Brindle asked.

"He is a Shouda warrior."

Ereben and his companions had traveled eastward for several hours, with no sight of Minkar Jarad. To his surprise, Minkar's still unnamed horse stood alongside the trail, grazing, yet Minkar himself was not there. Minkar's gear was still tied on.

"Minkar," Ereben shouted. There was no reply.

His horse happily joined the other horses, without needing to be encouraged or led. They continued forward on the trail for another half hour, periodically calling out Minkar's name. When they finally came upon him, they found him sitting against an oak near the trail. He waved to them, but said nothing. The party dismounted, and tethered the horses.

"What happened, Father?"

Minkar looked up at his son, then eventually said softly, "I have named my horse Wiser. I saw a serpent in the path, and chose to chase it away with Wiser's hoofs. But Wiser showed greater wisdom. He bucked, and threw me off, then ran back down the trail, rather than approach the serpent."

"Were you injured?" Brindle asked.

"I appear to have bruised my arm." He pointed to his right forearm. "So I decided to rest for a time. I slept poorly last night."

Ja No squatted next to him. "Let me see your arm." When he lifted it slightly toward her, apparently with some pain, she supported it with one huge hand, then gently touched it in various spots. She carefully tugged on each finger, exhibiting remarkable delicacy with her plump fingertips. "There are two long bones in your lower arm. You have broken the one that leads to your little finger."

Brindle approached with a handful of sticks, and tied them about his forearm with the twine. With the sharp edge of her steel mattock, she cut a generous corner from the bottom of her white caribou cape. This she wrapped about Minkar's forearm, then around his neck.

Minkar grimaced. "Thank you, Brindle Meadow. That feels much better. I am a fool."

Bahsa assisted his father in standing, and handed him his spear. "Committing an error does not make a man a fool, but failing to learn from it does. You have said that to me often, over the years, Father."

"Then I have committed an error, and learned a painful lesson. Help me to mount Wiser."

Bahsa supported his father in seating himself onto Wiser's back, while Ja No held his reins. Minkar motioned to his spear, which rested against the tree. Brindle placed Minkar's spear into his left hand, which also now gripped Wiser's reins. The party moved on, heading toward Timbul, without discussion of the implication of Minkar's injury.

Their passing from Oldwood Forest to the rolling grasslands of East Graze was not as abrupt as Ereben had imagined it would be: stately hardwood trees giving way to the drier climate. Instead, Ereben observed a belt of increasingly sickly trees, until the final margin consisted of nothing but dead and broken tree trunks. The eastern edge of Oldwood was dying.

East Graze appeared as drought-stricken as the worst areas that Ereben had seen on this increasingly grim journey. Carcasses of small animals, and occasionally those of larger ones lay sparsely scattered over the grassy hills. These were plentiful enough that many had completely desiccated before any predator or carrion fowl had noticed it. All day, fresh, dry winds blew from the East.

There had been little conversation among them. Just prior to sunset over the hills west of them, they halted on a rise. Below them, in the distance to the North, the complex, multi-story architecture of the Troll city of Timbul glowed as a golden vision of timeless stability and civilization. Ereben and his companions collectively and silently had chosen this rise to camp for the night.

While Brindle and Ja No cared for the horses, Bahsa took it upon himself to prepare a meal for the entire party. Ereben and Yassar wandered together to locate dead scrub brush with which to build a cooking fire.

"After all this, I feel that we haven't accomplished anything, Yassar." Ereben paused with an armload of small wood. "I don't have any idea how to fix the imbalance of nature, and I can't really see how the Glaive of Brenden can help me with all that."

"But, Ereben Leaf, we have assembled all but one remaining component of the Dragon Armor. You will still need to forge the pronged ax, but you could do that in many towns."

"The pronged ax is completed. I forged it years ago. I carry it within my pack. My walking staff is its blood locust haft —already sized and shaped as my grandfather's drawing indicated. So we are missing Jasper's helmet."

"That is a surprise! And Minkar Jarad has finally come around to recognizing that at least one of the dragons must be killed."

"So we are closer to killing a dragon, but no closer to salvaging the damaged bonds of nature."

"But you have learned of a way to enclose an entire island within the protection of a field of magic."

"You mean the giant columns of Jadeite for the Northwest Island?"

"Yes. If all of the lands are ravaged, there is no purpose in returning to Valand, or for me to return to Shouda. Lamblar, the home of my birth, cast me out. And the land surrounding the shrine deteriorates further each year. Yet, I cannot resign myself to wandering endlessly, like the desperate people we have seen all along the roads."

"I don't know that I'm ready to give up on everything and everybody, just to cower on a remote island with a few, select friends. And the Jadeite. We have no idea if such huge columns of Jadeite can even be mined at all. One yard wide and five yards long...four of them. I think the monks were just imagining their required size, without considering how anyone might mine them and then...and then transport them. How fragile would they be? It seems beyond hope that four columns of stone would all arrive at their destination undamaged. At least in Rippleton, I have a place to be."

"You had a place to be. Is it still there? Has it already been pillaged or burned to the dirt? For how many more seasons will the land there produce enough food for you to eat?"

While the cooking fire burned down to coals, and Bahsa was about to begin cooking, a young couple called out to them, and approached slowly. They carried no weapons, though each bore an empty sack over the shoulder.

"I don't mean to impose on you folks," the man said. His female companion looked at him with an expression of worry.

"Come and join us," Bahsa said.

"No. No. We wouldn't do that. I was wondering if you might have some extra food supplies that you could sell to us."

"We have coppers," the woman added.

Ereben was puzzled. "Timbul is only a half day away. We're headed that way tomorrow, and you are welcome to accompany us."

The young woman grimaced. "They eat horses in Timbul."

The man placed his hand on her shoulder. "What my wife is trying to say is that there is no food for sale in Timbul. The city is nothing but vicious fighting by...factions, I guess you say...for the past year. They don't have a market any more."

"The Trolls are fighting with one another?" Bahsa asked.

"Trolls are just one of those...factions."

"What else are there in Timbul?" Bahsa seemed truly surprised. "Timbul is nothing but Trolls."

"They got the growers," the man said. "They're Albians, like us. But the biggest faction is the Clothheads. I think they're all criminals from old Sulalia. My father said they just slowly moved into Timbul after the kingdoms fell, when I was little."

Brindle introduced herself to the Albian woman. "What did you mean, when you said they eat horses?"

"I heard that the famine got so bad that the Clothheads killed two Trolls who were guarding their giant, white horses, then slaughtered every animal for food. Every one of them. And then the war started in the city. They couldn't even butcher all the dead horses, before some of them just rotted there in the paddock. Everybody's been fighting ever since."

"It's pretty dangerous as you get close to the city now, specially if you're carrying valuable stuff. You can sometimes find some regular food there," the man added, "but nobody will take copper or silver. They only take some other kind of food, or sometimes useful things, as a trade. Our harvest from last year was poor, and it's all used up. We didn't even bother to plant this spring, because it's too dry for the seed to come up."

"Look at that!" Brindle said, pointing into the dark sky to the North.

A spot of bright light soared northward across the dome of the sky, growing ever larger. Then is vanished a quarter of the way to the horizon.

"We're seeing a lot of those," Yassar said. "And another one!"

A second bright light nearly followed the path of the first, but became even brighter, with a visible tail of flame. Instead of just vanishing, this one burst into numerous flaming pieces, which individually fell in the same general direction, before vanishing well above the horizon.

After a pause, a brief but deep rumble sounded in Ereben's ears. He also could feel it in his body. No one spoke, but instead held their heads toward the night sky, waiting for more. The night remained dark, as his eyes once again accommodated to the soft glow of the cooking coals.

Ereben ushered the two Albian farmers to a place near the cooking fire. "We will not sell you food. We will give you a small supply of what we have. But only after you sit with us, and share the meal that Bahsa Jarad is preparing. And I would like to learn more of what you know concerning Timbul and Sulalia."

"If killing One-Eye," Ereben said to Minkar, "is important to you, my friend, then it's a task in which the rest of us can't help in any way. Only one can travel to the dragons' island, and only one can wear the Dragon Armor, and carry the two axes." Ereben had repeated and elaborated on the discussion that he and Yassar had the previous evening. Their guests had departed immediately after sharing dinner and further tales of harrowing events and circumstances. Now Ereben and his companions were striking their tents, with the golden glow of sunrise sparkling off the great buildings of Timbul, resting like a beacon on the northern horizon.

"I believe I must do this, Ereben Leaf. Will you return to Rippleton? Where will the rest of you go?"

"I've decided to go to Malagaro," Ereben said, "and see if it is possible to obtain the Jadeite that the monks described. If that is not possible, then I may wander back to Rippleton. But if it is possible, and a means of transporting the Jadeite can be arranged, then I will travel to the Northwest Island with them, and make an attempt to establish a place of safety against the corruption of Nature. With either possibility, I am not hopeful."

Minkar looked directly at Yassar Khayin. "And you?"

"There is nothing for me in Shouda. I will accompany Ereben Leaf, and continue to study the materials that we have gathered."

"Brindle?" Ereben asked.

"Naneland is no longer my home, and Rippleton was a good home for precious few years. I will go with you to either destination. The bond of friendship is powerful."

"Ja No?"

"As with the others, I no longer have a place to regard as home. I will go with you to find the Jadeite."

"And what are your plans, my son?" Minkar asked, seeming to avoid looking directly at Bahsa.

"Ha! You ask me, as you sit with your right arm in bandages, and still need help mounting Wiser." Bahsa chuckled. "There is also that matter of a certain someone, who is still living in Shouda, while we roam about the land."

"You laugh at your father?" Minkar asked halfheartedly.

"Yes I do, Father." He laughed again, this time with more exuberance and conspicuous affection. "Of course I will go with you to Emerald, to get the helmet. And I will return with you to Shouda."

"After the business with the dragons," Ereben asked Minkar and Bahsa, "do you plan to remain in Shouda?"

Bahsa answered. "I think that for both of us, it will depend on the conditions we find there. Agreed Father?"

Minkar closed his eyes and nodded.

"Minkar," Ereben continued, "I believe all of the parts of the armor, together with the axes, are too much to fit into your packs...both of your packs. I think you will have to wear most of it as you continue on."

Bahsa carried his Shouda spear to Ereben, handed it to him, and took the Blood Locust staff from him. "I will carry my father's spear. He will have the golden ax, if he needs a weapon. And you now have a new walking cane."

"Look what Moap has been carrying all this time." Ja No held up Sawney Burn's iron war hammer. "Should we keep it, or leave it behind?"

The reminder that Sawney had been washed away in the flash flood of the canyon reminded Ereben of the risks each of them had taken, by joining this endeavor. "Let's keep it, for now. We can decide later, if Moap's burden becomes too great."

The others unpacked the various components of the Chamberlain's Golden Armor, and rested them beside Minkar. For the first time, Ereben pulled out the thin, layered steel head of the pronged ax, and laid it there as well.

Minkar shook his head. "My dedicated son will assist me in strapping on all this shiny stuff that Yassar says I have to wear. At least I will look the part of a formidable opponent."

"We will carry enough food to get us to Shibam," Ereben said, "and the two of you will carry the rest."

"Thank you, Ereben Leaf," Minkar said. "We will avoid Timbul, and head directly for Emerald."

A day and a half had passed since Minkar and Bahsa had headed their own way. Ereben could not rid himself of the sense of loss. Over two decades had separated Minkar's surprise arrival in Rippleton from the previous time he had seen him, at the Battle of Four Armies. Now, he thought, he might never again see him. And Bahsa as well.

The mood among the four of them, as they headed southward, toward the port city of Shibam, felt somber, almost funereal. There had been little conversation while they traveled, and very little the previous evening. Ereben still felt uncertainty about his decision to bid farewell forever to the only real home he had ever know.

He fretted over what he imagined had happened by now to his house—the house in which he had been raised. In a strange way, it felt similar to his discovery that his grandfather's smithy had been destroyed, and Chrysanthus apparently killed, despite his death turning out to be not quite true. Although realities often differed from his initial conclusions, nothing in his life since had seemed reasonable, except for those stable and predictable years in Rippleton, since the Great War.

A fleeting image of Phaena crept into his consciousness. He shook his head, refusing it any purchase. They had talked of marriage, since their their teen years. When he had awakened following the final battle of the war, she was gone, and never again communicated with him, despite his messages. He had felt too insecure in his understanding of her to travel to find her and speak with her. It would have been agonizing to confirm his fears.

All that he had learned, several years later, from Yarnish Blen, was that she had remained permanently on the twin islands of the Dryads, and had given birth to a child of someone else. At that revelation, he vowed to himself to purge her entirely from his mind. He mostly succeeded, though a stray memory popped up uninvited from time to time.

"The sea!" Brindle Meadow shouted, from her perch on Turnip. She turned her head toward those behind her and repeated it. "I haven't seen the sea since leaving Naneland."

"I think we can reach the town in another hour," Yassar said.

"It's exciting," Brindle continued. "I've never ridden in a boat of any kind, not even across a pond."

"I know of no Beddu who has ever ridden in a boat or ship." Ja No's big voice betrayed no sense of concern. "I have been told, years ago, that a Beddu cannot float or swim. They just sink to the bottom."

"I have swum across rivers," Ereben said. "I've never ridden a ship. I've seen the sea only from a distance."

"That adds up to all four of us," Yassar concluded. "None can reassure the others of a sea journey. We are all babies. Bahsa was the only seafarer among us."

"Hamsa ibn Ishaq al Gawahirgi Jubaili, at your service. You may call me just Hamsa." The stately, middle-aged Sulalian ushered Ereben and his three companions to a semi-circle of luxurious cushions which lay upon an unusually large, elaborately knotted carpet, behind his carved, wooden desk. A tiny model of a ship rested in a stand at the corner of the desk. The plastered walls of his high-roofed office displayed maps and charts.

Ereben seated himself onto a cushion, then introduced himself and his companions. "We were told at the docks that you might have a ship that might be suitable for a special cargo of stone, that needs to be taken by sea to an island to the Northwest."

"I see." Hamsa looked about his walls, then went to a canister of scrolled maps. "Ah. This one," he said, as he unrolled it onto the carpet. "Show me the island you have in mind."

"It is not shown," Yassar observed.

Ereben opened his own map, drawn by the now dead monks. "Here." He pointed to the island shown in the far northwest corner of the map.

"Hmm. Our cartographers have not mapped that area. Whose map is this that you carry?"

"The monks of Moss Abbey created it over many years. They provided me with this original," Ereben explained. "So it's cluttered with corrections and notes. But they assured me it was accurate in all the major features."

"The seas beyond the southwest peninsula are turbulent, and plagued by frequent storms." Hamsa lifted a fine brush from his desk, then placed a tiny jar of black ink onto his own map. With precise strokes, he added details copied from the monk's map. "So a lengthy and perhaps hazardous journey." Hamsa returned his brush and ink jar to his desk. "Now, tell me about the stone you hope to carry to this island. Did you bring it to Shibam?"

"Well…" Ereben began to feel that their needs had outstripped reason. "The stone is to be mined on Malagaro, then shipped from there to the Northwest Island. And I'm not sure that pieces the size we need can even be mined. But Malagaro is its only source."

"I see." Hamsa smiled as he shook his head. "What kind of stone is this, and how large will these stones be?"

Ereben removed his dagger from its sheath at his hip, and handed it, handle first, to Hamsa. "The stone of the handle is what we will mine."

Hamsa's eyebrows went up. "Jadeite!" He hefted the dagger in his hand, then flicked a fingernail against the milky green stone handle. "I have heard about Jadeite, but have never seen it before. When I was younger, I worked as a jeweler with my two cousins. We spoke about Jadeite from time, but it was one of the few precious stones we were never able to obtain."

"Yes," Ereben said. "It is a rare stone, mined only on Malagaro."

"What weight of these stones do you expect to ship?"

"I don't know. We need four solid columns of the stone."

"Do you know the measurements and shape?"

"The columns are round cylinders. Each will need to be one yard across and 5 yards long."

"Yards. Yards. Hmm." Hamsa stood, walked to the front corner of his office, and consulted a long, vertical plank of wood, marked with various lengths of carved, straight lines, each labeled in Sulalic characters. "Hmm. Yes. Yards." He returned to his desk. "One yard by five yards?" He seemed alarmed by the numbers. He again hefted Ereben's dagger, then handed it back to him.

"The weight of the Jadeite is difficult to determine, because of the steel of the dagger. I suspect it is a bit less dense than marble." The tip of Hamsa's tongue protruded slightly from between his lips, as he pondered the matter. "My guessing suggests that it is not possible. Excuse me while I compute it more carefully."

Hamsa placed a large square of vellum on his desk. With his fine brush and black ink, he drew a column. He then added measurement lines and Sulalic characters to it. What followed appeared to be a lengthy computation. Then another lengthy computation.

"My largest ship, the Rashiq, is a two mast caravel. It can carry only two of your four columns. The length and the required space is not a problem, but the weight of such columns presents the limit."

"Only two?" Ereben asked. He had not considered that the monks would overlook so important a factor.

"Each column is as heavy as seventy or seventy-five horses. Two columns can be managed, while even a third column would exceed the ship's ability. The four columns will require two separate trips. If I knew of a larger ship that might fulfill you need, I would escort you to its owner myself. But the Rashiq is the largest ship you will find on the coast of Sulalia."

"Two trips." The obstacles to Ereben's plan seemed to mount. "How much would this cost? Two trips?"

Hamsa shrugged. "That is another consideration. Most merchants in Shibam no longer accept copper or silver. Everyone wants materials or food stores in trade. It is all confusing and unpredictable. Whatever seems to be in shortest supply is what is demanded most."

Ereben was stunned. He now had no idea how they might pay for the ship.

"Can you accept a piece of Jadeite?" Ja No asked. "A sufficiently large piece?"

Hamsa smiled, and lowered his head. He sat silently for a moment. "Agreed."

"How large a piece?" Ereben asked.

"I will go with you to Malagaro, and look at what is available from the mine, after you have taken your four columns."

Ereben was stunned at the suddenness of a resolution for this obstacle.

"Let us go together, and meet Captain Mahfud. Have you considered how you will reimburse the people on Malagaro for the Jadeite?"

ৼৡ

A surprising change in winds and rains over the past ten years has been a boon to Palladium, transforming the expansive swamps of old Paradise City into rich and productive farmland, fueling the prosperity of the city as well as that of southern Jakar. But then it all turned to cracked, dry clay.

Jasper of Nilwid: Economy of the Free Lands of Sulalia

"We have brought in two very strange Shouda men passing into our lands. They say that they are your personal friends." Atan spoke with Jasper, who was seated in what had once been considered the throne of Jelar. Years ago, the room had been filled with chairs, and converted to its current use as the Assembly of Sulalia. "One of them wears a full suit of golden armor, though his sword arm appears injured, and is held in a sling of white fur. They willingly surrendered their weapons."

The two Shouda men were escorted into the Assembly. Jasper did not recognize either of them. "Who are you?" he asked. As soon as these words were uttered, Jasper gasped. "Minkar?"

"Yes," the armored man answered. "And this is my son, Bahsa." He gestured toward Bahsa.

Jasper walked over to them, satisfied himself with shaking Minkar's left hand, then he hugged Bahsa. "Each of us has changed so much. Come and sit." Jasper ushered them to two of the chairs, and dragged a third one to face them. "You look as though you have traveled a long way. And," he said to Minkar, "you are wearing all of the Chamberlain's armor."

"The golden ax was left outside the chamber," Minkar replied.

"Actually," Bahsa said, "it is dragon armor. It is the armor one person must wear, in order to kill a dragon."

"You plan to kill a dragon?"

"One-eye." Minkar stared at the tile floor. "One person must wear it all, and carry two special axes."

Jasper noticed Bahsa's gaze had settled over his shoulder. Jasper glanced in that direction, and immediately realized that they had come to complete the suit of armor by requesting his own golden helmet. "Atan, could you please hand Minkar Jarad the golden helmet."

The Orkahti chief, Khumartakin, walked in, and hesitated on seeing Jasper engaged with two strangers. Jasper waved him over. "You may recall Khumartakin..."

❦

One plans a voyage. It is always with the understanding that it will never come about in accordance with that plan. A plan is an essential first step of hope and aspiration. A voyage without a plan is an assurance of failure.
Hamsa ibn Ishaq al Gawahirgi Jubaili: Journeys

Ereben Leaf watched dock workers lashing a wide ramp that reached from the dock to the deck of Hamsa's caravel, the Rashiq, as Captain Mahfud directed them from his position at the mid deck of the impressively long, two masted ship. The Captain's plan was to tether the four horses and the mule between the two masts, an area that extended from the face of the quarterdeck to just beyond the center of the main deck. He had arranged a fabric covering for that portion of the deck, and covered the deck planking with straw.

Blue sky, with a scattering of puffy white clouds rested above a quiet sea. A hint of Malagaro's mountain peaks could be seen on the horizon to the east of Shibam. Hamsa had predicted an easy voyage to North Port today, with a light, southwest breeze assisting in overcoming the usual current which flowed in the opposite direction.

A number of smaller vessels stood at nearby docks. To Ereben, these other docks and ships seemed inactive. Though he could see crew moving on the decks of some of those ships, they appeared to be engaged in scrubbing the decks or mending sails. Little evidence of trade or commerce buzzed about the docks, or even among the inns and other businesses of the city. There were people about, but with seemingly little purpose. Even the humble town of Rippleton had usually shown more activity. But, he reminded himself, those memories of his home town were from many years ago.

"Come on, boy," Brindle Meadow said to her horse, Turnip, as she led the gelding toward the ramp. "Easy...easy." But the horse refused to set even one hoof onto the ramp. She hitched him to a nearby post on the dock, then walked over to Fart. "Okay, baby." She scratched his forehead, and patted him affectionately along his withers. "Let's go to the ship." She led him toward the ramp, but Fart too refused to step onto the lashed ramp. She moved him away. "I don't know if we can do this."

Yassar draped a cloth over the eyes of his horse. Without a word of encouragement, he walked up to the ramp, facing the ship, and with his horse's reins held to their full length in one hand behind him, he simply walked up the ramp. The horse followed him up, and stepped onto the deck of the Rashiq. He walked him to the location indicated by Captain Mahfud, and tied the placid animal. "Ha! I name you *Shujaun*, because you are the courageous one!" He removed the cloth.

Ereben used the same technique with Starfire, and the horse easily followed him up the ramp. After tying Starfire, he descended to the dock, and was able to do the same with Fart. He turned and smiled at Brindle.

Brindle found that Turnip was now willing to follow her up to the deck, so long as he could not see the water.

"You can try that with Moap, Brindle," Ja No suggested. Then I'll follow him up.

Brindle placed a cloth over Moap's eyes. Moap immediately folded his back legs, and sat. Ja No came along side Moap, and attempted to coax him toward the ramp. No amount of cajoling or force would change his mind. Moap would not stand, until the cloth was removed. Then the mule simply would not approach the ramp.

"Ereben," Ja No asked, "do you need Moap on Malagaro?"

"I don't think so, but we might need his added strength to move the Jadeite."

"Then I will remain here with him. He may reach Malagaro, then refuse to board. He fears the sea. I have been too proud to say so, but I am not eager to board the ship either. Moap has given me his permission to stay at Shibam for a few more days. I will wait for you to return from Malagaro, while I gather my fortitude."

"If he won't board the ship when we return," Yassar suggested, "then perhaps we could sell him here, so that you can join us."

"I would fear that he would be eaten."

"I have no idea how many days are needed to mine the Jadeite," Ereben said. "It may be a week or many weeks, before we can return."

Ja No nodded.

"Because of their weight," Captain Mahfud was explaining, as he and Hamsa, along with Ereben and his two remaining companions shared a simple, evening meal in the Captain's mess, beneath one side of the quarterdeck, "my carpenter has added this port..." He pointed at a yard-wide, square port that opened inward from the stern wall. "...and will cut a hatch into the deck here..." He indicated the floor near the door. "...as well as another further fore of this one, through the lower deck. We'll have a rope rig, with tackle, so that the columns can be stored in the hold. There is no other way to get them down there, because of their length. If they ride too high, their weight will capsize us in the slightest wave."

"This is similar to designing how to fit a model ship into the narrow neck of a glass bottle." Hamsa seemed to be amused by the clever solution that the Captain and his carpenter had devised. "When will we arrive at North Port?"

"Although the wind has been ideal, we have fought the current all day." Captain Mahfud thought for a bit. "Likely tonight. We'll stand off until sunrise, to dock."

"I leave it in your hands, Captain." Hamsa appeared to enjoy all things nautical. "I am successful at managing a shipping enterprise, but my actual experience with ships has been limited to my attempts, as a young man, to build a ship suitable for sailing by the Faeries of Ternaria. Have you heard of them, Ereben Leaf?"

"We met some of them not long ago," Brindle exclaimed. "They are so tiny, but seem to master their situation."

"You have just met them?" Hamsa's face showed utter surprise. "They used to sail down the Nettle River to Shibam. We—my two cousins and I—built a special, tiny dock for them, and created an equally tiny, covered passageway into our shop. But they stopped coming to Shibam some years ago."

"The Faeries we met," Brindle said, "were living in Moss Abbey. The Monks had abandoned it, because they could not grow enough food there, and the water was too scarce."

Ereben continued. "There are about twenty Faeries left. Their leader, Wisfel, told us that Ternaria was destroyed, and that no more Faeries lived there."

"And Wisfel," Brindle added, "was a peculiar Faerie. He was smaller than the rest of them, and he had no wings."

"White hair, and red eyes?" Hamsa asked.

"Yes," Brindle replied.

"I once met such a Faerie, decades ago. His name was Gedzik. To our amusement, he called himself a "truthsayer". Hamsa smiled broadly. "We made clothing for them, and I even fashioned a tiny, steel breastplate for Gedzik. We sold them kaffee and other products that they had never before enjoyed.

One group of them sailed back to Ternaria in a ship that I had fashioned."

"Wisfel obtained a small copy of the map that the Monks had drawn—the one that shows the Northwest Island." Ereben paused to remember just what Wisfel had said about their plans. "I think they were considering traveling to that same island, where we will deliver the Jadeite columns, though I have trouble imagining how they'll travel so far."

"Tell me again, Ereben Leaf, why you are so interested in this island."

"Nature has become corrupted. We hope to establish a refuge there. The Jadeite will serve to protect the island, in a way similar to how the Monks had protected Ternaria." Ereben still found it difficult to feel hope about it. "I think the Faeries were considering it, because it is thought to be uninhabited."

"It would seem rare, indeed," Hamsa said, "for any habitable place to remain uninhabited in this day."

The sun had not yet risen, when Ereben and Brindle climbed up to the main deck of the Rashiq, which stood outside the bay at North Port. Captain Mahfud had chosen to anchor there at their arrival, since it had been after sunset. A member of the crew stood on the quarterdeck, nearing the end of his night watch.

They approached the horses, to verify that there were no problems with them. Then Ereben headed forward, to the prow, which faced the bay and the town. To his surprise, he saw not a single ship standing in the harbor.

"It doesn't look like a busy place," Brindle said, as she came alongside him.

"There is a little rowboat coming out. See it up by the shore?" Ereben could barely make out the vessel in the predawn light. He turned to the lone crewman at the stern. "There is a little boat coming toward us."

The sailor descended from the quarterdeck, to have a look, then went back, and knocked on the door to the captain's quarters. After an inaudible conversation, he climbed the ladder back up to his post.

By the time that Captain Mahfud had dressed, and walked forward, the little dory had neared. "Harbor pilot. Permission, please," the solitary individual in the boat said.

"Come aboard," the captain said. "Tie up here." He pointed to a location along the hull.

A sidelong glance at Ereben from the captain suggested that he too thought the "harbor pilot" appeared suspiciously ill dressed, in an ankle length gown that revealed no hint of having been recently washed.

"I am the harbor pilot," the man said to Captain Mahfud. "The fee for entry is two silvers. You pay me now, and I will go back to the port with your fee and your name and your purpose for coming to North Port. Then I will return and pilot your ship past the dangerous reefs." He repeatedly glanced back at the docks.

"You have dangerous reefs in the harbor?" Mahfud asked.

"Oh yes. Very dangerous. First you have to go one way, then then other, and so forth, to avoid them." Again he glanced toward the docks, but this time, his eyebrows lifted. "You pay now, and I will go."

Captain Mahfud drew three silver coins from his small purse, held them out to the harbor pilot. As the harbor pilot reached for them, the captain lifted them beyond his reach. "Wouldn't you like to learn my name, and my purpose for coming to North Port?"

Ereben could now clearly see a slightly larger, four-oar boat approaching.

"You have missed your chance," the harbor pilot said. "I will return later in the day." He spun about, descended to his dory, and rowed directly toward the coast south of the bay.

"Port Master requests permission to board," one of the three men in the larger boat said.

"Come aboard." Captain Mahfud looked at Brindle and Ereben, shook his head, then chuckled.

A tidy, middle-aged man, dressed in dark trousers and a matching blouse, climbed up to the deck. He briefly bowed to the captain. About his neck, he wore a medallion of office on a black ribbon. "I am Damti, and wish to welcome you to North Port. We saw you standing off, and wanted to learn if I can assist you in any manner."

"Thank you. I am Captain Mahfud. We have already met your impatient harbor pilot."

"We have no harbor pilot, and have no need for one."

"He spoke of reefs."

"Who is this that spoke of reefs?"

"He departed just before your arrival."

"I saw a dory move away south. But we have no harbor pilot, and we have no reefs. Unfortunately, we have had few ships since the unrest over the past few years, but all of that is over now."

"Is there any fee to enter?"

"There is an export fee, if you load goods from our port."

"Excuse me, Damti." Ereben approached the Port Master. "What did you mean by 'unrest'?".

"It is all ended now. It was the priests. They refused to pay the miners in Sur, so hundreds of them marched north, and murdered all the priests. Everyone became involved. The fighting went on and on. Now Sur is a ghost port, and the mines are deserted. People still go to the Shrine of the Doves to pray, but they say it has never been the same since the dragon destroyed the central dove many years ago."

"That all sounds tragic," Ereben said.

By now Hamsa had joined them on the deck, and introduced himself. "We have come to North Port to acquire some very large pieces of Jadeite, the milky green stone. Can you guide us to someone we might talk with about that?"

Damti's face went slack. "I fear that is no longer possible. It is the Jadeite miners who led the rebellion. Jadeite is mined in Sur, and there are no people living there any longer."

"Do you know who owns the Jadeite mines?" Hamsa asked. "Perhaps we could make some arrangement with him."

"Nobody owns them. The priests controlled them, but the priests are dead. And they were the only people who used the Jadeite. Everyone else is afraid of its power. I suppose the mines are just holes in the mountain ridge now."

"I have seen Sur on the map," Captain Mahfud said. "It is at the opposite end of Malagaro. Do you know which direction around the island offers the easiest sailing? I think we would like to sail there, and assess the situation."

"Oh, down the eastern coast, both the winds and current are usually favorable. But I am told there is nothing there."

"If we mined the Jadeite ourselves," Brindle asked, "who would we pay for it?"

"There is nobody there. Nobody owns it. There is no one to transport it to the docks. And I'm told that the docks were destroyed. The story is that a hundred miners worked for months to mine the Jadeite for each pillar used to make the giant dove statues at the Shrine. But that was generations ago, when the mines were maintained, and the sledge course to the docks was kept repaired. Your hope for mining very large pieces of Jadeite would not appear to be promising."

Two bright lights streaked through the sky, passing from the South to the North, and vanished beyond the northern horizon.

Damti shook his head. "We have seen these more and more. No one can explain them. The Governor has said that, so long as these streaks of flames go elsewhere, he will not worry about them. But I worry. They mean something. It cannot be good." The Port Master searched the faces of the visitors.

"I don't know what they are, or where they come from," Ereben said, answering Damti's tacit question.

"Thank you for assisting us," Hamsa said to Damti. "It seems as though we now have no purpose for docking in North Port." He placed three silver coins into Damti's hand. "For your family."

"We can sail now for Sur, if you wish," Captain Mahfud said to the ship's owner. "Depending on the winds, we should near the port by nightfall."

After Damti departed, the captain spoke with his first mate, who then directed the crew to weigh anchor, and set sail for the north point of the island.

"I suppose we have to directly inspect the situation in Sur, and the condition of the docks and the mines." Hamsa placed his hand on Ereben's shoulder. "It would be a pity if nothing could be salvaged of this journey."

As the sun was just setting, the Rashiq approached the port of Sur. Captain Mahfud chose to anchor outside the port, since the weather seemed fair, and the light was fading. But in that dimming light, Ereben could see what appeared to be an abandoned port. Two rotting ships rested near one half of a visibly damaged dock. With darkness, he saw no lights within the silhouette of the town.

〜⁓

When a predatory creature kills and eats its prey for its own nourishment, we usually do not call such activity evil.
                    Jasper of Nilwid: The Evil in the East

"I never saw much of Orkahtsk when I was little. It is truly beautiful." Bahsa rode his horse to the right of his father, with Khumartakin to the other side. Behind them rode Khumartakin's thirty Orkahti bowmen. They had just crossed over from Bur Nor into the southern highland of Orkahtsk.

Minkar Jarad, despite his right arm being bandaged, and suspended by caribou hide that wrapped over his neck, rode wearing the full set of the Chamberlain's golden armor—the Dragon Armor. With the addition of the golden helmet, the middle-aged Shouda warrior now resembled Menash, the armored Lamblari who fought alongside Minkar during the great war. In Minkar's left hand, he carried Barrow's golden ax, while his son carried Minkar's Shouda spear.

"The slavers captured me too when I was young." Khumartakin gripped his horse's reins in his greenish-yellow hand—a hand, like those of all Orkahtis, with only three fingers and a thumb. "It was not until after the war that I really came to know Orkahtsk. One never understands the wonder of the open space, unless it has been taken away."

A bright light flared in the eastern sky, then descended to the horizon directly to the East. After a moment, Bahsa sensed a deep rumble. The horses as well seemed to notice it. A brief time after that, he heard a soft, low pitch sound, possibly from the East as well. "We have seen more and more of this."

"It is the work of the Dryad Bane. It calls down burning stones from the sky, to strike at its foes." Khumartakin raised an arm, and signaled for his horsemen to follow him toward the apparent target of the attack.

"What is this Dryad Bane?" Minkar asked.

"No one can say," Khumartakin replied. He picked up his horse's pace. "I have spoken with two Dryads who escaped to Orkahtsk. They would not speak of what it was or where it came from. But they said that it was an evil, magical creature that has killed all the Dryads on the Twins. Every Dryad. They said it eats trees to grow stronger. And it has called up demons to serve its will. In Orkahtsk, the Dryad Bane has attacked the southeast coast, and eaten trees there. Fortunately most of Orkahtsk is treeless, until you reach the western mountains."

As they neared a lightly forested area near the coast, a scattering of about twenty Orkahti horsemen from a separate patrol fired one arrow after another at nearly a dozen human-sized creatures that ran toward them. Individual arrows seemed to have little effect on slowing their advance. Each one had two very long legs, and two equally long arms, with little torso separating them. Their heads harbored two huge eyes and a gaping mouth, filled with scores of pointed teeth. Their skin appeared to be a mottled, bright red. The only sounds they made were brief squeals when struck by an arrow. On the open ground between the horsemen and the demons, a shallow crater smoldered at its margins.

Khumartakin moved his thirty horsemen closer, and assembled them in two wide ranks, one slightly behind the other. "The demon on the right!" he shouted. Once every bow was knocked with an arrow, he said, "Now!"

Thirty one arrows launched into an arc toward the demon farthest to the right. Nearly every arrow hit its mark. The red demon squealed loudly, flailed its arms, then fell to the ground, writhing. After a moment, it melted into a puddle.

"Next!" Khumartakin called out. Again their arrows were launched, and struck the designated demon.

Beyond this mayhem, a far larger creature, with the gray color and deeply furrowed texture of poplar bark, occupied itself with eating one tree after another, growing larger with each tree it consumed. It seemed to ignore the combat.

A demon reached one unfortunate horseman who was closest to the trees at the beginning of the attack. A long, demon arm wrenched the horseman from his horse. The terrified mount galloped away. The demon then proceeded to eat the Orkahti man, bone and flesh, starting with one arm, then the next. With each bite of living flesh, the demon's size grew noticeably larger.

"Aim for the killer!" Khumartakin shouted. By the time that the arrows reached the vile creature, it had nearly doubled in size, and half the victim had been consumed. It squealed with agony, but continued its feeding. "Again!" With the second volley, the demon silently fell and melted. Little remained of its victim.

At a screech from the tree-eating creature, the remaining demons sprouted wings, lifted into the air, and flew away, in the direction of the Twins. With them, the tree-eater unfurled enormous, branch-like wings that were spanned by sagging gray skin, flapped them, and departed in the air as well.

Khumartakin rode down to the besieged horsemen, accompanied by his own thirty men. Bahsa and Minkar followed them.

"Khumartakin," one of the rescued horsemen said. "We are grateful that you came. We could not turn them. Two of our horsemen were lost. All of us have been ill."

"We saw the flaming stone fall from the sky," Khumartakin explained, "and could sense that it struck nearby. So we came."

"But you killed three of the demons. We seemed to only scratch them with out arrows."

"You must strike at only one of them, with all your arrows at once."

"And did you see the big one, the one that eats trees?"

"Yes. That is the Dryad Bane." Khumartakin glanced toward the damaged trees. "No arrows can injure that one. It seems to be the leader of the small demons. We have encountered them a number of times. Each time, there seem to be more small demons, and the Dryad Bane is larger."

"Maybe arrows with burning pitch could kill the tree eater," Minkar suggested.

"We tried that once. It plucks them out with its hands, and throws the burning arrows out into the dry grass. The arrow points hardly penetrate its gray skin. It seems to feel no pain."

"From what have you been ill?" Bahsa asked.

"It has not been serious. We have had coughs and chest rattles, but it does make it difficult to patrol the coast as we usually do."

Four of Khumartakin's horsemen rode off to retrieve the two panic-stricken horses of the Orkahtis who had died. While he awaited their return, Bahsa inspected the remnants of the three demons that they had succeeded in killing. Where each had died, nothing remained but a dank, brownish green puddle of goo. The grass immediately surrounding each puddle appeared burnt.

Once the wayward horses had been located and returned, all the horsemen gathered in a circle to honor the dead horsemen. There were no bodies to bury.

"The road through Cinnabar and Zink, to reach Shouda through the high pass seemed to be a dangerous path. I have considered crossing through Easlan Brae," Minkar explained to Khumartakin, as their party rode northward through the grasslands of Orkahtsk, two days after their encounter with the Dryad Bane and its demons, "then using the pass to its northwest, to cross the Ledge of Leopards, and on down to Shouda." He coughed.

A rain had blessed the plains all morning. Now, the sun from the mid-day sky dried their garments and horses, as the two Shouda men, together with the thirty-one Orkahti horsemen continued on.

"My advice," Khumartakin replied, "would be to avoid passing near Easlan Brae, but instead crossing farther north. Although the trail is a little more difficult, it would be safer."

"Is there a problem in Easlan Brae?" Bahsa asked.

"I'm sure you recall those of us who rode together with Jasper, during the Great War. The Dwarf, Slim Chance is rumored to have murdered his twin brother, Lucky, and now rules Easlan Brae. He often leads raiders toward Cinnabar, which is controlled by a Dwarf named Finny Burnewin. Finny has sometimes asked Gemel Masuh, our horse master, to aid him in driving off Slim's raiders."

"That all sounds like a bad dream," Bahsa said.

"These are people you know?" Minkar asked. He coughed again.

"Yes, Father. There was a time when we trusted one another with our lives. And Slim murdering his own twin brother? Things have changed more than I could have ever imagined. Very little makes sense any more."

"Da. In more ordinary times," Khumartakin said, "each of us would have changed. As I grow older, I become a different person than I was when younger. You are a different person than the slender boy I knew so many years ago. And I suppose that every evil man was not necessarily an evil boy. These chaotic times seem to offer too many opportunities to chose a hateful path."

"I will need a way to carry some of this armor in my pack," Minkar said. He coughed. "Riding in the sun has become a little too warm for me."

Bahsa looked at his father's pack, then at his own. "I can wear the breastplate. That should give you more air. There isn't space in either of the packs to squeeze it in."

"That would be helpful. Perhaps you could wear the helmet as well."

That night, Bahsa, Minkar and all the Orkahti horsemen camped at the western edge of the grassland, below the pass that he and his father would climb tomorrow. Sharing a tent with his father, he spent the night hearing his father's coughing, as well as the sounds of coughing coming from a number of the horsemen, all of whom slept under the sky.

Minkar awakened in the morning with sweat covering his forehead. "Father, perhaps we should wait here a few days, until you are feeling better."

"I can lie here while feeling ill, or I can move closer to home while feeling ill. Either way, I will recover or get worse."

"I would never accuse you of being stubborn, Father, but this is not an easy path to reach into the valley of the Shouda."

"It will be easier if you carry the golden ax, and I carry my spear."

"Yes, Father."

As Bahsa emerged from his tent, Khumartakin approached Bahsa. "I heard your father coughing. I have a number of horsemen who are also ill. How are you feeling?"

"I feel well. And you?"

"I too feel well. Do you plan to head up to the pass, or rest here until your father is well?"

"He wants to continue. So we will continue toward Shouda. What will you do?"

"Once everyone is up, I will have to judge by the capabilities of my men." Khumartakin clasped Bahsa's forearm. "It has been a good thing to see you."

"Yes. I'm not surprised that you are a leader among the Orkahti warriors."

After packing all their gear, Bahsa assisted his father onto Wiser, mounted his own horse, and waved a final salutation to the Orkahti horsemen. They headed up a steep, narrow trail indicated by Khumartakin as the correct path for the northern crossing into Shouda lands. Bahsa chose to follow his father, rather than to constantly look behind to see him.

Near the end of the day, they stopped, and Bahsa pitched their tent on a relatively level patch of brushy ground. He tethered the horses near the densest growth, though he knew it would be insufficient for them. One after the other, the horses drank water that Bahsa had poured into the golden helmet, and held for them.

Tonight there was no fire. Bahsa ate a meager, cold meal, while Minkar refused food, preferring only water with a bit of dried bread crumbled into it.

Minkar appeared to be growing more ill. He coughed more frequently, and with more force. Bahsa, by contrast, felt fatigued, but well, as he retired.

When he awoke the following morning, his own muscles and joints ached. His head throbbed. When he assisted his father in mounting Wiser, he could see that Minkar Jarad might not be able to remain on the horse. So he tied rope from one foot to the other, passing it beneath the horse, and padding it with a spare garment from his pack. With his father slumped onto

Wiser's neck, Bahsa positioned Minkar's injured arm, then passed another rope over his father's torso. He lashed the golden ax onto his own gear, took his father's spear from him, and held it near its head, in order to prod Wiser to precede him up the trail.

Light snow flurries began about mid day. Near the same time, Bahsa began to cough, sometimes painfully. He experienced difficulty catching his breath. He felt miserable, but kept climbing up the trail, keeping Wiser ahead of him. He satisfied himself with observing an occasional, intentional movement from his father.

Near the end of a seemingly interminable day of struggle and pain, goading the two underfed horses to plod upward through deepening snow, he found it difficult to focus his mind on what he was doing—where he was going. Twice, he was startled awake, and caught himself from toppling from the horse. The trail and the horses and his aches and cough faded into dream.

Bahsa became aware that he was supine, surrounded by warmth and bright light. His entire body ached, and protested at any movement, but he seemed to breath more easily. He opened his eyes.

A low, brush roof allowed sunlight between its small gaps and wisps of rising smoke. He turned his head to see low, stacked stone walls, mostly covered by hanging rugs, and a small cooking fire in the floor. A long loom stood against one wall. He looked at himself, and saw a finely woven, wool blanket. *Father!*

Bahsa painfully turned to the other side. There, sitting on a pallet, his father sipped a liquid from a clay bowl. The caribou skin that supported his injured, right arm appeared to have been neatly re-tied.

"You are awake," Minkar croaked.

Bahsa attempted to reply, but found his throat too dry.

Minkar leaned toward him, and sloppily poured a bit of broth into Bahsa's mouth, using his left hand. "Goat herders. I cannot remember it...," He coughed. "...but goat herders found us, and brought us here."

"Where are we?" Bahsa asked.

"I do not know. I awakened here yesterday."

"How long have we been here?"

Minkar shook his head. "These goat herders speak a strange language." He coughed, then sipped more of his broth. He offered more to Bahsa, who declined. "They appear to be Orkahtis with brown skin, and have all their fingers. The goats have long, long hair. And they have woolly cows that carry their burdens."

Minkar forced his feet into his boots, draped his cape about him with his one good arm, and wobbled his way out a rude, wooden door. Bitterly cold air rushed in.

Bahsa looked around the rectangular, stone shelter. In one corner, all their gear appeared to be collected. Nearby sat a heap of golden pieces of armor, as well as the clothes he had been wearing. He discovered that he was nearly naked, dressed only in undershorts. Beneath him, the thick wool of goatskins served as a mattress.

The sound of coughing outside the door signaled his father's return. To his surprise, a woman with a well-wrapped, deeply wrinkled, brown face followed Minkar inside. She smiled, on seeing Bahsa braced up on an elbow, then closed the rickety door against the cold. She carried a small, leather bag.

The woman wore dark but colorful layers of garments that draped to the floor. After rummaging at a shelf, she squatted beside Bahsa, poured a viscous liquid from the leather bag into a clay dish, then gestured for him to drink it, while uttering unintelligible words.

Bahsa sniffed the milky white liquid. It smelled like milk and goats, though not unpleasant. He sipped it, puckering at its sour note. Cold and smooth, it made him aware that he was hungry. Gradually, he consumed the contents of the bowl. "Thank you."

The woman nodded, then offered some to his father, using the same dish. Minkar, seated on his pallet, bowed slightly, then emptied the dish. Upon returning it to her, he also said thank you. She repeated the words, with a smile, and departed.

"Are the horses alright, Father?"

Minkar pulled off his boots, and stretched out, covering himself with a wool blanket. "They are well. They are penned together with a group of goats. They seem to like the goats."

"How many people are here?"

"I do not really know. Most of them seem to be off herding goats to different grazing areas. The snow here is a little too deep for the goats to find the grasses beneath it." He coughed.

"Can you tell where we are?"

"It was so peaceful while you slept, Bahsa. Now all these questions. You do seem to breathe easy. For me, breathing is still a labor, but better than it was."

"Yes. You look better."

"We seem to be just west of the pass. I see a broad valley far below. That may be Shouda land, but if it is..." Minkar coughed. "...then all the valley and the Shrine are covered with deep snow."

Bahsa was finally able to recognize the milky white columns and pyramids of the immense Shouda Shrine in the distance, and their village just beyond, both resting within the broad valley of the Shouda. He and his father had remained with the kindly goat herders for two more days, and had now traveled another day and a half. Only now had the sun shone itself, and cast shadows from the Shrine. He had never seen so much snow in Shouda.

Although Bahsa had mostly recovered from the illness, and his cough completely resolved, his father still seemed weaker, and with a persistent cough. Their path to Shouda Village was now broad enough for the two horses to walk side by side. Even then, Bahsa's conversations with his father were limited, since it seemed to reliably start a bout of coughing in Minkar. Bahsa chose to simply enjoy the cold, sunny day, as they finally approached home.

The nearer they came to the Shrine, the greater Bahsa's alarm at the dept its snow cover became. He also noticed a new encampment of impromptu tents and shacks, spreading from the northeast corner of the Shrine, toward Shardas Lake, reaching nearly half the distance to its shrunken shoreline. And his father's house. It was simply missing.

"Father, our house is gone."

"I see that." Minkar coughed.

"And the others seem to have snow-covered piles of rubble beside their doors. Can we check on Deena?"

Minkar nodded.

As they rode the horses toward the home of Deena Hidad and her father, a tall, young, Shouda woman stepped outside, and stood in front of the door, clasping her hooded cape tightly about her shoulders.

Beside Deena's house, two horses munched a pile of fodder that had been placed atop the snow within a makeshift corral. Horses had never before been kept by the Shouda people.

Bahsa swung his leg over his horse, and finally set foot again on the solid ground of Shouda, albeit snow covered. He then beckoned with a hand gesture for Deena to come and assist him with dismounting Minkar from his horse. "His arm was broken, and he is just now improving after a bout of chest rattles."

The two of them assisted Minkar to the ground. Minkar wrapped his left arm around Deena. "It is good to see you Deena," Minkar said, "And I believe my son may be pleased to see you too." He turned away, and coughed.

Deena then threw her arms around Bahsa. "Bahsa Jarad, you were gone so long, and things have become so terrible." She sobbed briefly, then sniffed it away.

Bahsa hugged her tightly. "I have thought of you every moment that I was gone."

"How is your father doing?" Minkar asked.

She sobbed again. "He has gone into the arms of Elloh. Just this last week."

"Oh, Deena," Bahsa said, hugging her more tightly.

"It was the day after your house burned."

"Burned?" Minkar made an effort at unpacking the gear from Wiser.

"Lamblari squatters moved into the empty house, and would not be driven away. They carelessly set it aflame. Two of them died there."

Bahsa and Deena then unpacked Wiser, and carried the gear toward her front door.

"What is all this?" Bahsa gestured toward one of the snow-covered heaps beside the door.

Deena kicked it gently with one foot. With a soft clang of metal, displaced snow revealed golden utensils, golden goblets, golden dishes and pots, all jumbled together. Bahsa looked at Deena, begging for an explanation.

"The Lamblaris. Lamblar has been mostly abandoned. They were all starving down there. The water stopped flowing, and the deep snows prevented their gardens from growing. At first, we thought it was wonderful to trade our food for pure gold.

But there were so many Lamblaris, and the food so limited, that they offered more and more. Then we just gave what we could spare, out of pity, and accepted their gold out of courtesy. So now it is mostly just piled outside our doors. Nobody bothers with taking any of it."

"So that is all Lamblaris?" Minkar pointed toward the encampment to the Northeast, then coughed. "They have cast themselves out."

"Mostly. And a few migrants from who knows where."

Bahsa recognized his father's bitter allusion to his being officially cast out of their pious community, decades earlier. "And the horses?" Bahsa gestured his chin toward the makeshift corral.

"Traded for food by two starving Valanders. They were the only ones who stole some of the gold from people's piles. But they died a few days later. We buried them with their stolen gold cups." Deena swung her door open with one foot, then led Bahsa and Minkar inside. "You will have to stay here. I think it was those two Valanders who brought the chest rattles to Shouda. My father was the only one in the village who died from it, but he had been ill for months already. Mostly the old and the starving became seriously ill from it. I think a lot of the Lamblaris out there died. I was sick for only a couple of days. Then a dragon came, and burned many of their tents, and killed more of them."

"Will you be my wife?" Bahsa felt embarrassment as soon as the words came out of his mouth.

"What?" Deena seemed disoriented by the question.

"I will care for the horses," Minkar mumbled. He coughed, and exited the door, looking back briefly to smile at Deena Hidad.

"I...So much is happening," she mumbled. "Yes." She hugged Bahsa tightly, then began to sob uncontrollably.

"I have one more thing that I have to do first, but when I return, we will marry."

She pushed him away. "One more thing? Return? What are you talking about?"

"There is no way to make this sound easy, so I will just say it. Father is determined to travel to the north wastes immediately, to kill one of the dragons—One Eye. He has special...magical armor that will protect him. But it will be many weeks before his arm heals, and much longer before it will regain its strength. I plan to go there in his place, and kill One-Eye."

Deena pounded on his chest with both fists. "No! Don't do this. There are many dragons, and you will just walk in and kill one of them. Then you will return to marry me? No!" she shouted, and stomped out of the common room, and into one of the two sleeping chambers.

Bahsa finished packing food, water and the head of the pronged ax into his pack, and carried it, along with the blood locust staff and the golden ax out to the corral. Neither his father nor Deena had spoken with him this morning. He wore the full set of the Chamberlain's golden armor—the Dragon Armor.

He entered the corral alone. The sun was up and bright, though the breeze chilled him. As he lashed everything but the golden ax to his horse, one of Deena's horses, an aging mare, nuzzled his arm.

"Her name is Goldie."

Deena's voice startled him. He turned to face her. He wanted to embrace her, but feared she would not allow him to do that.

"That one is Tallow. What is your horse's name?"

"I never named him."

"Then I will name him Hope." She cried, and put her arms gently around him. "If you don't come back, I will hate you forever."

"I will hate myself forever, if I don't come back. But I intend to come back. I will come back."

Minkar Jarad walked out to the corral. He appeared withered and frightened. Bahsa drew his father to the two of them. Minkar's eyes were filled with tears. After a brief embrace with his one good arm, he turned, and walked back toward the house.

"Father, Deena has named my horse Hope."

Without turning back, Minkar nodded, and disappeared into the house.

ৡৄ৶

When meeting a challenge appears hopeless, ordinary people may come together, with their generosity and their labor, and even at risk to themselves, to selflessly assist strangers. To see this occur during such dire times is a wonder.

Ereben Leaf: Chronicle of the Counterspell

Ereben stepped down the planking, onto one of the few undamaged portions of the dock, leading a blindfolded Starfire behind him. The other three horses were already beyond the dock, and tied near a grassy area. Ereben felt comfortable in the clear, warm morning in just his tunic.

Sur appeared to be truly abandoned. Numerous houses of various sizes and in assorted states of disrepair lined two crossing roads. But not a soul could be seen. Only the calls of sea birds and the voices of his own companions broke the silence.

"It looks as though we will need to locate the mine ourselves," Hamsa said, as Ereben approached his three companions, who had remained with the horses in their tall grass. "There appears to be a wooden walkway that winds up into the nearby mountains."

"It must go up to the mine," Yassar added. "Why else would it be there?"

"Sledgeway," a raspy voice said from behind them.

Ereben turned to see a well groomed, quite elderly man with a substantial paunch. He was dressed in an impeccably clean, white gown. Short, white fuzz framed his otherwise bald head.

"It was for bringing cargo from the mines down to the dock."

"I am Ereben Leaf. I had the impression that Sur was deserted."

"My name is Pomay. I am Mayor of Sur. I was born and raised here, and I have been Mayor for forty-five years...or is it thirty-five?" Pomay stared off into the distance, and made invisible hash marks in the air with his finger. "Thirty-five years. No, wait." He repeated the silent counting. "Forty-five years. I am certain. Forty-five years. I have been Mayor of Sur for forty-five years."

"Are there other people here, Mayor Pomay?" Brindle asked.

"Oh yes. Many people. Once they see that you folks have not slit my throat and stolen my purse, they will come out of their houses. No one comes to Sur any more. It used to be a busy port—hundreds of workers on the docks, and three or four ships at anchor."

Ereben looked toward the houses, but saw no one else. "Can we just follow this walk...this sledgeway up to the mine?"

"It goes up to all of them." He looked into Hamsa's eyes. "And you are?"

"You may call me Hamsa. Forgive our manners. This is Brindle Meadow and Yassar Khayin."

"Pleased. Pleased. Pleased. What interest do you have in the mines? You realize that they are all shut down. It has been that way for years."

Ereben considered how candid he should be with the Mayor of Sur. "We hope to carry four large pieces of Jadeite to an island in the Northwest. Are there any miners in Sur?"

"I see. Miners? All the miners are gone. They are all gone. I heard that all the miners who marched north, to North Port, were either killed, or just stayed up there. Of course, the road from here to North Port is a difficult one. What, between the swamps to the East and the steep mountains to the West, that is no wonder. Mostly, travel between there and Sur is by ship. Well, it used to be, anyway. But we don't see ships any more. Your ship is the first one in quite a while. And I am delighted to offer you whatever help I can provide. I have always wondered what it might be like to sail on a ship. When I was young, that seemed like a wonderful thing to do. But as I grew older, I heard more about storms and reefs and wrecks."

"Do you know who owns the mines," Ereben asked, "so we might speak with them?"

"I think nobody. I am not really sure. I understand that all the priests are dead. So nobody, I guess. Only the priests wanted Jadeite. And they are dead. So I suppose that the mines have no owner, in my estimation, at least."

"How many mines are there?" Brindle asked.

"Lots of them, I think. Every time one vein played out, they opened a new mine. There used to be just one mine, for years. Then they had to open a new one. After that, I never really kept track of how many mines they opened. One after another."

"Can you show us which mine was the last one?" She asked.

"I have never been up there."

"In all these years, you have never gone up to the mines?" Ereben found that difficult to believe of someone so old, who had lived his entire life in Sur.

"When I was little, Mama would not allow it. As I grew older, I had no interest in climbing up there. A mayor has no need to go to a mine. None at all. So, I have never actually seen any of the mines. I am afraid that is the one thing I am unable to help you with. I have just never been up there. I imagine all the mines look pretty much the same."

Ereben noticed an elderly woman, dressed in a tidy, print gown, topped with a bright white apron, walking toward them. Although she used a cane to walk, her pace was steady and brisk.

"Do you know how far it is to reach the mines?" Brindle asked her in a slow, conspicuously pedantic voice.

"Hmm. Well, all the miners lived in Sur, and went up there to work each day, and returned at dark. I was a miner when I was young.

"Have you finished your planning for the summer festival, Mayor Pomay?" the elderly woman asked, as she approached him from behind.

"Oh. Yes, yes. I do need to get back to working on that, Mahila." He turned to Ereben. "Again, welcome. And if you will excuse me, I have some important matters to attend to." He then headed toward a squat, two-story building at the corner of the intersection.

"My name is Mahila. What are your names, and where do you come from?"

"I'm happy to meet you, Mahila. I am Ereben Leaf, from Valand. This is Brindle Meadow, originally from Naneland. Yassar Khayin, from Lamblar in the land of the Shouda, and Hamsa, from Shibam."

"From everywhere. How wonderful. I have to apologize for Pomay being the first to notice you. Sur hardly has use for a mayor, so that sweet old fool is perfect for the job. He really has never learned to do anything particularly useful." She chuckled.

Ereben looked at his companions, and smiled. "Can you provide us with information about the mines?"

"Absolutely. That I can. I used to work as a miner and as a supervisor up there." She nodded. "That was a long time ago. I can tell you everything that is known about the mines. But...in exchange, the four of you will have to come to my house—in two hours—for a mid-day meal of cooked, garden vegetables and crunchy greens. Oh! And grilled beef. No arguments. That is the offer. Agreed? Ereben Leaf from Valand? Yassar Khayin from Lamblar in the land of the Shouda? Hamsa from Shibam? Brindle Meadow, originally from Naneland?"

"Well, yes!" Brindle said.

The others nodded their easy consent.

"Maybe I'll have another guest or two." She turned to depart.

"Where should we go?" Hamsa asked.

"How silly of me. I am in the light blue house. Hmm. It used to be light blue. Do you see the smithy there, with the big, open front? I am at the second house past that. I have a little, brass wind twirly near the door."

"Yes. Over a hundred of them, but they all retired from the mines years ago." Mahila served more roasted vegetables and grilled beef to each of her guests. She seemed to be delighted at having the strangers at her table, and at having prepared food for them.

"Here? In Sur?" Ereben had seen only a couple of other individuals outdoors. He placed a small chunk of grilled beef into his mouth. The meat was tender inside, but lightly crispy on the outside.

"It is good beef, isn't it? Lumo raises it, and trades it to us for the vegetables that he does not grow himself."

Lumo, Mahila's only other mid-day guest, besides Ereben and his companions, beamed a broad smile, missing one front tooth. "I can not really say that I *raise* the beef. The cattle just feed themselves, and grow." He appeared to be in his mid eighties, but remarkably fit, with a dense and broad neck, and conspicuously bulging muscles in his arms.

"Everybody has a garden," Mahila explained, "but few have the space for cattle. Lumo has all that pasture behind his smithy."

"You're a smith?" Ereben asked.

"For much of my life. Yes. I made all the tools needed for mining and woodcutting and making the sledges." His gaze wandered away. "But the forge has not been fired up for many years. No need any more. The leather of the bellows has rotted. And my tools have turned to rust. But that is the path that each of us who live so long have to accept as natural. Things become old, and fall apart. We all grow old, and fall apart as well."

"If you folks wish to mine the Jadeite that you came for," Mahila said, "we will need to repair the smithy. And yes. There are over a hundred of us still living in Sur. All of us are like the smithy—a bit broken down, but not yet dead. Nearly everybody used to work the mines many years ago. After we finish here, I will see who is interested in exercising their old bones."

"I too am a smith," Ereben said to Lumo. "Mostly tools and blades. Perhaps you and I can have a look at the smithy and the forge, and see what might need to be done. Is there a supply of iron or steel?"

Ereben could not recall ever having seen so many old people in one place. Women predominated, but there were many men among the scores of volunteers refurbishing the smithy. All of them had learned that these four strangers hoped to mine Jadeite, and carry it off to a far away island, in order to establish a refuge. And all of them seemed content to live out their last days in Sur. They were helping younger people to fulfill a hope that they simply could never share.

"Cut it to exactly the same size and shape." Lumo instructed two volunteers in replacing the large, outer boards of his bellows, while another volunteer marked a tanned cow hide for its sides. "We will fit the nozzle to your final shape, so they need to match."

"Yes," Mahila said to a small group of carpenters. "Those planks look pretty rotted. And that one as well."

Ereben gathered nearly a dozen volunteers to brush and clean Lumo's existing tools. "We won't know if they can be used, until most of the rust is removed."

"We found lots of good, iron bands on one of the rotting ships, Ereben." Brindle Meadow showed him one section, nearly two yards long, that had just been pried off. "Yassar and Hamsa have gone up to look at the mines with a group of folks, and inspect the sledgeway." She watched as both Ereben and Lumo looked at the piece of iron.

"What do you think?" Ereben asked Lumo. He was not impressed with its quality.

"It is perfect," Lumo said, then turned to Brindle. "Have them bring in all they can scavenge."

She turned to leave, then turned back. "I forgot. Captain Mahfud has the ship's carpenter and some of the crew repairing the portion of the dock at the end of the sledgeway. He said he's going to reinforce it for the weight of the Jadeite columns."

Ereben then followed Brindle out of the smithy. "Have you ever seen anything like this?" he asked. "All these people seem to love having something important to do."

Brindle smiled. Then tears came to her eyes. "Especially after all the horrible things that we've passed through. I haven't felt this hopeful for a long time now."

"We found the newest mine, with large veins of Jadeite," Hamsa explained to Ereben, "but the retired miners all agreed that they could not possibly mine pieces the size we need."

Yassar lowered his head. "They made a list of the parts of the sledgeway that will need to be replaced, and estimated the size of the sledge that would be required to move one column at a time." He looked from the newly repaired and reinforced dock toward the flurry of activity at the smithy. "If we cannot mine the columns, then all this may be without a purpose."

"Do you think the four horses can manage the sledge?" Ereben asked the three companions gathered about him.

"I think so," Brindle said. "It is a gradual downhill all the way. Everyone may need to push, to get a sledge moving, but I think the horses could keep it moving all the way to the dock."

"But how do we mine it?" Hamsa asked. "And how do we load a column onto a sledge?"

"I'll ponder that," Ereben answered. "We'll all go up to the mine tomorrow, and figure it out. We will find a way. All the rest is coming together."

Ereben Leaf placed his hand against a massive vein of Jadeite. He sensed its power. As his hand slowly sank into the pure mineral, he felt its connectedness to everything else. His vision blurred. Gradually, he began to understand, for the first time, the true nature of Jadeite—its past and its present. He weighed its forces and their range of effect. Ereben realized that four cylindrical columns were not ideal. The estimation by the Monks of Moss Abbey were valid as to the length and width of the columns he would require, in order to shield an area as large as the Northwest Island. But their power would be optimized if the profile of each column were triangular, like a long prism. He now also understood how to separate each five-yard long, triangular column from the vein in which it had formed.

Ereben reluctantly removed his hand from the milky green stone. His normal vision returned. He placed a dried, Munu mushroom into his mouth, savoring the caress of its healing properties. From the velvet pouch suspended about his neck, he carefully removed the finely filigreed, bauxium sphere, crafted for him by the Gnomish engineer, Brother Richit Mor. Placing three fingers of each hand onto six specifically selected Sarcite apex stones, he engaged the hinged rod that completed its structure as a pentalphic sphere, activating its power.

Evanescent strands of connections between all things flashed into his vision. With surprisingly small adjustments, he separated his first triangular column, and slid one of its ends out of its place of birth. The Munu mushroom had been consumed, and he now felt fatigued. He disengaged the latch of the Gnomish sphere, and sat down on the floor of the mine to rest.

Hamsa, standing nearby, initially appeared to be amazed at what he had just witnessed, but then the Sulalian jeweler slapped both sides of his head, and closed his eyes. "I have made a foolish error!" He too sat down on the floor, and began to furiously scribble undecipherable figures into the dust with his fingertip. After erasing his work, then repeating the scribbling, he shook his head. "I mistakenly used the width of the column to calculate its weight, instead of using the distance from its center to its wall. "

"What does that mean?" Brindle asked.

"As a round column, each one weighs one quarter as much as I had estimated, back in Shibam. And as a triangular column, the weight is further reduced by almost half. I feel so careless and stupid. The Rashiq can easily carry all four of them at once!"

While Hamsa had been doing his calculations in the dust, two groups of elderly, retired miners, both men and women, maneuvered two wooden derricks into position, and lifted the freshly separated column of Jadeite out of the mine wall, and onto their newly completed sledge. Starfire, Turnip, Fart and Shujaun had been harnessed, and were ready to haul the sledge to the dock.

"I think I can only manage to cut one column a day," Ereben said. "I feel pretty drained."

Captain Mahfud, standing at the rear of the quarterdeck of the Rashiq, directed his crew members, along with volunteer assistants in guiding the fourth column of Jadeite into the rear hatch of the Captain's Mess. Men and women tugged on ropes from the complex tackle that had been rigged to the yard arm of the main mast.

Ereben and his companions watched from a grassy area just off the dock. The four horses grazed leisurely beside them. The final column had been cut the previous day, and this morning, Ereben had cut four small blocks of Jadeite that Hamsa had requested, each a cube one quarter-yard to a side. His mood, and that of the others in his party, was lifted by the prospects of a successful outcome here, and the prospect of setting sail once more, tomorrow morning.

His experience with the pure Jadeite had reminded him of what the Jadeite handle of his dagger had originally looked like, before being merged with his grandfather, and with an ice leopard. Even after both had been released, the leopard and Chrysanthus had taken away some characteristics of the dagger, Jadeite and layered steel alike, and had left behind a trace of themselves.

"You seem to have had a useful visit to Sur." Mayor Pomay had approached them from the town. "I hope you and your friends will come back again soon. When will you be leaving?"

"In the morning," Ereben replied. "Thank you for your kindness." Beyond Pomay, he saw Mahila and the smith, Lumo, approaching.

Lumo grasped Ereben's hand in both of his strong, wrinkled hands. "You have brought our town back from the dead, Ereben Leaf." He wore a full length, cowhide apron.

"Tonight," Mahila interjected, "we will have a celebration for you and your friends, and any of the ship crew that would like to come."

"A celebration?" Mayor Pomay asked with delight. "What a wonderful idea! I would be happy to help you plan it."

"Why, thank you, Mayor," Mahila said. "You can be in charge of rounding up enough benches."

"Absolutely! I can do that." Mayor Pomay turned toward the town, then stopped. "Where will the celebration be?"

"At our newly renovated smithy," Lumo answered.

Smoke from a dozen fires floated in jagged columns above Shibam. Hamsa, Ereben, Brindle and Yassar hurried down to the deserted docks. Ereben carried Bahsa's Shouda spear.

"I will go to my office," Hamsa said.

"We will all go there with you." Brindle stepped up to jog beside Hamsa.

Ereben knew that Hamsa's son also worked in that same office, and conducted their trade business during his absence. Passing several cross streets, he saw few people about. And those he saw moved furtively, and carried at least a makeshift weapon. A number of dead bodies littered the paving.

When they reached the office, the door was wide open, and nobody was there. Hamsa located the map that he had copied from Ereben, and spread it onto his desk. There, he used a small brush with ink to circle the Northwest Island, and to write an unintelligible note. He pinned it to the wall.

"Perhaps my son may come back, and see where I have gone. I say that I plan to remain there, and that I wish him to find a means of reaching the island with his family." Hamsa sobbed briefly.

"Should we look for Ja No and Moap?" Brindle asked.

"Everywhere here seems mostly deserted," Ereben answered. "We could spend days looking. I'm not too worried about her ability to care for herself. I am worried about us spending more time here." He felt selfish and cowardly.

"I agree," Yassar added. "I will miss her presence and her strength."

"Okay." Brindle looked at the others. "Back to the ship?"

Despite everyone's agreement, Ereben felt no less responsible for bringing Ja No so far away from the lands that she knew.

They hurried through the streets, back toward the dock. When it came into view, Ereben witnessed the crew of the Rashiq driving off a gang of eight or ten marauders with nothing more than cargo hooks and belaying pins. With two Shouda spears and Brindle's mattock, Ereben and his three companions marched onto the dock.

"Leave, or you will die!" Brindle shouted.

The ragged group of men abruptly fled.

꼭◦어

Not one of us will be allowed to hear the end of the story.

Yassar Khayin: A Place of Peace

Bahsa Jarad, in his full Dragon Armor, had ridden as far as the northwest ridge above Shouda Village. As the path approached closest to the spot where he had witnessed his mother's death in the jaws of a pack of Silver Wolves, when he was a small boy, he dismounted, and climbed to the crest, to remember her.

He felt grateful that he could no longer envision the event itself. Its traces had faded to some inaccessible corner of his memory. "I miss you, Mother. I miss you every day. I am going now to try and kill a dragon. I may not return. But it has to be done. This one dragon continues to kill people who have caused him no harm. Father would have gone, but he broke his arm. That will take a long time to heal. So I am going to the far north now. I love you."

Bahsa headed back toward Hope, waiting patiently on the trail below. As he neared, Hope's nostrils flared, he neighed loudly, and fled toward Shouda Village, carrying Bahsa's supplies with him. Bahsa followed Hope, but at only a walk, discouraged by the delay. As the trail came out from the tree canopy, a dragon lighted gently in its treadway.

The dragon looked directly at Bahsa, who presently held no weapon other than Bat Slayer at his hip. "Bahsa Jarad," a profoundly deep voice rumbled, "please pause and speak with me."

Bahsa froze in his steps. Having been told of the size of a dragon since he was a boy had not prepared him for the truly massive size of the dragon standing before him. He instantly recognized Splendor by the ring of scar about his neck. His father had spoken often of his discussions with the dragons. His heart pounded. "I am humbled to meet Splendor." Bahsa's voice felt feeble.

"Are you the son of Minkar Jarad?" Splendor asked, with a proper, though low pitched Valish inflection.

"Yes, Minkar Jarad is my father. How do you know my name?"

"My ears hear everything, whenever I approach a village. I hear every conversation, even when whispered. I hear them all at once, yet can untangle them if I wish. And, of course, you wear Minkar Jarad's golden girdle, which I scratched with my own claw."

Bahsa sensed that his mission had been revealed. His chin trembled slightly, in the presence of the magical beast. "What would you like to speak with me about?" He could not control his rapid breathing.

"You require something that I can provide to you. And in return, you must provide something for me." Splendor settled down onto his elbows and knees. His unblinking eyes, each the size of a man's head, faced mostly forward, and directly at Bahsa. "Oh. Your father and your spouse to be have just discovered your horse outside their house. They are quite concerned."

"I do not understand your offer."

"You wish to kill my brother who is angry—One Eye, you call him. I and my other brothers have concluded that he must be stopped. But we will not kill him. Is that not your plan?"

Bahsa returned Splendor's gaze unflinchingly. "Yes."

"With the Dragon Armor and the two axes?"

"Yes."

"You have unique courage, Bahsa Jarad—unique among all men. But you cannot reach our island on your horse. I will carry you there on my back. But I wish only one thing from you."

"What is that?"

"Return to your village, and collect all the golden articles that all of your people have heaped outside their doors. Place them all in pile upon enough pieces of fabrics to support their weight. Just one pile, and tie it into a bundle. I will carry that with me, when we travel to the island. I want all of the gold that was brought up from Lamblar."

Bahsa thought about Splendor's bizarre proposal. "Yes, I will do that."

"Place the filled bundle well away from people and animals. Perhaps near the center of the Shrine. I will come when it is ready."

At that, Splendor sprang high into the air, and lifted toward the North. Bahsa sat on the trail to calm himself, before heading back, on foot, toward the house of Deena Hidad.

Before making it halfway back to Shouda Village, he was approached by Deena, galloping toward him on the bare back of Goldie. "What happened?" she asked, somewhat winded. "We were so worried."

"I stopped to remember my mother. A dragon came, and frightened away Hope."

"A dragon?"

"Yes. Splendor. He landed in the trail, and spoke to me."

"You go to kill a dragon, and one pays a visit, just to talk to you?" Her eyes were wide.

"They can hear everything spoken in a village, when they fly above it, and can understand everybody, all at once. Father has spoken of that."

"Climb up here with me, and you can talk while we ride back. Your father is worried sick."

With a hand from Deena, Bahsa vaulted himself onto Goldie, seating himself behind her. "Splendor already knew what I had planned."

Deena pivoted Goldie in the trail, then headed toward the village at a slower pace.

"He said that the other dragons had decided that One-Eye must be stopped, but that they couldn't do anything about it. He made me a proposition. Father has told of how Splendor likes to collect gold and jewels of all sorts. Splendor wants all the gold that he has seen piled up outside the houses in the village. All of it. And he wants it bundled in cloth, so he can carry it all at once. If he gets the gold, he has said he would allow me to ride on his back to the Island of Dragons."

"You just trust a dragon to help you kill a dragon?"

"That is what he said. He could have dismembered me right there on the trail. The only weapon I had was Bat Slayer."

"Bahsa Jarad, this all grows beyond reason."

When they reached Deena's house, Minkar Jarad stood outside the door. After hugs and explanations, the three of them seated themselves inside.

"Splendor is not evil," Minkar stated. "He is greedy, but has no moral rules that guide him." He coughed. "The only dragon that would have killed me without hesitation was One-Eye, but the other dragons would not allow him to come near me while I was there."

"Can I trust him?" Bahsa asked.

Minkar shrugged. "I suppose, in your place, I would trust his word. He never spoke anything to me that was untrue. To go there and kill One-Eye, yet come back alive, assumes that the other dragons will not kill you for having done it. So the words of Splendor are actually good news."

Bahsa turned to Deena. "Do you think everyone would give up their gold?"

"I think that they would not care. But I just can't explain to them your plan. Maybe I should tell them that the dragon has demanded all the gold in exchange for not harming the village. That is almost true."

"And a giant piece of fabric that can hold the weight of the gold?"

"They may be less willing to part with their rugs and blankets, but I will try."

The pile of gold came as high as Bahsa's shoulders. They had made the pile near the ruins of the black pyramid in the center of the paved, Shouda Shrine. It rested on three layers of stitched together rugs and blankets that had been wrapped up the sides of the pile, and were tied together at their corners, like a market bundle. Twenty men and women of the village circled it, then grasped the edges, and lifted it a short way off the snow, to confirm that it could support the weight of the gold. When it appeared to be satisfactory, they rested it down again. Everyone but Minkar, Bahsa and Deena, returned to the village to see the spectacle.

"Already, Splendor is descending," Minkar said. "He has been watching and listening. He even waited for everyone to leave, so that he would not frighten them."

The dragon circled lower, then lighted on the snow-covered Shrine paving near the three of them. Deena appeared stupefied.

"I greet you again, Minkar Jarad, and Bahsa Jarad," Splendor rumbled.

Minkar offered a bow in the Shouda fashion, amended by his bandaged right arm. Bahsa bowed as well.

"You must be Deena Hidad."

"Yes. Yes. I am... Yes. I am Deena Hidad. Minkar and Bahsa have spoken of you." Her voice trembled. Her chin quivered.

"Bahsa Jarad, climb onto my shoulders."

Minkar assisted his son as well as he could manage with one arm, then held his hand for a moment. Tears filled his eyes.

"I will return him here, if he is successful." Splendor spread his wings, and in a storm of wind, hovered over to the bundle of gold. With the claws of one front foot, he grasped the tied bundle, then soared into the air on his powerful wings.

๑๛

We were surprised at how suddenly so much of what seemed enduring had descended into general chaos before our eyes. For the rest, for the parts and places and people we could not observe, we assumed only the worst.

Ereben Leaf: Chronicle of the Counterspell

Ereben firmly grasped a railing for stability, as he watched the four horses struggling against their tethers, in a panicked effort to flee the pitching and rolling deck of the Rashiq. Brindle Meadow, who stood behind him had moved to calm the frightened animals, but Ereben had held her back.

The ship had set off from Shibam a week earlier, in both following currents and fair winds. They had traced the coast westward, and eventually passed the mouth of the Iron River, and now were making toward the southeast peninsula of the western lands. But the winds and currents had suddenly become chaotic.

The crew struggled to adjust the sails. Captain Mahfud clung to the rail of the quarterdeck, shouting orders. With an order to fall off, the Rashiq slowly changed its course, and headed northward. The rolling and pitching diminished.

Ereben climbed the short ladder to the quarterdeck. "What has happened?," he asked the captain.

"We continue southward, and the ship will hold together through this, but your horses will not survive. We need to find a place to release them ashore."

"But we will need them."

"There was a good place by the Iron River." Captain Mahfud shouted several more orders, then returned his attention to Ereben. "We have no choice. The seas all the way around the southwest point are even worse than this. We either release the horses ashore, or we cast them over to the sea now."

Ereben descended the ladder, and motioned for Brindle to follow him into the Captain's mess, where he had last seen Yassar and Hamsa.

"Captain Mahfud says that the seas are rougher further on, and that the horses either have to be taken back to a spot he saw near the Iron River, and offloaded...or thrown overboard now."

His other companions sat speechless.

"So he's heading back."

"Are we just going to set them loose?" Brindle asked.

"Don't we need them to haul the Jadeite when we get to the island?" Hamsa asked.

"Perhaps we should all just go over the land with the horses," Yassar offered.

Ereben sat on a bench, and rested his head in his hands. He tried to picture the map he had obtained from the monks. "If the map is correct, that journey would be as long as traveling from Shibam to Rippleton, except we don't know what we might encounter or who might be there. We really don't know anything about all that western land, except the outline of its shape. We might have to make long detours to locate passes or avoid swamps. We just don't know."

"I don't want to give up Turnip," Brindle stated.

"I don't know how to ride on a horse or how to guide one," Hamsa admitted.

"I say we depart with the horses," Yassar said, as he planted both hands on the mess table, "and meet the ship in the Northwest."

Ereben felt inclined to agree, but dreaded the thought of many more weeks of travel on land. His aching joints had benefited from the leisure of strolling about the deck only when he chose to do so. And he too had developed a bond with his own horse, Starfire. "Brindle?"

"We get off at Iron River."

Ereben turned to Hamsa, and waited for his decision.

Hamsa shrugged. "I could sail there. But I could also learn to ride a horse. I guess that would be Fart." He chuckled. "Alright. I will abandon my own ship, and travel with my companions. And you, Ereben Leaf? What is your choice?"

"I would be lying, if I said that I don't prefer the comfort of a sea voyage. And I suppose that you three could bring all four horses to the northwest coast. But I don't want to say more farewells. We have lost Sawney Burn, and Ja No and Moap, and Minkar and Bahsa." He paused, and looked into each of their faces. He felt a spontaneous smile. "I have come to love you all. I will go with you and with the horses. There may be wonders and unexpected dangers. But we'll be safer together. Let's do this."

Crew members fended off the low cliff with their boat hooks. The captain had found a mooring alongside the cliff, just west of the mouth of the Iron River. The water here was deep enough for the Rashiq, but remarkably quiet. The tide seemed to be mostly gone out. They would have a brief time to offload the horses. The anchor was dropped, and the stern roped to the shore. Planking was spanned over the gap between ship and shore.

Brindle was first to lead a blindfolded Turnip across the plank, and onto the rock of the cliff. She returned alone to lead Fart, since Hamsa was afraid to do so. Yassar and Ereben followed.

They had all said their farewells earlier to Captain Mahfud and his crew. Hamsa stood on the rock to watch his own ship prepare to return, without him, to its journey around the southwestern peninsula.

"I suppose we should find a location uphill a bit, to spend the night," Brindle said. "I'll try to locate some grass and water for the horses."

Ereben assisted Hamsa onto Fart, and offered some simple instructions and reassurance. He knew that Fart would just plod along behind the other horses, regardless.

As they selected an area in which to camp for the night, near a small spring and tall grass for the horses, Ereben realized that he had not considered shelter for Hamsa. Since the departure of Bahsa and Minkar, Yassar had crowded into Ereben's tent each night, until they had reached Shibam. But three adults would not fit. Brindle Meadow carried the only other tent.

"We will need to create a shelter from the brush, for one of us to sleep in," Ereben said to Yassar.

"The simplest solution," Yassar pointed out, "would be for Brindle to share her tent with one of us."

"You are all so dense." Brindle fussed through the pile of gear that she had just unloaded from Fart. She pulled out Ja No's tent-size rain cape that they had requested from the tent maker in Zink. "Just cut a few branches to support this." She tossed the folded cape at Yassar.

Once they all finally settled down to prepare an evening meal, the pressing question in Ereben's mind was which direction to head in the morning. He unrolled the map he had received from Maha Jalaj, and examined it in the light of their cooking fire. "I think the easiest route to follow is westward along the coast, until it swings southward. Then we go northwest, just east of these low mountains, and directly to the northeast coast."

"And we have no idea what to expect along the way?" Hamsa asked.

"No idea." Ereben looked at other possible routes. "If we go north from where we are now...right here, then cross the high mountains, the weather will be more difficult the farther we go north. Then we still have to pass through unmarked land."

"The southern coast looks shorter," Brindle said. "Why not just go the shortest way?"

"Then the shortest." Ereben rolled the map. "We will go along the coast. So two, maybe three weeks."

By mid-morning, Ereben noticed a vague trail in the scrub that headed in the direction they had chosen to travel. Although it didn't appear well packed, as might a cowpath, the scrub had been trampled enough to be conspicuous.

Occasional, isolated trees dotted the otherwise brushy and relatively dry landscape. Before long, they came upon the body of a recently deceased Dwarf.

"He was traveling east," Yassar observed. "That doesn't seem right. And his belongings are still untouched."

"People everywhere are making strange decisions," Brindle said. "Or maybe he didn't like what he saw farther west."

One by one, they rode around the body, and continued westward. At mid-day, they stopped beside a small creek, and dismounted, so both they and the horses could rest.

"Come look at this," Hamsa said.

When Ereben walked to the creek to see what had caught Hamsa's attention, he saw a plump bird, pacing within a carefully crafted cage trap that had dropped over it. "Someone is out here setting these,"

"Look more closely, Ereben Leaf," Hamsa suggested.

To Ereben's amazement, the partridge-sized bird had only one wing. "I've never seen such a thing. How can it fly?"

Brindle walked up to the cage, and lifted it. The odd, one-wing bird fluffed its cream and buff feathers, then ran on its two legs into the brush. "It does not fly."

Not long after their rest stop, they came upon two more bodies along the faint trail. These two appeared to be an Orkahti woman and a Nanish man. They too were headed eastward.

Ereben recognized visible wounds. "They did not die of starvation or cold. They were killed by someone else."

"Someone else, who did not rob them," Hamsa pointed out.

"This doesn't feel promising." Ereben turned to his companions. "Do you think we should turn back, and try a different route?"

"I have no weapon," Hamsa said.

Ereben handed Hamsa the Shouda spear that Bahsa had traded for the blood locust staff. "I have my dagger."

"But I have never used a spear...or a dagger...or any weapon. This is frightening."

"Just think of the spear as a sharp stick," Yassar said, "to fend off any threat. The very appearance of it in your hand will cause an adversary to pause."

"We have driven off attackers before," Brindle pointed out. "I think we should continue along this route. After all, the alternatives may be just as dangerous. At least the weather here has been cooperating."

"Continue," Yassar stated simply.

Ereben urged Starfire westward.

There was no inference or ambiguity to the reason for the two dead Valanders, one on either side of the trail. Each was tied to a wooden post by his feet, upside down. Their hands were bound. Their throats had been slit.

Without consulting the others, Ereben calmly pivoted Starfire, and headed back in the direction from which he and his companions had come.

෯ඏ

*One may be remembered throughout all time for only
a single decision, a single moment.*
                    Minkar Jarad: Thoughts of Dragons

Bahsa Jarad, in full Dragon Armor, and carrying both the layered steel, pronged ax as well as the golden ax, walked eastward through the main tunnel within the Isle of Dragons. Splendor followed him closely behind.

Unlike the joyous journeys that his father had related, of philosophical discussions with Graybeard, as that loquacious dragon had happily carried him over the northern lands, Bahsa had ridden on the shoulders of Splendor in total silence. Bahsa spent the journey deep in thought—thoughts of both victory over One-Eye, and the very real prospect of instant death.

Minkar had explained that the dragons did not speak with one another, but instead routinely exchanged their thoughts freely. So Bahsa assumed that all of the dragons knew of his arrival and his purpose. One-Eye expected him.

As he passed the individual alcoves of the other four dragons, they each watched him in silence. His father had told him that dragons do not cry, but do express their sadness by a slight droop of their otherwise upright horns. They all appeared sad to Bahsa, but having never seen the others before, he could not be certain. He had no doubt, however, about Splendor. The massive dragon who now blocked his retreat, and followed him through the tunnel seemed truly saddened by the situation.

Bahsa struggled to control his breathing, but could not control his pounding heart, which echoed in his head, beneath his golden helmet. Already, both of his arms and his grip felt fatigued. The two axes seemed heavier with each step he took.

Bright sky shone through the eastern opening of the cave. The alcove to his right glistened with heaps of gold and jewels— the alcove of Splendor, who had left his newly acquired bundle of treasure unattended at the western landing.

Bahsa took one final, deep breath, and turned into the alcove on his left—the last one before the daylight of the eastern landing. A mere ten yards in front of him stood One-Eye. Bahsa's vision was immediately dazzled, as a gout of flame from the dragon's mouth engulfed him entirely.

He felt no heat. He did not slow his gait. Bahsa took eight long steps directly toward the source of the flame, then lowered the golden ax to the floor of the cave.

The flame ceased. He now stood immediately beneath the breast of One-Eye. The dragon's eyes, both the good one and the blinded one opened wide. As One-eye spread his tooth-filled maw toward the intruder, Bahsa plunged the prong of the steel ax into the base of the dragon's neck, just above its breast bone, and drove it home toward the dragon's body.

One-Eye reacted with a deafening scream, and another gout of flame. Bahsa lifted the golden ax from the floor. It attempted to remove the pronged ax with a front claw, but the haft was now flat against its breast, and the razor sharp blade edge cut into its foreleg. One-Eye arched his neck downward, attempting to catch the unsharpened back edge of the blade in its teeth.

Bahsa brought down the golden ax onto One-Eye's neck, just behind its head. With surprising ease, the magical ax cleanly decapitated the dragon. Bahsa's ears rang with the instant silence. A massive dragon body tipped away, and fell to the cave floor. He removed the pronged ax from the dead dragon, then turned, trembling, toward the exit of the alcove, with an ax in each hand. He began to sob—not from sadness, but from the horror of having slain a magical being that had existed for eons.

When Bahsa lifted his head, he could see through his tears that Splendor blocked his exit. Bahsa stood motionless for a moment, then dropped both axes to the floor. He unbuckled his waist belt, and allowed Bat Slayer, in its sheath, to fall to the floor as well. He removed his golden helmet. Piece by piece, he unfastened the Dragon Armor, and abandoned it in a haphazard pile.

Bahsa stood, unarmed and unarmored before the gaze of Splendor. He sobbed.

ೀ✦ೀ

Faeries persecuted the Saracets, because they were not like us. They were strange and different. Many Faeries persecuted me, because I was not like them. I was strange and different. They called me "blighted." Yet some nurtured me and guided me and taught me. They called me "friend." And Kurash, the very last surviving Saracet, who had himself suffered so much abuse, nurtured me and guided me and taught me. Nurturance and assistance may give birth to an unexpected, sometimes wonderful flowering, and to new and lasting relationships that otherwise would never exist.

Gedzik the Blighted: The Gift

Wisfel was not sure if he was more fatigued from their long journey or the constant complaints from Timo and his advocates. Now they had stopped mid-morning along the southern coast of the western lands to argue once more.

"I nearly drowned on your wonderful raft!" Timo shouted at Wisfel. Timo's mate, Margarida, stood beside him, glowering at Wisfel and the twelve Faeries who stood with him. "This is madness to keep going. The weather here is wonderful, and the land looks perfect."

So far as Wisfel could tell, only five other Faeries agreed with Timo and Margarida. Even a mated pair had split their opinions over him, though they continued to speak with one another, and camp together.

"I agree," Wisfel stated. "The land here looks perfect, and the weather is wonderful...today. But the weather will likely change. And what creatures might come along and pluck us from the ground for dinner? And what humans might crush us all to death in one unknowing footfall? The Northwest Island is said to be uninhabited, at least."

"Wisfel," Albric called out from a short distance beyond the feuding Faeries. "There is a cage behind that shrub."

All of the Faeries suspended their discussion, and walked over to look. Wisfel saw a cage, made of twigs. It was more than ten times his height. "There are humans here."

"Come closer," Albric said. "There is a bird trapped in there."

Wisfel walked around the shrub to get a full view of the cage. Inside, a bird, buff and white in color, sat eyeing them suspiciously. It's size was that of a grouse—a bird that might happily eat a Faerie. "It has only one wing!"

"Aw...how can it fly?" Laia asked, pity in her voice.

"It doesn't need to fly to eat us," Margarida replied.

As Wisfel watched, the trapped, one-wing bird nibbled a green leaf from a tiny plant also caught within the cage. The action seemed awfully timely to Wisfel. "You want us to free you?" he asked the bird.

It turned to Wisfel, and stared.

"I think it is a special bird," Wisfel said, "and understands what we're saying."

"You are crazy, Wisfel!" Timo barked. "He is crazy. A bird that size is a lot safer inside the cage."

The bird turned to look at Timo.

"We should figure out a way to free it," Laia said. "Who will help me?"

"And you are crazy too, Laia." Timo folded his arms across his chest, his wings held high. "That cage is way too heavy to lift."

Wisfel studied the trap. A rope reached from one edge of the cage top, looped over the end of a branch of the shrub, and dropped down to a position behind the cage. The dangling end held a short piece of twig. He identified a cut sprig of berries on the ground near the rear of the cage, and a small stake beside it.

"Those berries were the bait, and that twig on the end of the rope was wedged against the stake, holding that rope end to the ground. When the bird moved the berry sprig, it released the rope, and dropped the cage. We just need to find a way to pull that free end of the rope."

"Or maybe the bird could pull that end?" Albric suggested. "If it understands what we are saying, that is."

The bird turned and looked at the twig dangling from the end of the rope.

"I think it does!" Timo said with amazement. "I think it does! We just need to swing that twig through the cage bars."

"And then place something under the lifted edge, to hold up the cage until it gets outside," Margarida added.

Wisfel, physically the weakest of all twenty of the Faeries, stood back in awe, as his most ardent opponents recruited those needed to carry out the trick of moving the twig at the end of the rope into a position where the bird could grasp it—if it even knew to do that.

In order to reach into the cage, the small amount of slack in the dangling rope needed to be removed, and the twig end swung toward the back side of the cage. By the time the slack had been removed, there were five Faeries clinging to the rope— their arms wrapped about its girth, and nearly all the remaining Faeries dangling from the legs of the first five. Then they began to swing back and forth toward the vertical bars of the cage. After prodigious effort, the swinging mass of Faeries brought the twig at the end of the rope between two of the bars.

It immediately slipped out. They swung away once more, then inserted the twig again. This time, the bird grasped it in its beak. For a long moment, it paused there, immobile.

"It wants you all to let go," Wisfel suggested. He wasn't really sure, but otherwise they would be scraped off the rope at the bars.

One by one, the three tiers of clinging Faeries dropped to the ground. When the rope was free of Faeries, the bird calmly transferred the twig from its beak to what appeared to be a small claw, where its missing wing might be. Leaning away from the rope, the bird struggled to take one step after another, slowly lifting the front of the cage.

Margarida, with the help of Laia and Albric, quickly shoved a branched twig beneath the raised edge. The bird examined the rope end and the branched twig, then slowly reversed direction, to remove the tension from the rope. When the rope end reached the rear of the cage, the bird released it. The branched twig held.

After seeming to inspect the situation for a bit, the bird approached the raised edge of the cage, squatted, and walked out. It turned directly to Timo, and softly, in a musical tune, said, "Thank you."

The mouth of every Faerie gaped.

"I am Jian. The people here have become more devious in hiding their traps." The bird seemed to speak Valish, but in a musical manner. Some of the crisper and harsher sounds of Valish were absent, but Wisfel found it perfectly understandable.

He gathered himself, and approached the bird. "I am Wisfel. I am pleased to meet you."

"I have never seen such tiny people before," Jian intoned.

Albric approached. "I am Albric. We are Faeries. We are the last of the Faeries. So when we have gone, you will never see others like us."

"You are kind Faeries." Jian sang a brief tune. "Where are you going?"

"Everything is changing everywhere," Wisfel said. "We are traveling to make a new home on an island far to the Northwest."

"How far away is it?" Jian asked, in a tune.

"Probably many weeks away." Timo introduced himself. "We have come almost as far already. We rode on the backs of our ringtails, but they were killed when we reached that wide river. So now we're walking there."

"That is sad that your ringtails were killed." Jian once again sang the same melody. "Perhaps you could ride on my back, and I could fly you there."

"But how do you fly with only one wing?" Wisfel asked.

"I have two wings when I fly."

The Faeries looked at one another. Wisfel had seen some unusual things, but that would top them all. He heard a rustling in the surrounding brush. A second, similar, one-wing bird walked out, and directly to Jian.

"Jian," Jian said, "These are Faeries, and they freed me from that cage. They did not have to do that. They were clever."

"Thank you," the second Jian said, its voice a shade fuller.

Wisfel then realized that the two Jians were missing opposite wings.

"I have offered to fly them to an island in the far northwest," the first Jian explained.

The two Jians strode beside each other, and locked their opposing, stubby claws. "We are Jianjian," the two said simultaneously, but in harmony, rather than unison.

Wisfel looked at his fellow Faeries, and shrugged his shoulders.

Margarida was first to speak. "If you think it would be safe, it would be a lot better than walking for months."

"We fly," Timo said.

"Quiri is smiling," Laia quipped, "so we both would like to fly."

Albric nodded. All the others, as a group began to nod.

"How should we do this, Jianjian?" Wisfel asked the birds.

"Half of you ride on Jian's shoulders, and the other half on Jian's shoulders," they sang in harmony.

❦

*Among the most ordinary members of a group, traits
identified as foreign, as having intruded upon the
sameness of the group from outside, engender dislike,
disgust, exclusion, and sometimes vehement hatred.*
                              Meriwa: A Land of Belonging

Bahsa asked Splendor to set down on the ridge northwest of
Shouda Village, in order to avoid the drama of a dragon landing
again on the paving of the Shrine. That request was the only
verbal exchange between them since he had beheaded One-Eye.

After he slid from Splendor's scaly shoulders, Bahsa,
dressed only in his tunic, turned away, and started toward the
village.

"You are a good man, Bahsa Jarad," Splendor rumbled. "I
see that you feel no joy in your deed. Only sadness. I too am sad.
Perhaps conflict between men and dragons will now cease, and
the sadness we both carry now may diminish with the passage of
time." The ring-necked dragon launched himself into the air,
and headed directly north.

Bahsa watch the massive dragon quickly recede into a
vanishing dot in the northern sky. Splendor's sad words had
somehow relieved a burden from his mind, which had replayed
his gruesome deed again and again. He turned again toward his
home.

Deena Hidad could only stand and gasp, as Bahsa stood in her
doorway.

"Father..." Bahsa called out, while motioning with his arm
to Deena. She approached him, and simply placed her forehead
on his shoulder.

Minkar Jarad stepped from a sleeping chamber, a puzzled expression on his face, his right arm slung in its caribou hide support. Gradually, a smile spread from ear to ear. He silently gestured for his son to attend to Deena, then sat on a bench to weep.

"This is Drusa," Deena said.

Bahsa stood inside the corral, grooming Hope. He turned to see a petite woman of middle age, wearing a simple, green tunic. Her pale, pink skin and delicate facial features were capped by mostly blond hair, but also a touch of leafy greenery.

"She came to the village alone yesterday," Deena continued, "so I provided her with some food, and showed her an empty house." She gestured toward Bahsa. "This is Bahsa Jarad."

"I am pleased to meet you, Drusa." Bahsa made a perfunctory Shouda bow, still holding a brush in one hand.

"Hello, Bahsa," Drusa replied. "I had heard about you, when you were just a boy."

Deena appeared as surprised as Bahsa.

"I was a close friend of Phaena. She spoke of you often."

"Phaena Corban?" Bahsa recalled Phaena's caring for him when he was little, and they had fled with Liddie Burn to travel to Cinnabar. A flood of emotions swept through him. It had been shortly after, that the slavers had captured him. Phaena had then gone to live with the Dryads, while Liddie and Jasper had continued the effort to free him from enslavement. "You are a Dryad?"

"The last Dryad, I suspect." Drusa lowered her head. "Kehl killed most of the others."

Bahsa set aside the brush, and escorted Drusa and Deena to a shady place where they could sit and talk. During the past few days, during which they all prepared for the journey westward, the snow that had blanketed Shouda Village had melted away completely, and the weather had warmed.

"She had been forcibly mated by a Kelpie—at least that's what she understood it to be, and eventually gave birth to what appeared to be a normal baby boy. She named him Kehl Corban. As he grew, he displayed an unusual hatred toward other children, and adult Dryads as well. By the time he was about five years old, he gained the ability to sprout wings, and to fly. As he grew older, his appearance began to change. He became truly evil, and would kill other children." Drusa spoke with sadness in her voice, but did not cry.

"Could nothing be done?" Deena asked.

"If a Dryad attempted to stop him, he would lash out with long, sharp fingers that resembled woody branches. He sought out, and destroyed the individual trees to which Dryads had been paired, so those Dryads would die. Our weapons could not hurt him. Once he had killed his own mother's tree, Phaena died. The remaining Dryads then attempted to find ways to flee the islands. It was all so frightening and meaningless. And he was relentless."

"The Dryad Bane!" Minkar said from nearby, where he had been struggling to bind steel points to two new spears that he had decided to make. "That is what Khumartakin had called it. We fought against its demons on the coast of Orkahtsk."

"As suitable a name as any," Drusa said. She turned to Deena. "Have you discussed with the others what we spoke of last night?"

"Not yet. Drusa would like to come with us to the Northwest Island."

Bahsa exchanged shrugs with his father. "I don't see why not. She could ride Tallow."

Deena smiled broadly at Bahsa and at Minkar, then at Drusa.

"Thank you all," Drusa replied. "I have traveled alone for too long."

"One request," Bahsa added. "If we should again meet up with Ereben Leaf, please avoid telling him that the Dryad Bane is Phaena's child."

"I will try. But that may be difficult to hide, without lying."

"And you must come to our wedding this evening," Bahsa added, "at Deena's house."

Deena winked at Drusa.

A crisp, sunny morning promised comfortable travel westward. Minkar had suggested that the best place to ford the Iron River might be just west of Jasper's birthplace, the now destroyed village of Nilwid. Minkar, with his right arm still suspended, rode Wiser. Deena and Drusa sat atop the two mares, Goldie and Tallow, while Bahsa straddled Hope. He felt that, at last, there might be hope.

Most of the spring plantings in Shouda Village had been damaged or destroyed by the unusually late frost. Even a few of the Lamblari Shouda immigrants were at least considering moving elsewhere, in search of a better place. But most of the Lamblari just huddled in their tents and shanties.

They approached the low ridge of hills, where their trail intersected with a seldom used one that came down from the western margin of the Ledge of Leopards. The view to the East, the direction from which they had come, still lay partially shrouded in a layer of morning fog, with the columns of the Shouda Shrine reaching above it, into the sunshine. Foothills and mountains to the Southeast shone in vibrant green.

But down slope, to the West, lay a blackened wasteland of dead trees, where fires had destroyed most of the vegetation.

Despite their distance from it, the site of the village of Nilwid could be plainly seen.

"Bahsa," Deena said. "Look up the trail." She pointed up the rude trail to their south.

Bahsa saw a small group of odd looking people descending toward them. Although each of them appeared to be dressed in a tunic, and carried a backpack, their skin and facial features seemed blurry in the morning sunlight. None seemed to carry a weapon or even a walking stick. They could clearly see Bahsa and his party, mounted on horses, and armed, yet continued to approach.

"Good morning," the blurry man in the lead said.

To Bahsa's amazement, all of them, three men and three women, were furry, and bore a strong resemblance to the Chrysanthus that he had known when he was a boy. They were leopard people. Their skin seemed to be light in color, overlain by a scant, white fur with ghostly gray spots.

As they neared, a leopard woman gently restrained the lead leopard man, as she stepped in front of him. "May we approach, and talk with you?"

To Bahsa's ear, the leopard woman seemed to speak with a mild, Nanish accent to her Valish. He noticed that the three women were dressed in white tunics, while the three men wore identically made tunics, but in a granite gray.

"Peace to you," Minkar said, offering a one-arm Shouda bow from the back of Wiser.

"I am Meriwa," she said to Minkar. "We are Icemen, and we are looking for a place to settle. The leopards have become increasingly hostile, and it is no longer safe for us at our home. We were told that the village of the Shouda might be welcoming."

"I have never heard of Icemen," Deena said. "I am Deena Hid...Deena Jarad." She then introduced her other companions.

"My name is Amaqjuaq," the Icemen man standing beside Meriwa said, and smiled broadly.

After a pause, Meriwa rolled her eyes at Amaqjuaq, then introduced the other four Icemen. "We are the only Icemen there are. It is a long and tedious story. Can you be kind enough to advise us about settling in the village of the Shouda?"

"It is in a condition of collapse," Minkar said bluntly. "We ourselves are traveling to find another place in which to settle."

"So it is a bad idea?" Amaqjuaq asked.

Bahsa did not know how to advise them. "We are traveling to an unknown island in the far northwest. It is a long and probably dangerous journey, with no assurance of discovering a safe place to settle, even if we reach it."

Deena looked imploringly at her new husband, then at Minkar. Bahsa turned to his father, who once again shrugged. "You are welcome to follow along," Bahsa said, "though we are on horses, and the six of you are on foot. That might be a problem. And we carry shelters for ourselves, as well as supplies for the journey."

"We would have no problem keeping up," Amaqjuaq said.

"Your offer to allow us to travel with you is truly generous, since we have just now met," Meriwa said. "If you could allow us a brief moment to discuss this, we will make a decision."

"Of course," Deena said. "It is a weighty decision."

The Icemen stepped away a short distance, and huddled together. After scarcely a pause, they returned.

"We will do it!" Amaqjuaq pronounced, clapping his hand together.

"What we will do," Meriwa clarified, "is to journey with you. We may find a suitable location along the way. We do have sufficient supplies with us for a week or more, along with other essentials. There is safety in numbers, and we are not without useful skills."

"Mother was from Naneland, and Papa from Orkahtsk." As the group skirted north of Rippleton, Hitty, one of the Icemen women, described their past to Bahsa and Deena, walking between Hope and Goldie, while easily keeping pace and still maintaining a conversation. "None of us remembers any of this, other than what Mother and Papa told us over the years."

"And so far as you know," Bahsa asked, "you were the first generation of Icemen?"

"The first. Seven generations earlier—that is in leopard generations, there was a wizard called Chrysanthus who mated with a leopard. No leopard offspring resembled him until our own generation. By then, the wizard had been long dead. Each of us is from a different pair of leopards. We were cast out of our litters, and left abandoned to die. Mother rescued us."

"All of us that same spring," Amaqjuaq added. He had been walking on the opposite side of Hope, though not contributing much to the conversation. "Papa said we are cousins."

"Distant cousins," Hitty clarified. "That is what Mother said we were. So all of us are more or less related to one another, but she said that there is no record. The leopards are just regular animals, and they pay no attention to that sort of thing."

Bahsa found it fascinating that the humanness of Chrysanthus had remained hidden in his descendants, until seven generations later. Then it just bubbled to the surface, and produced children who were more human than Chrysanthus himself had been. They were all capable of language. Two languages, in fact. Meriwa had explained earlier that their papa spoke to them only in the Orkahti language, while their mother spoke to them only in Valish.

As Minkar Jarad rode Wiser in the lead, the third Icemen woman, Alasie, walked beside him, to his left. Bahsa could occasionally overhear fragments of questions and chuckles being exchanged, in a casual, meaningless conversation.

The two other Icemen men, Inuksuk and Nootaikok, walked to either side of Drusa, mounted on Tallow. They, like Meriwa, who brought up the rear of the party, said very little as the party progressed along the path his father had chosen. Bahsa found that he could easily recognize the individual Icemen women, and he knew Amaqjuaq by his jaunty gait and somewhat more muscular arms, but the other two Icemen men seemed indistinguishable from one another.

The weather in northern Valand felt more like early summer. Minkar hoped to cross the great western mountain range at the lowest pass that he had occasionally spotted. As they neared the mountains, Bahsa's view of them had vanished. Low clouds shrouded the upper reaches. He could only assume that his father would simply guess where they might cross, and then clarify his course as they climbed higher. They had all agreed that dropping south, to pass below the mountains at the coast would be a significantly longer journey.

By late afternoon, they had reached the foothills. They halted beside a small creek. Grass for the horses was abundant. The Icemen, as they had done on the previous nights, each erected a one-person shelter, made by draping a cape over the branch of a tall shrub. Some had slept outside, under the stars, but rigged a shelter nonetheless.

"The weather makes me feel foolish, setting up my tent," Minkar said, as he did just that, irritably laboring with his one good arm. He had hurriedly sewn a dome tent for himself at Shouda Village, insisting that Bahsa and Deena use the three-person dome that he and his son had previously shared. Drusa had, of course, carried her own shelter for many weeks.

"You are just stubborn," Alasie said to Minkar. "You remind me so much of Papa." She grasped one corner of his tent, and held it to the ground. "Now you can worry about one part of it at a time."

The following morning, the weather began warm and sunny, but by the time that they had climbed only about two hours into the high foothills, the sky grew overcast and even foggy in places. For most of the way, the route allowed only a single file, so conversation had been minimal. With high mountains directly to their west, the hazy orb of the sun sank out of sight by late afternoon. At a grassy spot alongside a spring, Minkar halted them for the day. The temperature had fallen abruptly.

"It smells like rain or snow will come in tonight," Meriwa said. She selected a low rock formation against which to set up her cape shelter.

Alasie set hers near Meriwa, then hurried to assist Minkar in erecting his Shouda dome. Although it was clear to Bahsa that Alasie had more or less adopted his father, and seemed fond of him, Bahsa was amused that his father continued to accept the mothering.

At nearly the same moment that all the shelters had been erected, a light shower of ice pellets began. During the night, so far as Bahsa could tell from the constant patter on the tent he shared with Deena, there was little or no snow—just ice. When he arose in the morning, and looked out of the dome, he discovered a blanket of loose, crunchy bits of ice. The horses munched the taller grass, and seemed undisturbed by the ice, with only a scattering of ice in their manes.

"It looks like home," Amaqjuaq said, when he saw Bahsa.

"We don't know what is on the trail above us," Bahsa replied.

After their camp was struck, Minkar once again led the party, riding atop Wiser. The single file of horses and Icemen wound upward along a scarcely discernible path, until they were well above the tree line. There, a broad, snow-covered shelf stretched from north to south, with no path directly westward.

Minkar studied the misty outlines of the peaks to the West. "I believe the path we need for reaching the lowest pass is to the north of here."

"Southward," Meriwa said, "the snows will be easier."

"But the passes there are higher," Minkar replied. "We will go northward for a distance, and see what is there."

It was at mid afternoon, when they all looked up at a ball of flame in the sky to their east. As it grew larger, it silently burst in mid-air.

Bahsa turned to look at his companions. "That must be from the Dryad Bane."

Once the words had come out of his mouth, and before any of the others could respond, they were struck by a blast of air, and a thunderous, low pitched noise, which spooked the animals. While Bahsa struggled to control Hope, a deep rumble signaled an avalanche of snow that rushed down the mountain slope just north of them, completely blocking their path ahead.

They could not continue northward, and had found no practical path westward.

Minkar's head tipped down to his chest, as he shook it in discouragement. "Meriwa made a better choice, but I did not listen. We turn around. I will ride last, until we have crossed the mountains."

A loud clack against the stone ridge to Bahsa's left was followed by a gout of steam rising from the snow on the ground between Hope and Goldie. The two horses merely stared at it.

Amaqjuaq nudged his way between the two horses, and reached into the snow as soon as the steam had ceased. He lifted a fist-size stone, tossing it back and forth between his two hands. "It is still hot. It must have come all the way from that fire in the sky. The rock weighs more than its size." The rock seemed to be entirely black.

"I believe it was aiming for my head," Minkar quipped.

Alasie, who stood near Wiser, whispered to Minkar loudly enough that Bahsa could hear her. "Ask Meriwa to lead."

After a long pause, Minkar looked at Meriwa, who stood at the rear of the line. "I would be grateful, Meriwa, if you could lead us across the high mountains."

⤜⤛

Events we do not understand may be attributed to acts of the capricious gods that are believed to exercise control over nature as well as of our lives. If an unexplained event harms us, then we may assume those gods are angry at our behavior, and must be placated by our response, preferably a sacrifice of something which we cherish.

Meriwa: A Land of Belonging

Brindle Meadow rode Turnip in the lead, as they worked their way up the eastern foothills of the mountains. "The weather looks pretty bad, up to the North," she shouted over the steady, westerly wind.

"Do you see anything that looks like a pass?" Yassar asked.

"Maybe two peaks over," she answered. "Two hours ahead."

Ereben again scanned the range to their west. It all still looked the same to him—a succession of high peaks with very high saddles between them. "We should just pick a path, and follow it."

"I don't think we can make it over this pass and the next one," Brindle said. "The third one looks a little lower and wider. So that is the one I pick...for now."

Hamsa, riding passively on Fart, had not spoken for several hours. Whenever Ereben looked back at him, Fart was keeping pace, and Hamsa would simply nod his awareness. So far as Ereben knew, Hamsa had never really traveled anywhere, other than occasionally by ship.

They all moved on, within a rising valley between the foothills and the seemingly impenetrable line of high mountains.

"Look down the valley!" Brindle shouted, pointing eastward into a valley passing through the foothills.

Ereben saw, about a half mile away, what appeared to be a Giant, slowly walking up the valley toward him. Alongside the Giant walked a horse ridden by a Dwarf. He then realized that the horse was actually a mule. "Can that be Ja No?"

"I think it is Ja No...and Sawney Burn riding Moap," Brindle replied, with astonishment in her voice.

"How can that be Sawney Burn?" Ereben wondered aloud. "He washed away in the Canyon."

As the Giant and the mounted mule grew nearer, both the Giant and the Dwarf waved enthusiastically.

"Who is Sawney Burn?" Hamsa asked.

"He traveled with us into the Great Canyon," Yassar Khayin explained, "but a flash flood of the Death River swept him away. We searched for him, but never found him." He dismounted from Shujaun. "What a happy reunion!"

A fireball in the eastern sky caught Ereben's attention. It appeared to head directly toward him. "That looks bad."

"That is the brightest we have seen so far," Yassar added.

At that instant the growing globe of fire silently burst.

"I would expect that to have made a noise," Hamsa commented.

This was followed by a blast of wind, accompanied by a deep, loud rapport, startling the riders and their mounts. Ereben wrestled Starfire's reins, to keep him from fleeing.

"The times are strange," Hamsa mumbled. Fart had hardly stirred from the commotion.

"Tha' water come doon so fast an' deep," Sawney Burn explained, "Aa' what I could do wes keep my head oop." Sawney thrashed his arms to demonstrate. "Efterin' two hour, aa' o' the sudden, tha' wild water lay me gentle atop a big, flat stone, an' it wes gone. Barely a trickle remain."

"You were not injured?" Yassar asked.

They had decided to make camp here for the night. Ja No retrieved her rain cape from Hamsa, in exchange for a smaller tent that Moap had been carrying. After the shelters had gone up, everyone sat about a small cooking fire, and told their improbable tales.

"I wes nearly drown. I suffert a bump or two. When the sun come oop, I figurt to be nearer the mouth o' the Canyon. I walked fer I dunna know how many day, then I wes oot. An' I wes near starvin'. I ate many a horrid thing alang the way. Then, wouldn't ye know it, aff in the distance, there stood Moap an' Ja No, like they expectet me to be on time. An' look here, it seem the four o' you were jes waitin', expectin' me an' Ja No to mosey alang at this very hour the day."

The reunited party chatted around the small fire later than usual, before finally breaking up into their shelters for the night. Ja No and Sawney Burn lingered about the fire, whispering, as Ereben walked to his tent. It was only then that he realized that the small tent that Ja No had provided for Hamsa was Sawney's tent. The thought of a Giant woman sharing her own huge tent with a Dwarf man struck him as both amusing and hazardous. But Ja No was single, and Sawney Burn recently widowed.

Brindle Meadow again rode in the lead, as they headed upward along a snow covered drainage that seemed likely to reach the lowest pass they had seen. The single file of horses, followed by Ja No on foot, using her massive cudgel as a walking stick, and

Sawney Burn riding Moap behind her, snaked its way, gradually gaining elevation. Although Ereben could make out the silhouette of the range crest above him, the lightly falling snow and a bright sun cutting beneath the weather caused his eyes to ache if he looked away from Starfire's neck for longer than a moment.

"Look at that!" Brindle called to the others. She gazed directly up the slope.

To Ereben's surprise, the weather, within the span of a brief moment, had completely cleared. The light snowfall had ceased, and the clouds parted, to reveal a clear pass above them —one that was much closer than it had seemed through the gloom. Even the constant wind in his face had vanished.

His spirits lifted. They would be over the pass within an hour or two, and headed down the western slope. What had hovered as an arduous promise for so many days had now resolved itself in a sudden revelation.

"We will be sleeping in the western lands tonight," Ja No called out from behind.

Brindle halted Turnip at the high point of the pass. The trail widened there on the snow-covered scree. Ereben pulled Starfire alongside Turnip. The view westward seemed endless. Spread below him, the steep descent appeared interwoven with ravines that converged in the distant plain. Most of the streams emerging westward from the slopes joined to form a broad river, while a few seemed to end at pock marks in the upper plateau. Snow covering their trail ended just below him. The far western horizon vanished in haze.

Fart, carrying Hamsa, stopped beside Ereben. When Hamsa looked out at the panoramic view, he gasped, then covered his face.

"The western lands," Ereben said, feeling a sense of profound progress in their journey. When he looked again at Hamsa, the Sulalian appeared to be deeply distressed. "Once we reach the plain, it should be much easier travel."

Hamsa nodded, without looking up again.

Morning dawned bright and sunny, as Ereben crawled from his tent. They had camped at a small stream in the low foothills of the western slopes. He suspected that the day would be a hot one —the first truly hot day in a long time. Others were rising, and disassembling their shelters.

"Any idea which way to head?" Yassar asked.

Ereben pulled out the now tattered map that the monks had given him. "I guess we should just follow this river...here." He pointed to a collection of streams that that issued from the western slopes, and converged in a generally northwestern direction, leading to a delta in the far northwest. "At least there should be water all along the way."

Hamsa appeared to feel better today. "How are you doing today?" Ereben asked.

Hamsa smiled. "I have never ridden a horse, until this journey. I have never seen snow. I have never gone up a mountain. I have never gone down a mountain. This has been the hardest thing I have ever done. The view from the pass terrified me. Today, I am proud of myself for having achieved those things, although the recollection of it still disturbs me. I am happy to now be beyond the great mountains."

"You have done very well," Ja No said. "The Beddu feel no fear, but we do recognize a risky situation."

"And I am happy that you chose to travel with us," Brindle added.

"Try washin' doon a river." Sawney quipped. "Tha' wes a wee bit risky. An' bein' it wes a river bearin' the name 'Death River' offert nae comfort."

Ja No chuckled in her distinctive contralto. "That is truly a tale requiring no exaggeration, yet few will really believe it years from now."

"If we survive to tell it," Sawney cautioned.

"We each have tales to tell," Yassar said with a nod.

Within the deep ravine, Ereben could ride Starfire alongside a second horse, as they followed the gentle stream flowing to the left of their path. Beyond the far bank of the stream, no passable ground offered itself between the stream and a rising cliff. Although the water was barely more than a trickle, the stream bed contained numerous enough rocks to make it unsuitable for the horses.

Near midday, while still enclosed within the high, sloping walls, Ereben became aware of the unmistakable sounds of weeping and wailing, punctuated by a single, louder, male voice. He assumed that a funeral was taking place beyond his view. He motioned for his companions to remain silent, and wait, while he proceeded forward on Starfire. After forty yards, the ravine opened.

Before him spread a wide plateau, just beyond an abrupt, cavernous hole in the surface, into which the stream along which he had been riding swung to its left, and cascaded as a waterfall that dropped beyond his view. The hole was apparently so deep that he could barely hear the rush of the water below.

Standing on the far side of the hole and its waterfall, scores of people stood, all expressing great sorrow. They were clothed in well-crafted, heavily decorated garments of animal skin. Along the near rim of the hole, a man dressed in the costume of a great cat, perhaps a leopard, danced alone slowly.

The dancer held a scepter fashioned to resemble an animal leg, with long claws. Though he faced away from Ereben, the dancer apparently had his head covered by a large mask, with fur tufts where its ears might be. After a series of steps, he would wag his clawed scepter in the air, then beseech the gods to show mercy.

Ereben observed the dancer for a short time, then noticed that at the far right margin of the hole stood one silent man, wearing a feathered headband. Beside him, six children stood at the brink of the hole. They appeared to range in age from three or four years, to ten or eleven. Their hands were bound behind their backs, and their eyes were covered by a band of dark cloth.

At that realization, Ereben experienced a deep sense of dread at what might happen. Someone in the weeping crowd pointed directly at him. The dancer pivoted to look, revealing a leopard head mask.

"Kill the intruder," the dancer shouted. A small group of men with spears separated from the group of mourners, circled the rim of the hole, and advanced toward Ereben. When the spear bearers abruptly halted in confusion, Ereben saw that Ja No, holding her massive cudgel and stepped alongside him. His other companions gathered behind him.

The feathered man beside the blindfolded children then spoke. "Stop this, now." Ereben gathered that this was their head man or chief. The chief affectionately squeezed the shoulder of the closest child with his hand, then stepped toward Ereben.

"They will further anger the gods!" the dancer shouted.

"What is your business here?' the chief asked. His eyes were red and tear stained.

"We are traveling westward, and have just crossed the great mountains," Ereben explained.

"Then pass by quickly," the chief stated, as he turned again toward the great hole.

"I fear what you are about to do," Ereben said, uncertain of how to approach the issue.

"We must kill these intruders, before the gods grow angrier," the dancer said emphatically.

The chief turned back toward Ereben, while lifting his hand toward the angry dancer. "Our crops have failed for the second year, and we are starving. Only days ago a fire lit the sky in the daylight. Our god-speaker has learned that these are signs that we have failed the gods, and that they will continue to punish us all, until we make a cherished offering to them. These children are from our leading families. My own son is among them. There is nothing we cherish more." His chin briefly quivered.

"Changes in the weather have come from people in the Eastern Lands doing things that they should not have done. They are at fault. That has corrupted the earth and the winds, and changed the rains."

The animal-costumed dancer approached Ereben, while motioning for his spear bearers to join him. "Our chief has lost his reason in his grief. The gods demand that these intruders be destroyed." He drew his own knife.

At that moment, the spear bearers as well as all the weeping people standing on the far side of the great hole dropped to their knees, and bowed their heads to the ground. When the chief turned about, his eyes widened, then he too fell to his knees and bowed his head.

The costumed dancer backed away from Ereben and his companions, and dropped to his knees, though he did not bow. "We have delayed too long!"

Thirty yards to Ereben's right, a figure emerged from another ravine. Ereben gasped. His initial impression was that his grandfather, Chrysanthus, had appeared—in human-leopard form, the way he looked when Ereben had released him from his confinement within the dagger. But this new leopard person was clearly youthful and female, dressed in a white tunic. And Ereben believed Chrysanthus to be long dead. The leopard woman calmly walked toward the costumed dancer.

A short distance behind her, five other leopard people followed. Two were also women, and three were men.

The costumed dancer pulled off his cat-like head mask, and lay it carefully on the ground beside him. His face expressed both fear and pleading.

ക്ക

We go about our daily struggles for shelter and food and security, and our efforts to fulfill our personal goals, while usually remaining ignorant of the narratives that others may construct about our past and our future.
                    Ereben Leaf: Chronicle of the Counterspell

"I am Meriwa. The man you threaten," the leopard woman said softly to the now unmasked, kneeling dancer, "is Ereben Leaf, last Guardian of the Ruins. He rides upon Starfire." She glanced briefly at Ereben. "Beside him stands Ja No, last of the Beddu of West Graze."

The god-speaker trembled, looking back and forth between the leopard woman who stood before him and Ereben. "I...how could I know? I wished only to please..."

Meriwa interrupted him. "We are not displeased with your people. They have committed no wrong. They have simply suffered from the unexpected weather. Your guests, whom you have not welcomed, have likewise committed no wrong."

"Forgive me," the god-speaker replied.

"But," Meriwa continued, "if you harm these children, we will be indeed angry." She motioned to the other leopard people.

Each of the leopard men and women stood behind one of the six bound and blindfolded children, and gently led them a short distance from the edge of the great hole. "We are your friends and guardians," she said warmly. "We don't look like you, but don't be afraid. You will soon rejoin your families."

Each held one hand on the child's shoulder, and deftly parted the blindfold with a silver fingernail. Ereben could see the surprised expressions on the faces of the children, as well as the loving smiles of the leopard people.   Only one girl momentarily attempted to flee, but was held firmly by one of the leopard men, until she relaxed.

"We will unbind your hands," Meriwa continued, "but be careful of the cliff. Run around it, and return to you family."

Again, with a metallic fingernail, the bindings were cut from the wrists of each child. The children stayed well clear of the margin of the hole, and ran to their families. The boy nearest the chief ran directly into his waiting arms.

Ereben watched all of this in amazement. He had no idea how Meriwa might know who he was, much less know the name of his horse, and the name of the Giant Beddu woman.

"But the fire in the sky?" the god-speaker said. "We saw it!"

One of the leopard men walked toward the god-speaker and handed him a black stone. "It was a great, falling rock, that burst into pieces. This is one of the pieces." He handed it to the god-speaker. "It is just a heavy rock. It was still hot when I picked it up from the ground."

The god-speaker looked at the rock, then dropped it as though it were still hot. He stood, and turned toward his chief, who appeared angry. In a rapid movement, the god-speaker lifted his knife, ran toward the edge of the great hole, and with his blade, slit his own throat, just before toppling into the abyss.

Ereben's gasp of astonishment joined in unison with the gasps of everyone present.

"The Kas believe that you are gods." Guardian, the head man, appeared pained, as he sat on a woven rug within his small, stone home. While the other Icemen wandered through the village, teaching new games to gleeful children, as their dumbfounded parents looked on, only Meriwa and Ereben had joined Guardian for this peculiar conversation.

"Each of us was born of ice leopard parents, but we carry the human features of Ereben Leaf's grandfather, Chrysanthus." Meriwa had previously explained some of this to Ereben, after her party, which turned out to include the three Shouda, as well as a Dryad, had joined in following Ereben and his companions to the Kas village, to which this "last Guardian of the Ruins" had been invited. "I had not intended to deceive you. I only wished to spare your children from needless harm."

"It may be that every god is ordinary in his own house," Guardian replied. "I am perplexed by all of this. It is all new to me. But I will be always grateful for the sparing of my son and the other children. Going Down The Ladder had said that children can be replaced, but that the gods must be appeased. He was wrong about the children. He was wrong about the gods. At his end, he did not go down the ladder, but dropped into the great pit, like a discarded stone."

"Perhaps it would be best," Ereben proposed, "if you continue to allow all your people to believe that the gods favor them, and came among them, and blessed their children."

A middle-aged Kas woman opened the door of the stone house, and entered with a teenage girl.

"This is my wife, Snake Flower, and my daughter, Flute Girl," Guardian said. Then to his wife, he said, "We are speaking of important things, so you will have to go back outside."

Snake Flower's eyebrows lifted. "You go outside, you old fool. Flute Girl and I have work to do." Seemingly as an afterthought, she turned to Ereben, and added with a sly smile, "The two of you are welcome to stay and help, or you can go outside with my important husband."

Guardian frowned, then shrugged. "We will go and speak with Weasel and his son about the water idea."

Meriwa and Ereben left Snake Flower and Flute Girl to their work, and followed Guardian out the door, into the bright sun of a hot afternoon.

"Snake Flower treats me with great respect when we are outside the house." Guardian rocked his head. "Inside, she is the ruler. And a stern one. But a good one." He pointed toward a square, stone house just beyond what appeared to be a stone granary. "Weasel lives there."

"Are you a god?" a young voice asked from behind Ereben.

Ereben turned to see a boy of about ten, tugging at the hem of Meriwa's white tunic. Ereben recognized him as one of the children bound and blindfolded at the brink of the great hole.

Meriwa looked down. "I am Meriwa. We call ourselves Icemen."

"Are Icemen gods?" the boy persisted.

"Mud Mound!" Guardian scolded. "I apologize for my son's ill behavior," he said to Meriwa.

"He is welcome to ask," Meriwa responded. "Only by asking can we learn and grow." She grasped Mud Mound's hand with her furry one, and seated the boy and herself on a low, stone wall. "We come from the high mountains far beyond these high mountains." She pointed to the peaks on the eastern horizon. "Although we have knowledge that you do not, you know things that may be a mystery to us. You and I may be gods to one another. It depends on where you stand and in which direction you look. But even a god must always try to be kind and generous."

The wisdom of Meriwa reminded Ereben of Grandpa Chrysanthus. Tears welled in his eyes. He had not heard his grandfather speak since he had left Chrysanthus' smithy in Rippleton, on a bright, sunny day so long ago—the same day that he discovered that his family had been murdered. It was the day his entire life had changed its course.

Meriwa turned directly toward Mud Mound, staring into the wide eyes of the boy. "Are you a god?" she asked with apparent sincerity.

Mud Mound smiled broadly, hopped from the wall, then said, "Maybe." As he started to run off, he stopped, turned a joyous face to Meriwa, then hurried toward some of the other children playing a new game with another of the Icemen.

Guardian silently stared at Meriwa for a moment, then nodded his head. With one hand, he motioned for her and Ereben to continue walking with him toward Weasel's house beside the cylindrical, stone granary.

A young man squatted near the house, repairing a stone fence. He looked up in surprise, when he saw Guardian approaching with Ereben and Meriwa, rising to his feet, and standing respectfully when they neared.

"Eagle Hunter," Guardian asked, "is your father in the house?"

"Yes he is, Guardian." He led them to the wooden door.

Beyond the house lay an expansive mud flat, dry and deeply cracked. Although vegetables and some short grains, which Ereben did not recognize, were planted in the soil surrounding the mud flat, the plants closest to it appeared stunted.

"Come inside, Guardian," a male voice shouted from within the house.

Ereben followed Guardian and Meriwa into Weasel's stone house. Weasel, a middle-aged man, apparently a bit older than Guardian, looked up from a miniature replica of the Kas village, in a corner of the stone floor. When he saw that Guardian brought guests, he rose to his feet, his eyes fixed on Meriwa.

"Weasel, this is Meriwa and Ereben Leaf." Guardian seated himself on the floor, and gestured for the others to join him. "We have come to you to discuss water."

"That will be a short discussion, Guardian," Weasel replied. "The wells continue to go dry, one by one. Our land is so dry that the River People are no longer interested in taking it from us."

"Is there anyone who recalls the lake?" Meriwa asked.

Weasel perked up. "There was once a lake, a long time ago. When I was a boy, my grandfather told me about it being there when he himself was a boy. A small river came into it from the mountains. He said that the river always flowed. Then one day, the great pit stole the river, and it never again flowed. By the time he had grown to a man, the lake had nearly vanished, and its water became salty. There is no Kas alive today who remembers the lake."

"One of my companions, Nootaikok, said to me, as we walked down from the great pit," Meriwa continued, "that he could see where a river had flowed long ago. He saw how the wall of the great pit had broken away, and stolen the river. More importantly, he pointed out to me how the river could be taken back from the great pit, and could then flow in its old course."

"Can we talk with your companion?" Weasel asked.

"Yes. Nootaikok seldom has much to say, but about rivers and creeks, he can speak endlessly."

"Eagle Hunter," Weasel shouted.

"Yes father?" a voice from outside the house replied.

"Go find one of our visitors, named..." Weasel looked back at Meriwa.

"Nootaikok," she said.

"Nootaikok," he shouted. "Ask him to come here and talk with us."

"Yes, father."

"Water flows all the year from the mountains," Weasel said to Meriwa. "But it goes into the big river, where the River People guard it. Or it pours into the great pit. That also must go to the big river, or the pit would fill up."

For a short time, Weasel and Guardian spoke about the gardens and withered crops of grain, as well as how long that and the stored food would last them.

When the door opened, and a male Iceman, clad in a gray tunic, was guided into the house, he simply stood in silence, with no discernible facial expression. His eyes turned to Meriwa.

"Nootaikok," Meriwa said, "this is Ereben Leaf, Guardian and Weasel." She pointed to each of them as she spoke. "Weasel would like to hear of your observations about the river that flows into the great pit, and how it might be restored to flow once again into a lake."

"The river?" Nootaikok's expression remained blank.

"Yes, Nootaikok. Tell him about what you told me."

"Oh!" Nootaikok's face lit up. "It is not really a river, but a large creek that flows from the crevices of the foothills below the mountain range. Many tiny tributaries feed into it, until the last few miles, before it reaches the pit. The pit was once a hidden, underground river, passing through a tunnel dissolved into the layers of rock. Over many, many years, part of the roof of the hidden river eroded enough to collapse. That made the pit. Many, many years later, more of the roof collapsed, and diverted that large creek to the waterfall, where it now joins the hidden river. There is a solid layer of rock immediately south of the pit that appears capable of carrying the large creek into its original bed, and down to the low area where it used to collect. Diverting the large creek to that area south of the pit would require a small, stone wall be built just before the large creek turns toward the pit. Then the water would once again form a lake down here." Nootaikok then stood expressionless once again, and silent.

"Thank you," Meriwa said. "Would you be willing to walk back up there, and show these people where to build that small, stone wall?"

"I would," Nootaikok answered without expression. "Now?"

"Tomorrow morning?" Weasel asked.

"Yes."

Ereben, on Starfire, decided to accompany Weasel and Eagle Hunter, as they followed Nootaikok. The reserved Iceman spoke this morning without prompting, as he led them along the former shore of the dried lake bed. and then up the now dry "large creek," toward the great pit. He explained to the two Kas men what he understood and guessed about the soils and rock layers.

Minkar Jarad soon caught up with them, and rode Wiser alongside Ereben. "Ereben Leaf, I have heard a curious story from an old, Kas man." He spoke softly, without interrupting Nootaikok. "He told me he knows of an ancient hermit who lives on the top of a cliff island in the center of the western lake that we see on the map."

"An ancient hermit?" Ereben repeated.

"This ancient hermit, he said, looks like me—tall, with dark brown skin and pointed ears. People say he brings storms to drive away any visitor who attempts to cross the lake to reach the island, and that he controls birds to bring him food."

"An ancient Shouda hermit? Can there be such a thing?"

"The old Kas man told me that when he was a boy, the brown man and a young Valand man traveled through the Kas village, and continued westward. He never saw either of them again, but has heard the tales of him from other travelers."

"That lake is not really along the shortest path to the Northwest island."

"Perhaps it could be our path," Minkar said with a smile.

"If the others agree, then it would add only a few more days."

"Along the outside of this curve, you will need to build a wall within the drainage, so that it is at least equal in height to the opposite bank." Nootaikok pointed out the location, as all of them walked or rode within the dry drainage, just below the waterfall into the great pit. "Once that is in place, then you must remove the rock, here, to divert the flow into the old channel."

"That might take only two weeks to do," Eagle Hunter said to his father.

"We will do it," Weasel proclaimed.

"You may not have reliable water in the old lake bed this season." Nootaikok seemed to have an intuitive sense of land and creeks and rocks and water flows.

Weasel patted the Iceman on the shoulder. "Your understanding of what needs to be done, by our own hands, is as if the gods have been appeased.

"I am just an Iceman, and the least of us."

"Do you have any knowledge of any member of your Shouda village ever traveling to the western lands, Minkar Jarad?" Yassar asked. "There is no record of a Lamblari traveling there, at least that I ever found or heard of."

"Beyond the Shouda lands," Minkar replied, "a Shouda stands out among other men, and is always remembered. The tale could be an invention, but the old Kas man seemed to recall such a visit during his childhood. That would have surely left an impression. The legends of magical powers may or may not be meaningful, but I believe we should travel to the western lake and see if we can reach the island. It may turn out to be wasted days of travel. But tales say that he was still living there recently."

All the members of Ereben's rejoined and expanded party of chaos refugees sat on a circle of square-cut stones that surrounded their communal cooking fire. Beyond them, their assorted sleeping structures had been erected in a large circle, just west of the cleanly paved village of the Kas. Ereben had expressed his feeling to all of them that evening that if even a single member of the party objected to detouring toward the cliff island, to chase the rumor of an ancient Shouda hermit, then they would all continue along his previously selected path to the Northwest.

"Even if such a person still lives on this cliff island," Ja No said, "it seems only a curiosity that would lengthen our already long journey."

"I agree," Drusa added. "That would be extraordinary, but of little consequence."

Every time Ereben looked at the Dryad who had just joined his party several days earlier, he felt the urge to ask her if she knew Phaena, and what had come of her life. But his profound aversion to hearing things about her that he did not wish to hear prevented him from asking. His deepest desire was to shield his love for her, and leave that part of his life sealed in the past.

"Perhaps," Bahsa offered, "such a person might posses a trove of knowledge that could be helpful or even crucial to our goals."

"It seems like a pointless detour to me," Brindle Meadow added, "but I would not oppose traveling there."

Meriwa spoke for the first time that evening. "Each of the Icemen has expressed to me their desire to stay with this party, regardless of your choice of routes. A few more days, or a few more weeks makes little difference in the end."

"It does make a difference," Amaqjuaq blurted. "It is a lot more walking!"

"Do you have something better to do?" Meriwa asked him.

Amaqjuaq wrinkled his furry brow. "No." He then laughed aloud, which generated laughter and head shaking around the circle of friends, both old and new.

Sawney Burn slapped both knees. "I say let's go there."

Heads began to nod in affirmation. One by one, Ereben looked directly at each of the fifteen other members of his party.

When he looked at Deena, she said aloud, "Yes, yes, yes."

"In the morning," Ereben concluded, "we will pack up, thank our Kas hosts, say our farewells to the children, and then set out for the cliff island in the western lake."

"How will we cross the lake?" Minkar asked.

There was silence. Ereben considered their eight horses and a mule. There were among the party a Valander, a Nane, four Shouda, a Sulalian jeweler turned ship owner, a Dryad, a Dwarf, six Icemen and a Beddu Giant. He could not imagine a better suited group to solve any problem. "I'm sure we will find a way."

❧

The extraordinary is, for some, merely ordinary. Discovering the extraordinary may simply require examining what should have been evident to us all along, had we bothered to look closely enough.

Meriwa: A Land of Belonging

"Ereben, have you noticed that people are following us?" Brindle Meadow asked, as she rode Turnip alongside Ereben on Starfire. "They are way out to either side, just out of sight—or mostly out of sight."

"Yes. We've been followed ever since we forded the river two days ago. I don't know if it's the same people the whole way, but somebody is always there, on both sides...if I look long enough."

"Do you think they are afraid of us?" she asked.

"I would be. Just look at us. A bunch of mostly armed people." Ereben twisted himself to look back over the improbable group. "Eight of us on horses. One on a mule. A Beddu Giant, and six Icemen. We certainly look like a war party of some kind."

"Maybe once we've passed on through their territory, without causing any trouble, they will just go back home, wherever that is."

"A lot of these groups seem to have picked the kind of land that suits their needs, and don't seem to spread into other land types. We'll be climbing those high hills up ahead, maybe tomorrow, and I'll bet they lose interest in us."

As the hills rose, and their views of the horizon to the West, and on either side slowly closed in on their party, Ereben became aware that those who incessantly watched their movements were closer than in the open plain. He could also see their features more clearly, though still from a considerable distance. They appeared to have painted their faces in many-colored patterns. Each individual seemed to display a different, unique design, in differing colors. The painting was limited to just their faces, as bare chested men left the light bronze skin of their well-muscled torsos undecorated. And their numbers seemed to be increasing as well.

"Ereben Leaf," Minkar said from behind him, "I suspect that we may be nearing a village."

When Ereben turned to reply, he saw a bright light descending toward him from the East at a steep angle. "Take cover!" he shouted, pointing upward, as he quickly dismounted from Starfire. The horse would not come down to the ground.

Those of the party who were also mounted, looked up, briefly transfixed by the sight, then jumped down from their mounts, and scrambled for any nearby depressions in the rising land. But before Ereben or any of the others had thrown themselves to the ground, the clearly fiery object passed over them westward. It then burst into countless, flaming shards, just before passing out of view. The horses and Moap, their only mule, remained where they had been. As Ereben headed toward Starfire, a sudden blast of air knocked him to the ground.

Ereben awakened to find himself lying on his back. He hurt everywhere. Moap stood nearby, but all eight of the horses were nowhere that he could see them. All of his companions lay scattered about on the ground—some unconscious, others lying awake, feeling their extremities or head. Sawney Burn lifted himself onto one elbow, and spoke something to Ereben, but Ereben heard nothing. The wind was silent. Everything was utterly quiet, other than a high, ringing note. Both of his ears felt as though they had been poked with a sharp, thin object.

Ereben pointed to his ears. "I can't hear," he said, but even within his head, his own voice was nothing more than a distorted rumble. He looked himself over, and found only scrapes and bruises from striking the ground. Slowly, he rose to his feet, his head pounding. He sat back down again.

Nootaikok rose with surprising ease, stretched his fur-covered arms and legs, felt his neck and head, then assisted his fellow Icemen to their feet, one by one. He flashed hand signals to them, including a gesture toward his ears.

Meriwa looked about, then pointed to various directions, which she and the other Icemen scattered toward, at a run. Within a brief moment, all six of them had passed beyond Ereben's sight, in six different directions.

The last of Ereben's companions to awaken was Ja No, who suddenly sat up in a daze, staring blankly ahead. Sawney Burn walked to her, and remained standing, his eyes level with those of the seated Giant. When he placed his stubby hand on her massive shoulder, Ja No slowly rotated her head toward him, though her facial expression remained blank. Sawney spoke to her. Ereben again heard nothing. Ja No showed no reaction at all.

Of the local people following them to either side, Ereben saw only one, a young, painted-faced man, immediately sprinting out of sight, heading directly westward through the steep hills.

By the time that Ereben and all his companions had risen to their feet and cleared their heads, the Icemen straggled back to the group, bringing the reluctant, though apparently unharmed horses with them. No one seemed able to hear much, though Ereben noticed that he could now detect muffled, unintelligible rumbles.

Everyone slowly, spontaneously reassembled into their habitual travel arrangement, and wordlessly resumed the trek westward, up the steepening slope. Ereben could not see anyone following them. He was uncertain if that was simply because of the closer terrain, or because they were no longer being tracked and escorted by the local inhabitants. When Starfire carried him to the top of a gently rolling plateau, he was halted by the scene before him. Other members of his party spoke, though he could not understand. Ereben said nothing. One by one, the others ascended to the open plateau, and spread out to either side of Starfire. They too were silent.

Ten or twelve individuals, all with uniquely painted faces, frantically lifted and cast aside slabs of sandstone from as many heaps of what appeared to Ereben to be the remains of shattered, stone houses, all the while calling out to the silent mounds of rubble. None of them paid the slightest regard to the arrival of Ereben and his companions. One tribesman dragged the limp body of a child from one heap, then fell to his knees and wept.

The Icemen were the first to rush toward the rubble of the ruined village. Ereben and the others followed. Ja No examined the limp child, gently palpating obvious injuries, then shook her head, and cried.

Each of Ereben's fellow travelers assisted at a different heap, lifting slabs of stone, and eventually assisting in cautiously removing a victim or two. Nobody spoke a word.

"Lakaa!" a tribesman shouted.

Yassar Khayin had extracted a young woman from one of the heaps. He had been assisting a young man whom Ereben recognized as the single individual who had been following them, who sprinted westward following the passage of the flaming rock that had exploded.

The rescued young woman was clearly alive, and shouted back to the young man, "Ibara!"

Ereben could once again hear, though his ears still rang incessantly.

Ibara briefly hugged Lakaa, then pointed to another heap, so far unattended, and ran toward it. Lakaa, her left leg bloody, limped after him. Yassar followed.

The man whom Ereben had been assisting cried aloud, covering his face in his hands. He had just uncovered a woman who appeared to have been crushed to death. Ereben stepped toward him, and placed his hand on the man's shoulder. The tribesman turned his painted, grief stricken face toward Ereben, briefly nodded an acknowledgment, then gestured with a single wave of his hand for him to help someone else.

The setting sun glistened from the surface of a distant lake to the West, highlighting its stony island—a towering, flat-topped spike in its center. The bodies of all the dead from the village had been extracted, and laid out in a long row. Some had been covered, others left exposed. A small girl with a switch chased away any birds that landed on them. Nearly a hundred had died: old and young, male and female, adults and children. More of the villagers were now dead than those still alive. Few spoke; many softly wept.

After assisting in any way they could, Ereben and his companions set up their camp just west of the destroyed village. None of them spoke much to one another. Ereben made a ring of stones, and began to prepare twigs for cooking dinner.

"Where you are going?"

Ereben looked up to see a young man with the dark-colored, angular daisy painted on his face. It was partially obscured by sandstone dust. Ereben recalled his name: Ibara.

"I am Ereben Leaf. We have been traveling for a long time. We hope to find a safe place to live, on an island to the Northwest."

"Me, my sister, my friend can go away with you people?"

Ereben felt tired, and still ached everywhere. He glanced to either side, and caught Brindle Meadow in his gaze. She lowered her head.

"You would need your own food supplies and provide your own shelter," she said to the stony ground. "Most of us are mounted, so you might have trouble keeping up with us."

"We have food," Ibara explained, a hopeful note in his voice. "We make shelter if we need. We come with you."

Brindle looked back to Ereben, and shrugged.

Ereben reluctantly nodded. "Yes, Ibara. You may come with us."

Ja No squatted along the trail, inspecting Lakaa's swollen left calf muscle. "Can you spare some munu, Ereben Leaf?" she asked. Lakaa, had been slowly falling behind all morning, as the party trudged westward.

Ereben's heart sank.   His precious pouch of munu mushrooms was not at his belt. He tried to remember the last time he had used it. So many events fogged his recollection of it. He replayed in his mind packing his gear this morning. He was certain that he did not pack the munu. He could not imagine where it might be, if he still held it among his few possessions. "It's gone. I've lost it."

"Lakaa may ride with me, on Shujaun," Yassar Khayin offered.

Ereben had learned from Yassar that Lakaa was the older sister of Ibara, and that their mother was among those killed. Their father had died years earlier. Yassar, together with Ibara and Lakaa had helped to rescue a girl, named Meesi, whom he believed was romantically connected to Ibara. Both of Meesi's parents had been killed by the blast—her father in a nearby field;

her mother within their collapsed stone house where the uninjured Meesi had been rescued.

Ja No grasped Lakaa with two massive hands that nearly encircled the young woman's waist, and effortlessly lifted her onto Shujaun's back, in a position behind Yassar. Yassar turned to offer her a smile, then placed Lakaa's hands at his own waist.

Ja No approached Starfire. "Ereben Leaf," she said softly, "I have no wish to visit the island cliff with the hermit wizard. So I will walk around the lake. I could lead the horses and Moap around as well."

Ereben's right hand involuntarily slapped his forehead. "The horses! I forgot about them. Will Sawney go with you?"

"I have not discussed that with him, but that would be welcome."

"I guess that when we arrive at the lake shore, we can see who wishes to cross to the island, and who would rather walk around the lake. And I don't know if we can find a boat, or will have to build one."

"I will certainly visit the island," Minkar said, from atop Wiser.

"Visit an ancient Shouda on a cliff island in the center of a lake?" Deena chuckled. "Of course Bahsa and I will go, won't we."

Bahsa simply smiled at his new bride.

"Fish boats," Ibara called out. "People at water have many fish boats. I go there one time. Very different."

Once the party reached the final rise of rolling, parched hills, before descending toward the huge lake, Ereben understood what Ibara meant by "very different." A warm, moist breeze swept up the slope with the late day sun. It carried scents that reminded him of the jungle plateau, before it had perished in the fires that swept across it.

The following morning, they began the descent toward the lake. As they progressed lower and lower, the heat and humidity steadily increased. The sound of distant flutes and whistles and reed horns filtered through the breeze and the more tropical plants along their path.

A large town of wicker-walled, thatch-roofed buildings came into view. Approaching the town, Ereben realized that hundreds of inhabitants were gathered in its central street, dancing in circles and lines. All were costumed as birds or fish or other sea creatures. Spectators, including scores of small children, stood to either side, waving their arms and hands in synchrony with the music. Smiles were everywhere.

One dancer, dressed as a huge fish noticed Ereben's party approaching. Bringing several other costumed dancers along, he danced his way toward the odd assemblage of visitors. The fish encouraged Ereben to ride Starfire into their parade, while a crayfish took hold of Turnip's bridle, and danced the horse, carrying Brindle Meadow, alongside Starfire. Soon, Ereben and all of his companions—including the six furry Icemen—were the center of the celebration. Eyes of parents and children alike were wide with delight. People clapped their hands and sang to the music being played by dancing musicians.

Ereben, feeling a sense of joy for the first time in months, turned his head to look back. While those who were mounted appeared gleeful, all of his companions on foot, including a Beddu Giant, the bare-chested Ibara, a more modestly dressed Meesi—both with painted faces, and the six improbable, fur-covered Icemen, were dancing their way along, all in step to the raucous music. The fearsome teeth of smiling Icemen, smiles he could not recall having seen before, seemed to fit in perfectly, as they danced about.

A sour yet sweet aroma of fermented fruit filled his nostrils. Villagers passed bowls of liquid to one another, and even to some of the older children. From the increasingly wobbly parade of the masqueraded dancers, and the progressively disjointed sounds coming from the musicians, Ereben assumed that most or all of the performers had partaken of the fermented beverage at the start.

A sudden, sad thought swept away his joy. The destructive disruption of nature, of the order of all things, had not yet reached this more innocent part of the land. How soon would it destroy them? Would even the older children among the village spectators reach adulthood?

One village woman approached Starfire, and lifted a shallow, glazed pottery dish of liquid toward Ereben. She smiled and nodded.

Ereben accepted the dish, and swallowed a sip from it, before allowing himself to sniff its tart aroma. Smiling back at the woman, he returned the dish, and thanked her. She then carried the dish to offer to each of Ereben's companions.

The celebration seemed to last for several hours of increasingly raucous laughter and dancing and drinking and dissonant musical instruments. Then, as if on a silent signal, all of the people of the village melted away into their homes, leaving Ereben's party alone in the center of the deserted, main road. The only sounds were the muffled voices of small children.

"Tha' barley brei, or wha'e'er it wes, hes laid them oot flat," Sawney commented.

"We can set up camp," Minkar said, "beside the lake. Then we can wait in the morning for them to crawl back out."

Ereben finished his breakfast of dried biscuit and dried fruits, washed down with sweet, slightly sulfurous lake water. The others were also done eating, and now beginning to strike their tents and assemble their gear, with the realization that, for many of them, there would be no horse to carry it. So those who intended to cross the lake to the cliff island separated most of their gear from the single packs that they would keep immediately on hand.

Whenever the gentle lake breeze drifted northward, the air filled with an aroma of raw fish. A short distance down the lake shore, dozens of wooden racks shimmered with the cleaned flesh of drying fish. Well crafted wooden boats, each painted a different, bright color, lay upon the beach, just above the water line. Aside from Ereben and his companions, the shore appeared to be deserted.

Ja No, Hitty, and Nootaikok had already brought in the horses and Sawney Burn's mule. Those three, together with Sawney and Drusa, planned to follow a land route northward around the lake, and meet the others at its western outlet.

Everyone loaded the horses with bags and sundry packed items, and bid good journey to those taking the land path, while reaffirming their plans for meeting again on the western shore. Once the land route group departed with the horses and mule, eyes turned toward the scattered backpacks, then boats resting on the beach.

The heat and humidity of the day rose rapidly. Ereben wondered aloud how they would locate the boat owners who, along with all the adults in the village, seemed to be sleeping away their previous day of revelry. His best guess was that they would need three boats to carry them across to the island, and an arrangement for the boats to carry them to the lake's western shore the following day.

One bronze-skinned, middle-age man, wearing only a simple loin cloth—a stunning change from the sea-life costumes of the celebration—wearily approached a bright blue boat. After looking back toward the village several times, and paying no attention to Ereben and his party, he shook his head, and began the chore of sliding his boat toward the water's edge.

Ereben saw this as an opportunity. He and Brindle Meadow silently jogged to the boat, and assisted the struggling fisherman.

The man paused, raising both hands toward Ereben. "I am Matrincha. Who are you strange people?" His voice held no emotion but fatigue.

Ereben introduced himself and Brindle. As he was explaining his hope to arrange several boats to carry him and his thirteen other companions to the island, and then be picked up the following day to go to the western shore, Ereben noticed a young woman, dressed in a coarse, short tunic, walking among the wicker huts of the village. Around her neck, and supported by both hands she carried what appeared to be a half-yard wide pentalphic sphere made of wood. "Who is that?" he asked, pointing toward the woman.

Matrincha squinted. "That is just Doqui. She cleans the road of trash, after we celebrate."

Doqui lifted her sphere, then fell clumsily to the ground. Throughout the village, debris of all sorts lifted as a cloud into the air, then arced away eastward, vanishing beneath the canopy of the jungle trees and vines that climbed the slope.

Ereben sensed her use of magic, though he did not fully understand how she accomplished her cleaning chore with the pentalphic sphere. Or how she might have learned to use and possibly even make it, so far from the roiling centers of wizardry to the East. Then, for the first time, he noticed that, although cleaned, drying fish were evident on the nearby drying racks, the area was nearly free of fish bones and fish entrails. The lakefront was a remarkably tidy place for a fishing village.

A young man in a loin cloth walked from one of the wicker huts toward them. He gazed downward, occasionally kicking a small ridge of muddy sand with a bare foot.

"Arowana," Matrincha shouted. "Go wake up Tambaqui. We need three boats to carry these people to the island." With that, Matrincha reached into his bright blue boat, and removed a folded fishing net.

"We can pay you for your trouble," Ereben said.

"If you pay me fish, then I will accept it." Matrincha flashed a wrinkled smile. "I have everything else that I need. We travel to the island every week, to take fish for the old man and his friend. But some of you will have to row, with so heavy a load."

"The old man has very dark skin?" Brindle asked.

"Yes. Like some of your people. Very dark. And he is very old. For two generations, a family from the village has lived with him, to help. Now only Arowana's father remains to help. At harvest, some others of his family go out to bring in the food."

When Tambaqui, an older man, emerged from a hut, and slowly walked with Arowana down toward the boats, he inspected the strangers. Matrincha introduced Ereben Leaf, and explained the need.

"Let me bring everyone here to help," Ereben suggested. "We'll be right back, with our gear."

All three of the boats rode low in the water, heavily burdened with their passengers and gear, but the lake surface lay calm before them. The sun had risen brightly above the eastern slope. Four of the passengers of each boat knelt on the interior ribs of the hulls, facing the stern, as they gently rowed with crude oars that each rested between two wooden pins serving as rowlocks. Matrincha, Tambaqui and Arowana knelt at the stern tiller of their respective boats, guiding them toward the cliff island.

Ereben sat in the bow of Matrincha's boat, studying the unusual island, as he rowed toward it. He concluded that the island, as well as its surrounding lake, was an ancient volcano. That, he felt, might explain the central island, the surprising warmth of the area, and the slight taste and aroma of sulfur.

Black clouds swept in over the eastern hills. Wind picked up precipitously. The previously placid lake developed a chop.

"Should we turn back?" Arowana shouted at Matrincha.

"To the island," the middle aged man shouted back. "The wind is behind us."

With the boats riding so low, lake water began to splash inside the hulls. Those who were not rowing, frantically scooped out handfuls of water. The boats had crossed only about one third of the distance to the island. Heavy rain poured down on them.

⟋⟍

A distant goal seen only on a map serves as an almost mythical objective. Through physical hardships and increasing chaos, the mind's eye holds only that vacant scribble on a square of vellum.

Ereben Leaf: Chronicle of the Counterspell

Squinting through the rain that dripped into his eyes, Ereben saw no likely landing point along the rocky coast of the cliff island. He briefly thought of his Ice Leopard cape, that now was being carried around the shore of the lake with the land party. Matrincha, at the stern tiller of his boat, seemed well in control, and heading toward the abrupt cliffs at the island's southern end. There seemed to be no visible structures of any kind—just rock rising from the stormy lake.

As the three fishing boats struggled closer, a bay opened to his view, and soon a narrow beach below a cluster of small, stone buildings. He shivered. The temperature continued to drop. To his surprise, the rain transitioned to large, wet snowflakes. Looking back, his view of the eastern lake shore vanished in the blowing snow.

Entering the mouth of the small bay, the wind dramatically diminished, and the snow became a light drizzle. He hopped from the bow of his bright blue boat, when the steep, stony beach was near enough. Using the bow rope, Ereben dragged the boat ever so slightly onto the beach, and held it steady, while Brindle, Bahsa, Deena and finally Matrincha disembarked. All of them joined in hauling the boat up the pebbles of the steep beach.

As the two remaining boats, side by side, approached the stony edge, Meesi abruptly stood, capsizing the overloaded boat.

She grasped the gunwale of the adjacent boat, tipping it over as well. Twelve of them splashed into the water, and disappeared beneath the murky surface.

Four Icemen heads immediately popped up, all vigorously shaking them, then scanning the water. Tambaqui and Arowana, followed by Minkar, Yassar and Hamsa surfaced as well. The small backpacks of the three travelers had remained on their backs. Ereben realized that the slope of the beach was so steep, that it provided little assistance to those in the water. When Minkar climbed to the stony beach, his right arm no longer rested in the caribou hide sling. He left the white loop of hide hanging freely about his neck.

Three of the Icemen—Ereben could not tell which—dove under, and pulled up Lakaa, Ibara and Meesi, who seemed unable to swim. Their meager belongings, which consisted of hand-carried parcels of food, were lost.

"It is snowing on the village," Arowana said to his father, Piraiba.

"Like up on the mountain?" Piraiba asked, astonishment in his voice.

Piraiba, after his initial shock at seeing so many visitors walk into the simple plaza of the compound, had hurriedly escorted them into two empty, stone homes—two of the total of four small, stone, single story buildings arranged symmetrically about the square plaza. The late-middle aged, somewhat stoop shouldered man now sat with Ereben and Arowana within his own home.

"I cannot really tell, father. It may be no more than snow in the air, that melts before it lands."

"Even if that is true," Piraiba said, "I have never seen or heard of such a thing here. Snow is only rare on the mountain."

Ereben lowered his head. "The weather..." He wondered to himself how much he should reveal to Piraiba and his son.

"The weather has been changing across the land. Sometimes suddenly."

"Why would this be?" Arowana asked.

Ereben sighed. "Magic. Too many people have become careless with magic. It has disrupted nature."

"I have seen magic," Piraiba said dismissively. "It does not disturb things."

"Imagine a small cooking fire on the hearth. With careless handling, the house—perhaps the entire village—may burn to the ground."

Both Piraiba and his son sat silently on their short stools. The older man seemed visibly distressed.

"Your sisters and their families?" he asked Arowana.

"I will return to the village when the wind falls, Father, and be certain that they are well."

"And I will go with you." Piraiba stood. "I am worried."

"What about Yaddie?"

Piraiba looked at Ereben. "Can you and your people watch after him, until I come back?"

"We have not yet met him. How long would you be gone?" Ereben asked.

The older man shrugged. "If my children and grandchildren are in no danger, then Arowana will bring me back tomorrow."

Ereben reluctantly nodded. "How old is...Yaddie?"

Arowana smiled. "Nobody knows. He came here over 60 or 70 years ago. Different elders say different years."

"Some of our people were infants when he arrived, yet died from age," Piraiba said. "But Yaddie remains. He no longer can climb to the fields above the cliff. And hauling water from the seep is difficult. I visit him every day, and sometimes prepare his dinner and help clean. He tells many strange stories. I have lived with him here for almost thirty years, yet he still can tell tales I have not heard. I will take you to him when I fetch the water, in a short while."

Ereben thanked Piraiba and his son, then left them. On exiting Piraiba's door he found most of his companions gathered on the plaza, around Lakaa, who sat on the stone, appearing dazed. Kneeling in front of her, an ancient man with dark brown skin applied a salve to her swollen, now red left calf. He touched her brow.

"She must rest. Apply this again in the evening." The ancient man handed a tiny crock and a glass jar of what appeared to be tree leaves in a liquid to the nearest person. "Bathe her with lake water, to lessen her fever." His voice, though soft and overly sibilant, was clear. He held out a hand for someone to assist him in standing. Minkar Jarad took both of the old man's hands, and steadily raised him upright. When he looked at the man who had assisted him, he spoke words that Ereben could not understand—except for the word "Shouda".

Yassar Khayin spoke up. "He says that he has not seen a Shouda for a long, long time. He is speaking Shadae. He is from Lamblar!" Turning to the old man, Yassar added, "The others do not understand Shadae. Only Valish."

The wrinkled old man then gracefully, with arms spread, elaborately bowed in the Shouda fashion toward Minkar, then bowed in a similar manner toward Yassar, then to the remainder as a group. The Shouda among them returned the bow. "I am Yadelloh Khayin. But everyone calls me just "Yaddie." His back seemed to Ereben to be remarkably straight for someone of great age. And he had apparently walked into the plaza without the aid of a cane.

Yassar's eyes widened with amazement, his mouth agape.

"When my son, Arif, had started his family, and my wife had passed into the arms of Elloh," Yaddie explained to the group joining him inside his small home, "I decided to adventure for a short time with a brilliant young, Valish wizard named Chrysanthus. The elders of Lamblar did not regard magic in the fairest of light." All four of Ereben's Shouda companions, together with Brindle Meadow, listened to his soft, toothless voice.

"My grandfather was named Arif Khayin," Yassar interjected. "I know of no other Arif."

"I must then be great grandfather to you, Yassar. I offer my apology for hiding from you your entire life. The time just slips away."

"May I call you Great Grandfather?"

"You may, if you wish. But if you address me as Yaddie, then I will recognize that you are speaking to me."

Behind Yaddie, from floor to roof, shelves held countless books and scrolls. There was also a collection of small sculptures, and even a tiny ship within a glass bottle.

"Chrysanthus was my grandfather," Ereben whispered aloud.

Tears appeared in Yaddie's eyes. "I have allowed so much to fade. Chrysanthus was much younger than me, but I have somehow lived to be ninety-eight. Has he passed?"

"Yes and no. It's a long and strange story. It includes the furry Icemen you met today. I'll explain it when they come in to visit later. But for now, do you know anything about the island far to the Northwest? That is our destination."

Yaddie gestured with his hands for his guest to remain seated. He slowly rose from his cushioned stool, and stepped to his doorway. As he returned to his seat, he said, "Right about now is the time of day to climb to the top. You will reach it just before sunset. Look to the Northwest at the farthest horizon. That is the highest peak on that island." He again slowly stood, and encouraged them to go. "Keep one hand on the cliff wall as you come back down in the darkness. It will be safe."

Ereben, together with the three boat pilots and all of his companions except Lakaa, stepped from the brutally steep trail— a combination of slopes and stone steps—onto the remarkably flat plateau atop the cliff island. The winds had stopped, and the clouds had vanished as quickly as they had appeared. He moved away from the edge, then sat on a small, stone bench to catch his breath. All the others chattered about the dramatic views in every direction. Most of the plateau appeared to be fallow gardens interspersed with the leafless forms of fruit trees. A small pond sparkled near the center. When he again stood, the sun was just above the horizon to the West. He looked to the Northwest, far up the sweeping coast, but could see nothing at the horizon. As he considered sitting once more, a brilliant light flared at the horizon in the Northwest, and glowed brightly for a long moment, then vanished. He felt an upwelling thrill. After so many miles and hardships and hopes, his objective had finally revealed itself to his eyes.

Arowana, who stood beside Ereben, gasped, and placed his hand onto Ereben's shoulder, pivoting him to the East. Ereben could hardly believe what he saw. His view of their starting point this morning was now clear. The entire eastern shore of the lake glowed a bright orange, all the way up the jungle slope. It was all covered in snow that reflected the sunset, save for one broad shadow cast across the lake and onto the shore by the height of the cliff island.

"I must go now to carry my father back to the village." Arowana, along with Matrincha and Tambaqui, immediately headed down into the shadows of the cliff trail.

"We should probably head down now too," Brindle suggested, "before it gets completely dark."

The upper portion of the descent passed quickly, but as the light faded, the line of hikers slowed. Ereben remembered to keep one hand on the stone wall rising beside the trail. But the switchbacks were frightening in the dark. When he felt his foot stepping down the first of the stone stairways, his recollection of their proximity to the bottom end of the trail eased his mind.

Yaddie had planned to meet the other visitors after dinner. Even though none of Ereben's group had eaten yet, he suggested that Hamsa, Alasie, Meriwa, Amaqjuaq, Inuksuk, Ibara, and Meesi join him in directly visiting Yaddie.

"I will go there shortly," Hamsa said, heading back toward one of the other stone houses.

"Descendants of Chrysanthus," Yaddie said, as he smiled, and shook his head. "Trapped within a dagger. Took an Ice Leopard as a mate. That is all so remarkable."

Ereben had just related, in as brief a manner as he could, the scarcely credible story of his grandfather's later life. "So all of these Icemen, as well as the two who are leading the horses around the lake, are related to Chrysanthus, related to one another, and related to me. We have journeyed from places scattered across the lands, and have traversed all the way to this spot, only to witness how much we all share."

"May I enter?" Hamsa asked from the doorway.

Yaddie motioned him in with one hand.

Hamsa nodded an acknowledgment, and entered, his eyes scanning the remarkable items displayed on the shelves. When they spotted the tiny ship within a delicate, glass bottle, he walked immediately to inspect it. "This is a truly beautiful thing."

"A long time ago," Yaddie explained, "Chrysanthus journeyed with me to a beautiful city in the East."

"Bur Nor?" Hamsa asked, his eyes widening.

"Yes, yes. Bur Nor. In Jubail. On the Eastern Sea. So many things are tucked inside my head. It is sometimes difficult to reawaken them. A jeweler made this for me."

"Do you recall his name?"

"Hmm. His name. His name. Oh! His name was Ishaq al Gawahirgi. Why would I remember that?"

Hamsa gently wept. "My...my father made this. Thank you, Yadelloh Khayin, for keeping his memory alive." Hamsa briefly touched the tiny bottle with a fingertip, then found a place in the center of a beautiful, small, knotted rug to seat himself.

"A child brings together the many divergent fibers that make up childhood," Yaddie mused, "and from that begins to form a solid yarn. Then many different yarns. It is from those yarns of experience that an adult weaves a life." Yaddie scratched the scant, white fuzz that grew from the margins of his head. "At my age, the fabric has long ago frayed, and the fibers unwind. Speaking with you all has helped to bind the hems."

"The salve." Ereben interrupted him. "What is the salve you used for Lakaa's leg? I have lost all of my munu."

"Ah. Munu. I do miss munu. I call that smelly salve 'balm.' It is made from onion, garlic, wild grape wine, and pigeon bile. A pickled hazel leaf is used for a dressing." He scanned his many shelves. "I have more of it somewhere. Oak leaf works well, or grape leaves. Any tart leaf."

"If you can tell me the proportions," Ereben said, "then I can just make some. Does it need to be pigeon bile, or can any bile work?"

"The greater the variety of things that a bird eats, the more effective its bile becomes in drawing out the festering. Pigeons eat nearly anything."

Amaqjuaq descended the cliff trail, and jogged over to where Ereben stood on the plaza. The sun was not quite high enough to clear the cliff of the southeastern point, and shine directly into the little community. "It is still snow covered on the eastern shore."

"Yet it is comfortable here." Ereben recalled his notion that the lake had formed over a volcano. And the previous evening, Yaddie had referred to the lake as "the cauldron".

"And there is no sign of boats coming out today," Amaqjuaq continued. "There must be hardships in the village."

"I would leave our gear packed, as much as possible, in case they do come today," Bahsa said. "But we will have to hope they can return tomorrow."

Yaddie approached from his house. "If they cannot come today, I am certain they will sail tomorrow. He held out a cloth bag to Brindle. "Root tubers. For stew. I have dried fish behind the house."

Brindle accepted the bag, thanked Yaddie, then promptly handed it to Minkar. "Be sure to make enough for Yaddie too."

Yaddie looked at Minkar's expression of surprise, then at Brindle Meadow. With a nod, he said, "I like your courage. How is the young girl...mmm...Lakaa doing?"

Brindle looked to Yassar.

"Better, Great Grandfather." Yassar said. "Her fever has broken. Her leg is still red and painful."

Yaddie scratched his deeply wrinkled chin, which was emphasized by his lack of teeth. "She should not be traveling until the leg has fully healed. Healing is a delicate process."

"We would like to live here, and help you," Yassar said. "Lakaa has agreed to marriage."

There was silence for a short moment. Bahsa slapped Yassar on the top of his shoulder. "That is wonderful. We should hold a wedding today, while we are all still together. And celebrate with my father's stew of root tubers and dried fish."

"I will officiate," Yaddie said, with unrestrained delight on his face.

Ibara hesitantly approached the ancient man. "Me and Meesi wish to live here, and to wed. We can grow much food for you."

Yaddie smiled, and nodded, an expression of satisfaction on his face. "You are welcome here."

Ereben was stunned by the sudden announcements. "Two weddings and a feast!"

The gifts to the two newly married couples were simple, personal, useful items: a small knife, a pouch of dried peas, a flint. Lakaa and Yassar were married at the pallet on which she had been resting, while Ibara and Meesi were wed in the stone plaza.

Two of the Icemen, Amaqjuaq and Inuksuk, joined with Minkar Jarad to prepare a manly stew of root tubers and fish, seasoned with some wild berries and grape leaves that Alasie and Meriwa had gathered that morning. Yaddie provided clay bowls for Ibara, Meesi and Lakaa, while everyone else carried their own ceramic or wooden bowl. The ancient Shouda appeared as energetic as any of his much younger visitors, and seemed to be overjoyed at being able to observe and participate in all the activities.

Brindle, Bahsa and Deena scoured the narrow, stony edges of the bay for dried heath twigs, which Ereben used to build a small campfire for evening story telling. After feasting, most of those on the island sat in a circle about the fire, and, one by one, they told a story—humorous, frightening, amazing, legendary. It didn't matter. Hardly a breeze stirred, allowing the smoke of the fire to rise up nearly vertically. The weather was perfect for just sitting around the small fire. Lakaa's pallet had been carried out, so that she could join in the listening and the telling.

As Yaddie began to recount one of his adventures with the young Chrysanthus—one that involved Rock Gnomes and hilarious embarrassments—he extracted a stubby, wooden pipe from his robe, along with a pouch of dried leaf. Continuing to speak, he packed his pipe, then sparked a flint to light it.

Ereben stoked up a pipe of his colts foot leaf, and puffed as he listened.

Yaddie interrupted his story to ask Ereben what he was smoking.

"Colts foot."

Yaddie smiled, then gestured with his own pipe. "Sumac. We could trade some?" He winked.

৩৵৶

Sometimes we describe a placid setting as beautiful. But the beauty may come not so much from its aesthetic as from its absence of perceived threat and tumult.

Meriwa: A Land of Belonging

Ereben Leaf stood on the gentle slope of the western lake shore, watching Matrincha, Tambaqui and Arowana turn their boats about, and head back to the calamity that had befallen their village. The fishermen had found frozen crops and shivering townspeople, none possessing clothing adequate for freezing weather. One elderly man had been found dead inside his wicker house. Piraiba had decided to remain with his daughters' families in the village, rather than return to his lifelong dedication to assisting Yaddie.

Skies to the east, as well as he could see them beyond either end of the cliff island, appeared lovely in the mid-day sun. Alongside him, Minkar shook his head.

"The reach of this upheaval in nature," the Shouda said, almost to himself, "seems beyond any bounds." He flexed and rotated his recuperating arm. The white caribou hide now served as a wrap about his neck.

Ereben rested his hand on Minkar's shoulder. "I can't say that it's worse than we feared, but watching its effects does take a toll on the spirit. I had hoped that Yassar might find a possible remedy or defense among the ancient books, but he has found another place to be."

"All of his books are still among the packs on the horses."

"I really can't translate the Shadae myself," Ereben lamented. "Yassar was my only hope of understanding much more of that."

"I guess we just start walking north," Brindle said, "until we run into the others."

Ereben squinted into the distance northward. "We spent an extra day with Yaddie. I think it's about two days of walking for us to reach the northern end of this peninsula. But even on horses, that trip around the lake may take them a few days."

"Perhaps," Bahsa said, "they encountered some difficulties along their route, though I would imagine that a Beddu Giant with a cudgel, a Dwarf with a war hammer, and two Icemen would be intimidating enough. I don't know if a Dryad would frighten anyone not familiar with their skills."

The sky suddenly darkened. Ereben looked up to see a low, rapidly moving, nearly black cloud sweeping westward, blocking the mid-day sun. A black funnel dropped from its underbelly, and extended toward the surface of the lake, just northeast of them, lifting a water spout upward. It cruised onto the broad peninsula, then continued westward as a violent finger of wind, uprooting vegetation along the way.

Heavy rain pounded Ereben and his party, then just as quickly, ceased, as the black cloud moved beyond their view. Ereben's soaked clothing chilled him in the brisk wind. A moment later, the mid-day sun again shined down on them.

"Does anyone besides me," Brindle asked, "feel as though all this terrible weather and the flaming rocks are following us?"

"Who would guide such things?" Ereben asked in response. "All of the petty wizards care only about their tiny places."

"The Dryad Bane," Minkar said. "We witnessed that when we were among the Orkahti horsemen."

"How would this Dryad Bane even know about us, to follow us?" Ereben searched the faces of his companions. Bahsa and Deena seemed uncomfortable with the subject. Minkar shrugged his shoulders.

"We have heard about this Dryad Bane," Meriwa said. "but we know few details with any degree of certainty."

"It eats trees!" Amaqjuaq blurted, with an expression of amusement.

"Trees?" Ereben asked.

"That is what is said." Amaqjuaq looked to his fellow Icemen for affirmation, but the others seemed to ignore him.

"I think we should start walking," Bahsa said, "since we have only a half a day left, before the sun sets." His suggestion seemed to be directed at his father.

Ereben sensed a conspiratorial undercurrent. But the mere term, Dryad, deflated any eagerness he might have had to pursue the matter. There were so many unanswered Dryad questions roiling beneath his consciousness. He knew they were there, and that they always led to painful thoughts of Phaena. "Yes. We should start moving. No better way to dry out than a hike in the sunshine."

It was evening of their second day of walking that they reached the northern extent of the lake, still with no sign of their companions who had escorted the horses and mule. The weather had cooperated, so far. Ereben had been confident that if that group had completed circumventing the lake, they would be camped at this very spot. With only low brush and an occasional tree, his view was unimpeded for at least a mile in every direction.

Meriwa huddled with the three other Icemen. "We will continue along the northern shore of the lake into the night, and attempt to locate them," she announced to everyone.

"We are all tired from a day and a half of walking," Deena said. "In the morning, we could all travel together to find them."

"Our worry," Alasie replied, "outweighs our fatigue."

"I worry," Ereben said, "every time our group splits into smaller, separate groups. But I recognize your concern. For my part, I will need to rest overnight, before walking any farther. I no longer have the stamina to push beyond my endurance."

"I understand, Ereben Leaf," Meriwa said. "We will return with the others to this spot as soon as we have located them. Some unexpected event has clearly interposed itself into their plans."

Minkar and Hamsa returned to their lakeside camp at about mid-day. Dangling from the center of a horizontal Shouda spear that rested on the left shoulder of each of them, an odd, fur-covered animal swung lifelessly to either side as the two men walked.

To Ereben, the dead animal appeared to be about the size of a wild pig, but with a plump, blunt-nosed head. "What is that?" He asked.

"I killed it myself," Hamsa boasted, "with this very spear."

"He learned quickly," Minkar said, "with the proper instruction."

"But you do not know what it is?" Brindle asked, with a smirk.

"It was eating plants near the lake," Minkar said, "so we will eat *it* near the lake. Build up the cooking fire, while I show Hamsa how to skin it and prepare it for roasting." The Shouda man looked about. "That small tree there will have to do."

"Maybe farther away from here," Bahsa suggested, "so that something bigger does not smell the scent of its entrails, and come to eat *us* near the lake." He pointed to a runted tree a hundred yards away.

Minkar glanced imploringly at Ereben, who smiled and shrugged. "Young people," Minkar grumbled, as he and Hamsa headed toward the distant tree.

"I suppose we should go with them," Deena said to Brindle, "to make sure it is fit to eat by the time they are done pretending to be great hunters."

Everyone laughed, including Minkar and Hamsa. Brindle nodded, and joined Deena in catching up to the two men.

Bahsa turned to Ereben. "You and I have the honor of locating more firewood."

"And a spit and two supports," Ereben added. His thoughts briefly drifted to the other half of their party, and the Icemen who had departed the previous evening.

Eventually, Minkar and Hamsa returned, each carrying a skinned, split half of the mystery animal's body. They rigged one of the halves onto a spit above the coals, then set up a higher scaffold above the fire. To this, Brindle and Deena added, one by one, small segments of the other half, in order to dry and smoke the pieces for preservation.

As melting fats began to drip into the coals, a mild aroma filled the air. "It smells like roast pork," Ereben said.

"No. It is more like a wild bird," Hamsa conjectured.

"Either is good," Brindle said, "since I think it is some manner of giant lake rat."

"The pelt is rather attractive," Deena added, "but we don't have any easy way to cure it. So we just left it hanging on a branch."

Ereben squinted toward the distant tree. "Jasper would dash out its brains, mix them with ash from the fire, then smear it over the back side of the pelt. If you are interested. That's how he cured a wolf skin cape. And he was still just a boy then."

Deena pursed her lips. "Brains and ash?"

"We can do this!" Brindle stated. She turned Deena about by her shoulders, laughing all the while, and the two of them headed back toward the pelt in the tree.

Night had just fallen, when the six Icemen, Ja No and Sawney Burn arrived, with the horses and Moap.

Ereben noticed immediately that Tallow bore no rider. Drusa, the Dryad refugee, was not among them. He then sensed the somber aura of the entire group.

Sawney Burn dismounted from Moap, and watched as Ja No and six Icemen unloaded all the gear from the animals. Ja No and Hitty then led the livestock to graze a short distance away, along the lake shore. Sawney's eyes never met Ereben's gaze. The Dwarf pulled a small knife from a pouch, sliced a sizzling piece of meat from the half carcass roasting on the spit, then seated himself on a nearby stone to eat it.

Deena Jarad approached him, and squatted there. "What happened, Sawney?"

"A day ago. Drusa screamt. We hed been ridin' alang a day ago, an' she screamt. An' then she raspt oot the word, '*my tree*', an' jest oop an' died. Dropt right off the horse an' died on the spot. We buried her yester eve. The Icemen helpt when they come across us."

Deena covered her mouth with one hand, then began to weep.

"Drusa told us that each Dryad," Bahsa explained, "is bound to an individual tree. When the Dryad dies, the tree dies. If the tree dies, then the Dryad dies."

"So," Minkar conjectured, "the Dryad Bane must have found her tree, and killed it."

"That is so sad." Ereben paced about. "I wonder if the Dryad Bane was able to sense Drusa's location, by identifying her tree."

"Is such a thing possible?" Hamsa asked.

Ereben seated himself near the fire. "Probably. But not once it had killed her tree. I really don't know. We don't know enough about this Dryad Bane, or the kinds of forces it controls."

"We understand", Bahsa continued, "that a kelpie, in the form of a human, forced itself upon a Dryad. This produced a child that was bonded to the same tree as the Dryad. But this child was half magical. Once it killed its mother's tree, the mother died, but the child did not. It displayed more tree-like properties within itself. But like a kelpie, it could sprout wings at will, and fly." Bahsa seemed to be choosing his words with care. "Father and I witnessed this Dryad Bane and its demons during an encounter in Orkahtsk. It eats trees to grow larger, destroying entire stands of trees."

"What are these demons?" Ereben asked. He pondered why these revelations about the Dryad Bane had not come up earlier in their journey.

"They are hideous, blood red things," Minkar said, "that eat people. Each is the size of a man, but with very long legs and long arms. Only a short body. Their heads are mostly two great eyes and a gaping mouth of sharpened teeth."

Bahsa nodded in agreement. "Individual arrows had little effect on them, but many arrows at once could kill one. Then it would melt into a foul puddle."

Minkar picked up the description. "When the Dryad Bane commanded them, the demons sprouted wings, and they all flew away together."

"So the demons seem to be entirely magical?" Ereben asked.

Minkar and Bahsa looked at one another. Both shrugged.

"And now this Bane thing...and its demons...are tracking us for some reason." Ereben shook his head. "Fleeing the chaos doesn't seem like so clever a plan any more."

"Maybe it was just hunting the Dryad. Looking for Drusa," Hamsa offered. His face brightened. "It might not be looking for us."

"I think he should know," Deena said to Bahsa. "It seems important now."

Bahsa turned toward his father, who nodded in assent. "He should know," Minkar said.

"Know what?"   Ereben could sense his heart rate increasing.

"The Dryad Bane," Bahsa began. "The mother of the Dryad Bane...the mother killed by her own child..." Bahsa swallowed, then looked again to his father.

Minkar looked directly into Ereben's eyes, and with a steady voice, said simply, "The mother of the Dryad Bane was Phaena Corban. Your Phaena."

Ereben felt tears welling in his eyes. Somehow he had known for decades, within his heart, that something unusual accounted for Phaena's having broken off contact with him. Now, he recognized that he should have overcome his insecurity long ago, and reached out to her. *The Dryad Bane.* Through his tears, he said softly, "Thank you...my friends. It is important that I know." He rose from his seat by the glowing coals, and wondered alone into the darkness of the scrub.

"I saved the sinews from your lake rat." Brindle Meadow showed Minkar a handful of partially dried sinews, then tucked them away. "And I've saved some bones to make needles. May I?" She gestured toward Minkar's neck.

Minkar slumped his shoulders, removed the large triangle of white caribou hide from around his neck, then returned it to

Brindle. "You were kind to allow me the use of it for so long." He was turning to resume his packing, then looked back at Brindle. "It didn't taste like a rat."

"Besides, when it gets cold again," she continued, "you have your brown caribou cape in your baggage. It was truly tasty...but it was a big rat."

Hamsa climbed onto Fart, then said to Brindle, with mock indignation, "When you have hunted and killed food for everyone to share, then you may name it whatever you like."

"But you never named it," Brindle replied.

"In all my experience as a hunter," Hamsa added with a smile, "this beast was unique."

Meriwa turned toward a fellow Iceman, and mouthed the word, "rat."

Ereben enjoyed the unusually playful banter. He understood that it was probably a release from the heavy burden upon the group, of Drusa's death and burial. Only his own, inner world had been shaken by what he had learned the previous evening about the Dryad Bane. It is not his own child. *Phaena's child. Killing so many. Damaging so much.*

Once everyone had completed packing, and for those who had journeyed to the cliff island, retrieving desired items from the horses' packs, Ereben climbed once again onto Starfire. He decided to follow the others, rather than lead. That would allow him to browse through one of the books that he had located in Yassar's pack, left on Shujaun, who now served merely as a pack horse. He would need to work harder at understanding the ancient Shadae in which it was written.

"I will lead today," Hamsa proclaimed.

"Do you know which way to go?" Ja No asked.

Hamsa looked to the East, and to the West, then pointed his entire arm northward.

"May I walk alongside," Meriwa asked, "to keep you company?"

"Of course."

Meriwa turned her head back toward the group, and winked her fur-rimmed eye.

"Fart shows us his pride," Ja No said.

Ereben realized that he had been dozing, as Starfire leisurely followed the loose line of animals and people. He still held an ancient tome in his hands. His dread of wrestling with the Shadae translation had kept the book tightly closed within the grip of both hands, which also held Starfire's reins. The sun beat down directly from above.

"How might a horse show us pride?" Sawney asked from atop Moap.

"He has always been left to the rear of all the rest of the animals," Ja No clarified. She and Sawney were immediately in front of Ereben. The Icemen had dispersed alongside the other riders. "Now he looks about with attention. Sometimes he looks back down the line in disbelief that he is leading. Anyone can see that."

Ereben leaned his body to bring Fart, with Hamsa riding him, into view. Fart indeed appeared to show a different personality than he had previously seen. "Fart does look proud."

"I am happy to see that you are awake," Ja No said. "I've been waiting to reach back and catch you when you tumbled off Starfire."

"Following is more relaxing than leading," he replied. Ereben sighed deeply, then opened the book he had held through his nap. The pages were not as he had remembered them. He closed the covers, and looked at the spine. He opened it again. Scribbled between the original lines of ancient Shadae, all boldly hand-written, he now found a tiny, jagged script that was difficult to make out. He halted Starfire for a moment, and squinted. Between each of the original lines was an apparent translation, written in Valish.

"Yassar Khayin has translated the Shadae," Ereben said to no one in particular. He quickly flipped through the pages, all the way to the end. "He translated it all." When Ja No turned her head back toward the lagging Ereben, he asked, "Did you ever see Yassar writing as we journeyed?"

"I did not," she replied. "Now that you are awake, you have to keep up with us."

Ereben went back to the beginning of the book, and tried to read it while Starfire was moving. He found he simply could not. He paused Starfire briefly, to stow the translated book into one of his pack bags. A hopeful warmth filled him. He wondered if Yassar had translated any of the other books. And his admiration of Yassar's dedication swelled.

When they halted for a short while beside a small pond, Ereben retrieved the book, and sat against a stunted tree to read it. The scribbled translation required him to work for each word. By the end of the first page, he developed a better sense of Yassar's script.

"You seem amused," Minkar said. He moved to a location from which he could see the pages.

"I am," Ereben replied. "When I couldn't understand it very well, it was all an awesome mystery. Now, I can see that there are valuable details and notions. But there is also a lot of total nonsense in here. The wisest people among the Lamblari Shouda were still trying to understand magic. Here, it says, 'Each act of magic exists only because of its connection to *The One Magic*, from which its descent to the human realm has emanated'. It's like there is a Magic god, who shares his power with people."

Minkar cringed, then raised both hands as well as his head, in a Shouda gesture of reverence toward Elloh.

"We all just take baby steps, trying to understand all of the connections." Ereben marked his place in the book with a thin twig, closed it, then carried the ancient tome to a dry place within one of Starfire's pack bags. He missed the wisdom of his grandfather, Chrysanthus.

Although he had decided that reading Yassar's scribble was too difficult while riding, he recognized that he rather enjoyed bringing up the rear of the group. There no longer seemed to be any doubt of their course toward the northwest coast. A weight had been lifted from his aging, fatigued shoulders. Even his knuckles and knees ached less, when he shed the mantle of leader.

As they proceeded northward through the afternoon, easterly wind increased, and an overcast sky seemed to grow lower and darker, with occasional, black, roiling clouds below the rest. The wind grew colder. Toward sunset—what he could discern of it, the party halted near a trickle of a creek, and set about erecting their various shelters.

Ereben looked about for anything that might serve as shelter for the Icemen, but saw nothing promising—only a runted, crooked tree with little foliage. "Meriwa," he shouted over the rasp of the cold wind, "you will need to share our tents tonight."

Meriwa scratched a fur-covered ear, and returned glances from her fellow Icemen. "We are Icemen."

"Good idea," Ja No said. "Two of you can fit in my tent."

"The weather looks like it's getting worse," Ereben added.

Those who had tents offered their available space. Ereben tapped Nootaikok's shoulder. "You can sleep in my tent."

Nootaikok appeared confused. Meriwa pointed a clawed finger at him, then at Ereben's still-collapsed tent. Without further hesitation, Nootaikok began to set up Ereben's tent so rapidly and properly, that Ereben could hardly assist in the process.

Ereben was awakened in the middle of the night by a loud groan from Nootaikok, who had been sleeping beside him. The interior of the tent was totally dark. He heard the sound of heavy hail striking the tent, and the noise of Nootaikok shuffling nearby. The rumble of thunder seemed muted, but offered no visible flashes of light. After a short while, with no indication of the hailstorm diminishing, Ereben dozed off again.

Ereben Leaf opened his eyes. The storm had passed, and daylight shined outside. Beside him, Nootaikok, seated with his back braced against the oiled canvas of the tent, snored softly, his head drooped to his chest.

Ereben carefully contorted himself, and managed to lace his boots without disturbing his Iceman guest. But when he began to unfasten the tent door, Nootaikok abruptly lifted his head, and blinked.

"Were you comfortable sleeping that way?" Ereben asked.

In response, Nootaikok shifted his torso to reveal a hole in the tent fabric. "I was not comfortable. A large hailstone tore through the wall of the shelter, and struck the middle of my thigh. With the continued storm, and no reasonable method for closing the hole, I blocked it with my back. I am certain that I now have many small bruises on my back from the hail. That seemed preferable to allowing the shelter to be torn apart entirely."

Ereben smiled, and patted Nootaikok on the knee. "Thank you, Nootaikok. I believe Brindle has some sinew for me to use for applying a patch."

Nootaikok seemed uncertain about how to reply. He gathered his belongings, and opened the tent. To Ereben's surprise, ankle-deep hailstones covered the ground. The air seemed warm enough to melt it.

He stepped out into the brightness of the morning. The sky was still overcast, but only with thin, high clouds that seemed barely to drift. Although the ground everywhere appeared snow covered, he could see at his feet only hailstones—mostly small, though some were as large as a walnut. Ereben found movement along the ground easiest if he simply shuffled his feet beneath the hail, rather than stepping above it.

Nootaikok walked to the side of the tent, near where he had slept against the fabric. He reached down, and retrieved a remarkable hailstone that nearly filled his palm. Several points projected from it. "This is the hailstone that struck the middle of my thigh. I would keep it if it would not melt. I have never seen hail so large—large enough to kill a person." He then snapped upright, and gazed toward the horses and the mule.

Ereben followed his gaze. The horses leisurely grazed beside the now hail-obscured creek. Moap stood beneath the scant protection of the solitary, runted tree, not bothering to uncover the meager grass below the hail.

"The storms have been backwards," Nootaikok said.

"Backwards?"

"In my home, the storms would come from many directions, probably because of the great mountains of Leopard Country. Since we left, most of the storms appear to come from the East. That seems backwards to me."

Ereben considered that for a moment. "I think you're right, Nootaikok. Now that I look back on all the horrible weather, it has come from the East. When I was young, in Rippleton, it seemed to always come from either the North or the West." Ereben could discern no response from the awkward

Iceman. "You have a sharp eye and a remarkable mind for observing details and analyzing their significance. Why do you suppose the weather has been backwards?"

Without a pause or facial expression, Nootaikok said, "All weather swirls, and moves eastward. When the swirls are small and tight, it is a storm. When they are larger swirls, that is the ordinary weather in between storms. A force has disturbed their normal movement, so they follow a different, less predictable course. The burning stones in the sky may be a cause or a consequence. That is the limit of what I can conclude."

Ereben smiled broadly at the expressionless Iceman, and nodded his head. "You are a treasure."

Ereben began to take down his tent, hoping to avoid its becoming soggy from melting hail. Nootaikok joined him in the effort.

"Tallow is not carrying much. Would you like to ride her?"

"Yes. I have never ridden a horse." Nootaikok remained without expression.

"That is a great idea," Deena said. She and Bahsa were folding their tent not far from Ereben. "Come with me now. We'll go and meet Tallow." She abandoned Bahsa. Walking up to Nootaikok, she locked arms, and escorted him to where Tallow was grazing.

"I think that is more about Tallow than Nootaikok," Bahsa commented. "She doesn't want Tallow to become a pack horse, and lose the feel of responding to a rider."

"If he doesn't frighten the horse," Ereben replied, "and he can learn to ride, then maybe the other Icemen will give it a try. Not that they need to ride. They seem to have more stamina than the horses."

"The horses...and Moap...have become accustomed to being led by the Icemen," Bahsa added, "every time something causes them to bolt."

"And there is Shujaun," Ereben said. He crunched his boots on top of the accumulated hail. "Should the horses be ridden on all this stuff?"

"It just followed us back." Minkar rubbed the stray stallion on its forehead. "Nothing but bones. But he still has a bridle." Minkar gently removed the stallion's bridle. "His mouth looks very sore."

Minkar and Hamsa had spent the morning on a hunting excursion, while everyone else waited for the hail to melt in the warmth of the sun. The animals had been allowed to graze and drink from the creek.

"No luck?" Bahsa asked his father.

"Other than this poor horse, we saw almost nothing. It is a barren stretch of land east of here. No animals, few birds, and no signs of people."

"Have you named your new horse?" Brindle asked.

"Bones." When Minkar walked toward the creek, where the other animals were grazing, Bones willingly followed. Bones then squeezed himself between two of the other horses, and remained there, grazing and drinking, as Minkar returned to the campsite.

While everyone was discussing when to resume the journey, Nootaikok walked about, collecting an armful of long, brown blades of grass. When he returned to the campsite, he began braiding the grass, eventually making what was clearly a halter for a horse. Then he walked among the horses, and calmly approached Bones. The stallion paid him little attention, as he gently placed the braided grass halter onto Bones' head.

"I will look after Bones," he said bluntly to Minkar.

Minkar nodded. "I think he would like that. He looks so frail that he may have difficulty keeping up with the other horses."

"I will look after him," the Iceman stated again.

Brindle Meadow approached Bones, and carefully tied a large, white triangle of caribou hide around the stallion's neck. "He needs to feel some dignity," she said to Nootaikok.

The Iceman glanced blankly at Brindle. He touched the white fur of the stallion's new neckerchief, then smiled broadly at Bones, and rubbed her forehead again. Ereben had never seen Nootaikok smile before.

As she returned to the group, Minkar smirked at her. "That is indeed a much better use."

"If you no longer need your sinew," Ereben said to Brindle, "I do need to patch my tent, where the hail punched through."

Brindle looked back and forth between Ereben and Minkar. "I have always cherished my caribou cape, but it works perfectly well with a corner of it missing. The sinew is yours. Do you need my bone needle as well?"

"Thank you, Brindle."

Not only was the day warming rapidly, but a dry wind swooped in from the East, melting the remaining hail stones, and drying all of their gear. Moap and the horses were brought into the camp for packing up. Nootaikok gently led Bones by his new, braided grass halter to join them.

Ereben quickly stitched the tear in his tent wall, while the others completed their packing. It would still need better waterproofing, but he decided that it would have to suffice for at least one night.

Hamsa again rode Fart in the lead, as the party trudged northward again. By late afternoon, the warm, dry breeze had brought in more humidity, and with it, clouds of gnats. The animals shook their heads repeatedly, while their riders as well as those on foot waved their hands continually across their faces, to find respite from the gnats.

As they searched for a suitable site to halt for the night, Ereben noticed that most of the areas that appeared promising from a distance were instead slightly boggy. Finally, just before the sun set, Hamsa proclaimed that he had found a dry spot that also offered an abundance of dry, twiggy branches usable as firewood.

Ereben invited Nootaikok to once again join him inside his tent, but the Iceman stated simply that he preferred to sleep under the sky. Nevertheless, Nootaikok assisted Ereben in erecting the tent, for which Ereben thanked him.

Near their eventual campfire, the gnats either avoided the smoky area, or momentarily hovered above the light of the flames, then dropped into the coals.

"Look at this," Deena said, bending close to the ground. "Hundreds of tiny frogs. They are everywhere."

Ereben saw no frogs in front of him, but when he turned around, he could see them in the shadows. Not hundreds, but thousands—each the size of his little fingernail or smaller. They climbed about the plethora of dry branches scattered in the shadowy boundary beyond the fire circle and those seated about it. They seemed to be attempting to climb as high as possible, in an apparent quest to consume gnats.

Nootaikok glanced at all the tiny frogs. "I will sleep in your tent tonight, Ereben Leaf."

✂

Even a goal within clear view can be snatched away in an instant by an unanticipated challenge. We plan only for what we know.

Gedzik the Blighted: The Gift

"This is insane!" Margarida shouted. She stared through the pike fence that they had hurriedly set up at the mouth of their rock shelter the previous evening, to keep frogs from entering. Now, beyond the pikes, frogs were everywhere. Frogs on the ground, frogs on the plants, frogs on the rocks, frogs on top of frogs. "We really should have stayed at the Abbey. We're all going to die here!" Her wings stood erect above her, in an unmistakable sign of alarm.

For once, her mate, Timo, did not immediately amplify Margarida's dismay. "They're not that big."

"They come up to my waist," Margarida replied, "and they swallow bugs my size. At least all those gnats weren't trying to eat us. How are we supposed to leave here?"

Wisfel tried as best he could to ignore the conversation. He knew they were within a day or so of reaching the northwest coast. Yesterday afternoon, before Jianjian had descended through the menacing clouds of gnats, he had actually seen the Northwest Island—their destination—rising above the horizon. "Jianjian!" he called out.

After a moment Jian and Jian walked separately into view. As the two unique, one-winged birds walked toward the pike fence, the frogs scattered. "We have eaten a generous meal this morning," Jian sang melodiously.

Standing beside Jian, Jian agreed. "That is a rarely encountered opportunity."

They joined their stubby, wingless claws. "We are not likely to see that again," Jianjian sang in harmony. "Where there are so many frogs, the lizards and snakes soon come to feast on them. And larger birds then come to eat the lizards and snakes."

"Take down the fence, and pack up!" Wisfel shouted to the group.

For a moment, Margarida stared at the broad bodies of Jianjian, and the fleeing frogs, then relaxed her diaphanous wings, and joined other Faeries in retrieving the pikes that had formed the impromptu fence.

Timo came alongside her, and kissed her with a smile. "Wisfel said he had seen the island island yesterday. It won't be much longer."

"Timo is correct, Margarida." Jianjian intoned in a beautiful harmony. "We will reach the coast today."

Twenty Faeries scurried about, packing their gear onto Jianjians' two, broad backs, then climbed aboard in their accustomed places. As Jianjian spread their wings, and lifted from the damp ground, their good fortune became apparent.

Just to their east, a trickle of lizards and snakes seeped westward. Wisfel could see more and larger lizards and snakes following behind them. Clouds of gnats rose from the grasslands, but appeared to him to be not as dense as the previous afternoon.

Albric, seated immediately behind Wisfel, shouted into his ear. "Margarida's complaint was just a little early. Those snakes would have had no trouble passing through our fence."

Wisfel turned to see Margarida, on the adjacent body, smirk at him with satisfaction. As he thought about all the dangers they had thus far encountered and avoided, since leaving the tenuous safety of Moss Abbey, he wondered if he would have been so confident about leaving, had he known then what they would face.

So far, nobody had died, though his beloved ringtails, Headie and Tailer, had lost their lives to a larger predator. If all of the Faeries successfully reached the Northwest Island, then unlike the now-extinct Thistlepix, Faeries would have a chance at rebuilding a growing colony. There would be nine mated pairs, plus Albric and himself. He knew—had known most of his life— that he would never mate. Blighted Faeries, in addition to displaying conspicuous abnormalities, were invariably sterile. And he was forced to always wear Gedzik's long sleeved, deeply cowled cape, whenever he might be exposed to the sun.

But Albric, though a young adult, would be quite old by the time any newly born female finally came of age. During this entire journey, Albric had supported and encouraged him. Wisfel could not recall ever having so loyal a companion. He cherished the friendship, and could not help but wonder if it would last beyond their arrival at their final destination.

Wisfel deflected a gnat the size of his head with his left arm, almost unseating himself. He immediately felt the hand of Albric on his shoulder, assisting him. "Thank you."

His deep purple, cowled cape was tucked snugly about his torso and legs. Early in their initial journey aboard Jianjian, he had learned to draw the string of the cowl tightly under his chin, and to tie the generous cuffs of its sleeves with pieces of spider silk twine. All of these measures prevented the cape from flapping and inflating in the steady air that flowed over Jianjian during flight. He usually sat with his chest nearly flat against the birds' feathers.

Even the normal Faeries, those with wings, could not really fly, but only use the weak, filmy things to break their fall from not too great a height. But he had envied them their wings all of his life. With the generosity of Jianjian, even his blighted, wingless body could experience true flight. Although none of the others had mentioned it, he was certain that they were all just as thrilled—despite their bickering and outbursts of complaints about the difficulty and dangers of their migration to the Northwest Island.

Late in the day, as they continued toward the northwest, Wisfel noted a wave of seagulls moving eastward, and descending to the ground. *And larger birds then come to eat the lizards and snakes.* Just north of the path followed by Jianjian, he saw a small group of humans, accompanied by a few domestic animals heading in the same direction, toward the coast. He had seen very few humans below them for the past several days.

Jianjian seemed to instinctively avoid humans, both in their flight path and where they chose to land. A river below them and just south of the humans reached directly to the coast. As he expected, Jianjian descended south of the river, toward a rocky area in the otherwise open plain of marshy grass.

What he could see of the Northwest Island, still in the distance, was a large, mountain peak near the center, and several smaller peaks toward different edges of the coast. They would be there tomorrow. Then would begin the challenge of locating the safest spot for Faeries to settle—safe from humans and animals, and safe from storms. He had no idea how to identify such a place, though he knew that nineteen other Faeries would expect him to lead them to it. They might have to fly all about the island to decide.

Another unknown was whether or not Jianjian would be content to drop them all at the nearest spot of solid land on the island, then return to their home in the Western Lands. Wisfel had not discussed the issue with the birds.

As daylight dawned on what might be the final day of their journey, Wisfel strode from beneath their rock shelter to find an overcast sky, with a strong, northerly breeze. He felt chill in the air. When he called Jianjian, the birds approached him, then joined. "Do you think it is too windy to fly?"

Jianjian replied in a tuneful harmony. "We will need to hop along the chain of islands, in order to reach the largest island. That may require a number of days. If the wind blows too hard, we will turn back."

A number of days. He sensed a deflation of his hope. As he seriously considered the distances among the islands, which had always been plain to see on his map, he recognized that Jianjian were, of course, correct. It might be a number of days or even a week or more to arrive. He had been ready for this ordeal to end. "When we finally arrive," Wisfel asked, "will you stay with us, or return to your home?"

"That cannot be answered until we have arrived," Jianjian sang. "Will Jianjian find sufficient food? Will Jianjian be safe from the creatures that live there, and the humans that are traveling there? And nesting time will come."

Wisfel had given very little consideration to the risk to the Faeries themselves from creatures that might already inhabit the island. It had been only by magic that Ternaria had existed for so many generations. Once that magic by the Monks of Moss Abbey had failed, the Thistlepix were exterminated in the blink of an eye, and all but twenty Faeries, including himself, had perished.

He was startled by Albric's hand on his shoulder. "Everybody and everything is loaded up. Time to go."

Wisfel had been lost in thought, staring westward into the blustery sky for longer than he realized. He climbed aboard the base of Jianjians' neck, and offered a hand to Albric, who seated himself, as usual, immediately behind him. He tied the sleeves of his cape, just before they lifted off into the northerly wind.

Once aloft, Wisfel noted a huge sailing ship off the coast. He had not seen it the evening before. He wondered if the

Northwest Island might have become populated with humans, after the Monks had considered it to be deserted. Surely humans had visited there in the past. If the island has continued to remain unpopulated, what was it about the island that was so inhospitable? The thoughts of too many unfortunate outcomes seemed to be crowding into his joy at having nearly completed the journey—farther than any Faeries had ever traveled.

Jianjian were repeatedly buffeted by wind gusts, as they crossed the delta of a great river, and aimed toward the nearest of the islands. He hugged himself against the nape of Jian's neck. Looking back over the nine Faeries behind him, and the other ten riding Jianjians' other half, he could see that everyone perched themselves more snugly into Jianjians' feathers. Though the twin birds seemed to be expending more effort than usual, their course never altered.

With now open water below him, Wisfel could not judge the speed of their travel. Small whitecaps ruffled in several different directions. Judging from the increasingly distant western coast of the mainland, Jianjian were making only gradual headway.

By mid-day, Jianjian descended over a marshy area above the coast of the near island. A flock of about a dozen ducks rose up from the water. When they reached nearly the height at which Jianjian were flying, three of the ducks thrashed in mid-air, and fell again to the water.

It was then that Quiri shouted, "Hunters with arrows!" He pointed to the edge of a small pond.

Jianjian dipped away from the pond, and cruised along the island's western coast, passing a human settlement. About midway up the island coast, Wisfel saw that they were finally landing on a ledge below a modest cliff.

Stopping here for the night meant that there were three more islands to reach, prior to arriving at the much larger

Northwest Island. Wisfel counted four days in his head. *Four more days.*

Timo and Margarida bickered with one another about the presence of humans. Sixteen other Faeries seemed to have their individual interpretations of its significance, and voiced them all nearly simultaneously. Albric simply looked at Wisfel, and rolled his eyes, as he began to unpack.

Jianjian separated, and walked in opposite directions along the ledge, apparently in their search for dinner. The two of them conspicuously moved with more fatigue than usual.

"You look tired, Jian," he said to the nearest.

"The wind is difficult over the sea," Jian sang at a slower tempo, and in a lower pitch. "I have never flown over the sea. I am afraid of the remainder of the journey. I am afraid of human hunters."

"We have gone a long way," Wisfel reminded Jian, "and it's not too much farther."

Jian slowly, silently walked away.

"Maybe we could rest here for a day." Albric offered.

"An entire day of this?" Wisfel nodded his head toward the eighteen bickering Faeries.

"Do you think we need to put up the pike fence tonight?"

Wisfel stepped toward the outer edge of their rock shelf, peered over. Far below him breakers dashed against the base of the cliff. "Just to be safe. We don't know what crawls around here."

Laia screamed, and bolted away from the just completed pike fence, and into the protective arms of Quiri. A huge bird landed on the rock shelf, and awkwardly walked toward the fence. It pecked at the fence with a long, curved, black beak. The sun had already fallen behind the nearest island to their west, though the sky had yet to significantly darken.

Soon, the entire shelf beyond the fence filled with nearly identical birds. Each one seemed curious enough about the fence to approach it, and peck it a time or two, then would locate one of the increasingly rare empty spots in which to settle down for the evening.

Wisfel wondered about Jian and Jian. They had gone off in opposite directions. Without one another, they were unable to fly. But he had not paid attention to them while the pike fence was being set. If anything happened to either one of them, then he and the rest of the Faeries he had urged to join him in this journey would surely die here.

By nightfall, Wisfel could no longer see out of the inward-leaning, pike fence. The bodies of sleeping birds rose well above his height. He mused that a benefit of the birds' surprise arrival was that it had caused all of the Faeries to voice their complaints in guarded whispers. Another was that the interior of their ledge cave was comfortably warm, despite the sea breeze.

In a cacophony of flapping wings and bursts of air, Wisfel awakened to see all of the birds depart, nearly at the same moment. He examined the pike fence. Even the merest nudge brought down several of the pikes. He stepped beyond them onto the open ledge. Jianjian were nowhere in sight. He could not imagine how they might have escaped, or which direction they could have gone.

He looked over the edge, but could see only the pounding of breakers against the rocky cliff. "Jianjian! Jianjian!"

"What do we do if they don't come back?" Albric asked quietly.

"I guess we can look for a path to climb up to the top," Wisfel said, though he felt certain that there was no way to do that.

Without carrying any of his gear, Albric immediately located a small, vertical notch in the cliff, to the side of their shelter cave, and began to climb upward. Because of the contour of the stone above Wisfel, Albric soon vanished from his view. He stepped closer to the edge of their ledge, and looked up again, but could see only layers of rock.

After a short time, Wisfel faintly heard the voice of Albric calling, "Jianjian!" In reply, he heard only a susurration of sea breeze.

"What are we supposed to do now?" Timo asked.

Wisfel could see the eyes of eighteen Faeries upon him. He felt like simply weeping. Instead, he turned away from them, and carefully seated himself with his blighted legs dangling over the cliff edge.

Clearly a young and healthy Faerie could scale the cliff above. If Albric could do it, likely all the rest of the Faeries could do so as well—except for him. He gazed down at his pale, white legs. Far below his feet, breakers silently crashed against the island.

Laia seated herself beside him, and draped an arm across his wingless shoulders. "They'll all calm down pretty soon, and get to thinking about options."

"There probably aren't many," he replied.

She squeezed his shoulders briefly. "Time to move away from this gusty edge, or there won't be any options."

Wisfel and Laia both scooted backwards a bit, then rose to their feet. When Wisfel turned to face the anger of the Faeries that he had left stranded on a cliff face, he was surprised to see Quiri directly in front of him. Quiri smiled, shook his head, then shrugged.

"The two of us were worried about you," Quiri said. "Let's all sit down together, and figure out what to do."

With all of them but Albric, seated in a circle on the stone, Quiri's call for ideas initially silenced everyone. "With so much to say, nobody has any ideas?"

"Well," Margarida started off, "we can't stay here. So we either go up or down."

"There is no way we can go down." Timo asserted flatly. "And we would just end up drowning in the sea."

"So, up?" Laia scanned the group of downturned faces.

"Albric climbed upward," Wisfel said tentatively.

"How far up?" Timo smirked. "He's not here!"

"He climbed up to search for Jianjian. I heard him calling them at one point."

Every Faerie stood, and looked up toward the upper cliff. Several of them shouted Albric's name. There was no reply.

"Let's all call him at the same time," Laia suggested. "One, two, three then call." At her count most of them shouted his name simultaneously. Still no reply.

Then, as if on cue, and with an uncharacteristic fluttering of wings, Jianjian descended toward them. Everyone hurried to the safety of the overhang. Jianjians' landing was not as graceful as usual. When they came to rest, Albric hopped down.

"We need to gather everything immediately," he said, with command in his voice, "if you want to leave this island."

"What is this about?" Timo asked.

"Jianjian have an injured wing. They can no longer fly us across the open water, but they can fly us downward, to a sailing ship that is passing below us now."

"Where is the sailing ship going?" Wisfel asked.

"That doesn't matter. The ship can carry us away from here to some land somewhere. But we have to do so now, or the opportunity will be lost."

"Yes?" Wisfel asked of the other Faeries. When he saw general nodding in agreement, he added, "Albric says now!"

ஒஒஒ

A single, favored seed may appear to be an obvious choice for planting a new garden, but only the broadest array of possibilities offers a prospect of enduring success.

Meriwa: A Land of Belonging

Ereben, with some amusement, had been watching Nootaikok fussing over Bones, the emaciated stallion that he had adopted from Minkar Jarad. The Iceman smiled and rocked his head, as he spoke to the stallion as if speaking to an infant. He would repeatedly hide a handful of grain behind his back, then casually turn away from Bones, keeping the grain visible in his open hand. As soon as Bones would sweep up a mouthful from Nootaikok's palm, the Iceman would turn back around, to chortle, and rub Bones' nose or ears.

The stallion already seemed to be gaining in strength, while Nootaikok seemed to be gaining in confidence and engagement outside of his private thoughts. Each seemed to benefit the other.

A small group of people—what appeared to Ereben to be two or three families with children and goats approached their camp from the East. Two adults and two children were dressed in clothing similar to Ereben's recollection of Kasazi garb. Three individuals appeared to have the yellowish skin tones of the Orkahti people—two adults and a child. The Orkahti man carried two wicker cages containing chickens, while the child guided two goats with a switch. With a sudden recognition, Ereben realized that the remaining two children were, in fact, two Rock Gnomes.

The three children pointed with glee at the gathered horses, but abruptly lowered their arms when Nootaikok stepped around Bones to look at the children.   The adults took on cautious expressions.

Ereben came forward. "Welcome."

"Ereben Leaf!" the male Rock Gnome shouted, as he sprinted toward Ereben.

"Palmer?" Ereben asked. The waist-high Gnome looked familiar, but now dressed in more traditional garb.

"Brother Palmer, now," he proclaimed, as he gave Ereben's thigh a hug. "Come, come, come," he called to the other Rock Gnome, while flapping one tiny hand at her.

Dressed in a deep purple robe, with a sickle tucked into the side of the waist tie, the other Gnome scurried over. "Brother Palmer makes up stories," she said, with a sidelong glance, "so I am pleased that this one turns out to be true.   I am Sister Ariama." Ereben bent over, and offered Sister Ariama his hand. She replied with a perfunctory handshake. "So I understand that we are going to live on an island."

Ereben realized that, not only had Palmer—Brother Palmer—belatedly accepted his offer to join their party, but had successfully recruited eight others as well. And although Palmer had suggested that he might likely be the only surviving Rock Gnome, he had nonetheless found a partner—Sister Ariama—to comfortably guide and regulate his daily activities, in the tradition of the Rock Gnomes.

"It is looking like we are going to have quite a gathering," Brindle Meadow said from behind Ereben.

He turned to look at her. "Come help me greet our newcomers." He grimaced, out of sight of the Rock Gnomes, Orkahtis and Kasazis.

When he looked back at the new arrivals, Ereben was surprised to see Nootaikok spread his arms wide, and proclaim with a broad smile, "Welcome!"

As they all approached, Ereben's companions greeted them, and undertook a lengthy round of introductions on both sides. The Orkahti man and woman were named Batu and Kushi, respectively, and their seven year old daughter, Zaypo.

Zaypo then ceremoniously introduced her two goats. "This is Chaga, and he always wants to be the boss. And this is Chagala, and she is more gentle."

Batu laughed. "My daughter named the goats, and likes to care for them. My chickens have no names." He held up his two wicker cages containing what appeared to be a black feathered rooster and a brown and white speckled hen.

Nootaikok fondly greeted the two goats, and shook the hand of the Orkahti girl, Zaypo.

"I am called Kwahu," the Kasazi man said with a bow. "My woman is called Soyala. My two babies, Tocho and Tawa."

The kids appeared to Ereben to be four or five years old. When Kwahu mentioned that he carried seed for planting, Deena Jarad inquired as to what he expected to plant.

"Maize, barley, squash, brown bean and onion."

It was only then that Ereben realized how inadequate their own planning had been. He had given no though whatsoever to how they might provide for themselves on their new island. "You are wiser than we have been. Your seed is a treasure for us all. And the goats and chickens."

During the early morning, their ship, the Rashiq, had anchored on the nearby coast. Hamsa, its owner, had gone out to the shore to meet with Captain Mahfud. When he returned, he looked over the much enlarged group of passengers, and yet an additional horse, Bones. Hamsa took Ereben and Brindle aside.

"I count a total of nine horses, one mule, two goats, chickens, and twenty-three people, not counting the captain and crew of the Rashiq. And we still have the four, huge columns of Jadeite below deck. Captain Mahfud has already sailed to the

Northwest Island once, to explore the possible sites for landing and unloading the Jadeite. He says that the seas are rough, and the winds are strong. Without a proper dock, he believes that we will need two horses to assist in off-loading the Jadeite safely. But we will need at least two, perhaps three trips to carry all the animals and people."

"So the Jadeite has to be unloaded first?" Brindle asked.

"Yes. But two of the animals will go with us for that. And they will need to be left there."

"Ereben! Come quick! Quick! Quick!" Brother Palmer jabbered, waving both hands.

Ereben and Brindle Meadow had been sitting in the captain's cabin, beneath the quarterdeck of the Rashiq, discussing with Hamsa the issues of handling the Jadeite columns, once they reached the Northwest Island. Sister Ariama had joined them, while Captain Mahfud commanded the ship from the deck above where they sat. Sister Ariama rolled her eyes.

"What is it, Brother Palmer?" Ereben asked politely.

"You won't believe me if I tell you." He gestured some more, while almost bouncing on his toes.

Ereben drooped his head, then lifted it bearing a broad smile. "We will be right along." He realized that the Rock Gnome was easily amazed by the many new experiences he now shared. But the Gnome truly was becoming an annoyance. He glanced around the cabin. When everyone shrugged, he led the three of them out onto the main deck of the Rashiq.

Brother Palmer had already sprinted to the bow of the ship. Ereben and the others walked past Starfire and Turnip, both tied between the two masts, and on to the very bow, where a jib sail had been hoisted onto the bowsprit to aid in negotiating the winds and currents between the islands.

"See?" Brother Palmer asked.

What Ereben saw appeared to be two pigeon-sized birds sheltering beside one another on the deck, just aft of the bow rails. Neither bird moved at all, when Brother Palmer approached.

"It's two birds," Sister Ariama said, with a glimmer of ridicule in her tone.

"Yes. Yes. Two birds," Brother Palmer replied. "But look closer. A lot closer."

Ereben bent over. "Faeries! Is that Wisfel?" He crouched further, steadying himself against the rolling of the Rashiq.

"Ereben Leaf!", Wisfel shouted. "Is there a safer place for us?"

"The captain's cabin?" Ereben asked Hamsa, who crouched beside him, eyes wide with wonder.

"Of course," Hamsa said. "The birds as well?"

"Yes," the Faerie replied. "These are Jianjian."

Hamsa turned to Brother Palmer. "Go ask the cook for a bread basket."

"I assured our cook that they would only pick up scraps from the floor," Hamsa said to Wisfel, who had remained in the bread basket with Jianjian. "While their are no frogs, and not too many insects in the galley, they should find their dinner with ease."

The other Faeries had accepted a wooden nook along the planking of a buttress of the cabin's stern wall, beneath the hinged port that Captain Mahfud had created for passing the Jadeite columns below deck.

"Should I carry them down there?" Hamsa asked.

"No need," the blighted Faerie answered. "Just describe how to get there from here, and they can find it. I think they can even fit under the cabin door."

"Describe it?"

"Yes. They are quite intelligent."

After Hamsa skeptically explained the route, Jianjian joined their stubby claws, then fluttered out of the basket and silently vanished beneath the cabin door.

"The cook will bring some cracked grains for you and your companions, as well as some water from a cask. While we wait for that, can you tell me how you came to be wearing the cloak and armor and saber of Gedzik?"

"You know about Gedzik?" Wisfel exclaimed.

"I not only know *about* Gedzik, I knew Gedzik himself. I once worked with my cousins as jewelers in Shibam. I personally made the cloak and the other items specifically for Gedzik." Hamsa could hardly stop smiling.

"You made them yourself?" Brindle Meadow asked.

"Indeed. We made tiny furniture for children's toys. When Faeries would sail down to visit, they often found the tiny items perfect for their own use." Hamsa cautiously touched the hem of Wisfel's full-length cloak. "Gedzik was not like any of the other Faeries. He had white hair, red eyes, and completely white skin. He was smaller, and had no wings. I worked with a jeweler's eye piece to make these things to fit him."

"Thank you," Wisfel said softly, pressing tears from his eyes with his fingertips. "They fit me perfectly. The cloak has allowed me to travel in the sun. And the shine from the breast plate saved us more than once from certain death."

"And he got us this far, with all twenty of us still alive," a female Faerie said.

Ereben Leaf guided Starfire, while Brindle Meadow did the same for Turnip, as the two horses gently lowered the last of the four massive Jadeite columns to the hastily constructed pier. Each column had been rigged with lath and ropes, so that a yard arm of the Rashiq could lift each column from the ship's hold, out through the port created through the stern wall of the captain's cabin.

Captain Mahfud's crew had located their pier within a sheltered nook of the large bay at the southwest of the great island. After the last of the Jadeite columns had been offloaded, the crew weighed anchor, and set sail with their empty ship, across the turbulent straight, to transport another load of animals and migrants from the far coast, to their new home.

The Faeries and their Jianjian had been the first to disembark on their arrival at the island. Hamsa joined the two Rock Gnomes, Brother Palmer and Sister Ariama in also staying on the island.

The Jadeite columns would remain where they were, until Ereben had formulated a plan for their transport on the island, and their ultimate placement. Ereben stared at the resting Jadeite.

"Where will the Faeries go?" Hamsa asked Ereben.

"I don't know. Jianjian can't fly." He glanced at the small rock indentation beneath which the Jianjian could be seen. He assumed that the Faeries were also there.

Brother Palmer pulled on the edge of Ereben's cape. "We know rock. And most of this island seems to have a lot of deep rock...and peaks of solid rock."

"What Brother Palmer is suggesting," Sister Ariama stated, "is that the two of us spend a little time studying the lay of the land in the various features. Then we can make some useful suggestions for situating the Faeries and the rest of the people and animals."

"And the proper locations for the Jadeite columns?" Ereben added. "They will need to form a tetrahedron—one on each of the lower peaks on the corners of the island, and one at the very top."

"Lets go," Sister Ariama said to Brother Palmer, with a wave of her hand. The two of them walked to a nearby rock outcrop, and effortlessly vanished into it.

Ereben looked down at the four huge columns of Jadeite, in their lath and rope slings, and then glanced up toward the highest peak. "I don't think the Monks had thought about how to get these things up onto the peaks."

Brindle Meadow smiled. "They were good at notions, but not about practicalities."

"I think that all the people and animals pulling together can tow them to the three, low peaks." Ereben shook his head. "Even then, we'll have to figure out how to get them standing within the sockets that we dig at their summits." He rubbed his forehead with his hand. "I don't have any idea how to deal with the one on the big peak in the center of the island."

Brindle, Hamsa and Ereben labored together in constructing a human-size fence just to the east of the newly built dock. Brindle's idea was to instruct all newcomers, along with their various animals, to avoid heading in that direction. The fence could not possibly block off the miles-wide passage into the southeast, but, they hoped, would at least remind those who arrived on subsequent voyages of the Rashiq from the mainland, to not go there. Earlier, Ereben and Brindle had carried Jianjian and all the Faeries in their hands, to a location well beyond the fence.

"Wisfel said that it might take them a week or more to identify a suitable location where they could establish a community on the peninsula," Ereben explained to Hamsa.

Hamsa sighed. "I have the extra Jadeite to carve four small columns for their protection. They would be similar to your huge columns, but in proportion to their size. The Faeries could dig the sockets for standing the columns, but they would not be able to transport them to the places where they would be used." He shook his head. "A single human could easily carry the Jadeite there, and stick them into their sockets, but how can they be placed by a human, without trampling the very land the Faeries have chosen?"

"Do you think Jianjian could lift them?" Brindle asked.

Ereben turned to her. "We don't know how long it will take for the injured wing to heal...or if it will ever heal."

"People used to live here," Sister Ariama said. She and Brother Palmer had just emerged from the rock, after surveying the island.

"Are there any people still here?" Brindle asked.

"No."

"They were miners," Brother Palmer added. "They mined stuff from a cave about half-way North from here."

When Brindle and Ereben waited for some clarification, Sister Ariama continued. "We found a tiny, deserted village of dilapidated shacks near the mine entrance. Whatever they were mining must have been exhausted many years ago. Metals, I think. There are a few graves, with no markers, but not much else. And when they left, they must have taken away all their tools and such."

In Ereben's mind, a now useless mine might explain why nobody had recently braved the stormy straight to come and live here. "Did you identify the right locations for the Jadeite pillars?"

"Yes. Yes. Of course. The three low peaks will be difficult to climb, but the high peak doesn't have a trail of any kind that leads to the top." She adjusted the sickle tucked into her waist rope. "I can show you the exact spots, but you'll have to figure out how to do those pillar things."

"Are the spots for the Jadeite solid rock, or can we dig into it?"

"All solid rock," Brother Palmer answered. "Totally solid."

Ereben glanced at Brindle, then stared at his own feet. "Maybe this is all just not possible. Maybe this was all a bad idea from the start."

Ereben stooped, as he walked alone into the mine shaft just above the deserted settlement. He held a small torch of twigs, to light his way. To his surprise, the shaft ended after about 60 yards. The scraped walls revealed nothing in particular. He felt the fine rocks at the edges of the floor, guessing by its dark gray color and its weight that it contained iron.

Outside the mine, he scooted down the slope, and surveyed the small collection of collapsing shanties that comprised the deserted town. One small shack appeared to possess a disproportionately large, stone chimney. Upon opening the door, both its rusted hinges broke away from the doorpost. Then the door's wooden handle snapped off the plank that had anchored it. He entered.

There, he found a forge, with rotted bellows, but a large, solid anvil, mounted atop a section of tree trunk. There appeared to be no tools remaining, other than a single, iron mallet.

The remainder of the village consisted of structures that were likely too decrepit to be useful. There seemed to be no easily portable tools or vessels remaining. His thought of vessels raised the question in his mind of their source of water. Ereben followed the slope of a gentle ravine into a stand of forest. At the convergence of the ravine with another, similar ravine, he discovered a circular stone well. After dropping a small rock into its dark hole, he heard a distinct splash. He guessed the water was about five yards below ground.

He returned up the slope to the town, and scanned the nearby land. Much of it seemed suitable for growing food, and grazing animals.

Ereben located a small plank of desiccated lumber, then used his dagger to carve a sign:

Ereben Leaf

Smithy

This he hung above the empty doorway of the forge, then climbed back onto Starfire, and headed down toward the dock.

Partway down, he came upon Brindle Meadow, riding Turnip up the trail.

"Come see what I found," she called to Ereben, before he could say the very same words. Brindle turned Turnip about and led Ereben downward. She dismounted at the opening of a narrow, slanted cleft in the rock east of the trail, and pointed for Ereben to look in.

He hoisted his aching body off of Starfire, walked to the entrance of the cleft, then held his hand above his eyes, to block the glare of the bright sky. He gazed into the deep shadow. On the slender patch of soil about half-way back, his eyes fell upon a munu mushroom. He saw only one.

꒰ଓ꒱

Certain tasks which present the most daunting of challenges may surprise us with their truly simple solutions.

Ereben Leaf: Chronicle of the Counterspell

Hamsa and a single crew member from the Rashiq pulled the ship's small boat onto the shore at the very tip of the southern peninsula. He then climbed a low hill, dug a socket into the stony ground, and inserted the third, small Jadeite column that he had carved. The two of them packed the bottom edge of the column's exposed surface with small stones. He had not yet found a solution to placing the fourth column at the small peak at the center of the peninsula.

Upon returning to the Rashiq, Hamsa stood on the deck amid ship with Captain Mahfud and all the crew members. "Since all of the work of transporting the columns and passengers is complete," Hamsa said, "you now have to decide whether to return to your homes aboard the Rashiq, or remain here on the Northwest Island, to make a new home. I plan to stay. But if any one or more of you wish to return, then the Rashiq will set sail tomorrow with the full crew."

"Who wishes to stay?" Captain Mahfud asked.

The crew members looked at one another, but remained silent.

"Then I ask, 'who wishes to return?'"

Again, they looked at one another, and remained silent.

"We will sail to the new dock, to carry our ship's owner there. Tomorrow morning, each of you must decide. All must remain, or all must go."

"Maybe call it New Rippleton?", Bahsa Jarad suggested.

His spouse, Deena, shook her head. "I think simple would be better."

Zaypo, the self-assured Orkahti girl smiled broadly. "We can call the town Simpleton."

The circle of dozens of new migrants chuckled as a group. They had gathered at mid-day in the deserted and crumbling mining town, to give names to the town, the location of the dock at the shore, and the island itself. To Ereben's eyes, everyone was there but the Faeries, who had wisely vanished to the south of their designated peninsula. And everyone would, with the group's approval, select locations for eventually constructing their homes or farms.

"My crew," Captain Mahfud said, "already calls our tiny dock 'Blinkport', because if you blink, you will miss it. Most of them plan to settle near there."

"Anyone disagree with that?" Brindle asked. "Well...I think we've chosen a name for the port."

As assorted suggestions droned on, Ereben considered asking all the adults, horses and the mule drag to one of the Jadeite columns to the low peak on the west coast—the easiest of the hauls. That, he thought, might make the naming process a little less tedious.

"Oh, look at that!" Meriwa said loudly. She pointed her clawed index finger toward a small stand of scrubby trees. "Hazel! We'll have hazel nuts to eat in season."

"That's perfect," Ereben said. "Let's name this town Hazelton."

Nods slowly propagated through the group. Hazelton it was. Within a short time, they had agreed to name the island itself Newhome.

"Is it possible for you to just open a socket in the rock of each of the four peaks where the columns will be placed?" Ereben spoke with Brother Palmer and Sister Ariama.

Brother Palmer's eyes widened, while Sister Ariama's eyebrows lowered.

"We just came back from those peaks," Sister Ariama complained. "It's a long way to travel inside the rock."

"I suppose we can just have teams of people climb up to the peaks, and eventually dig them out," Ereben stated gravely. "Of course that would have to wait until I had forged suitable tools for the job."

"No need for drama," Sister Ariama replied. "We'll head up there again tomorrow. Give us a couple of days to get all four of them ready."

He smiled. "Thank you, Sister Ariama and Brother Palmer. Be sure to measure the dimensions of the column bases, and allow about a quarter of each column's length to rest inside the sockets."

Ereben selected the shack next to his smithy as his home. Brindle Meadow chose the shack behind Ereben's. The two families with children wandered out farther, to partially open areas suitable for agriculture. Bahsa and Deena did likewise.

Minkar Jarad looked over several of the remaining shacks, then sat on a rock beside Ereben. "These shacks will require so much repair, it may be better to build one from the start."

"Most of them look like they will keep you dry," Ereben replied.

"That sounds like a wise precaution..." Minkar turned to Ereben. "...yet we have not seen a single drop of rain in the weeks that we have been here. This has been some of the fairest weather of our entire ordeal."

"Minkar Jarad will take this house," said Alasie, pointing a clawed hand to one near Ereben's smithy. "It has two sleeping rooms. I will repair the house in exchange for use of the extra sleeping room."

Minkar appeared embarrassed. Ereben smiled. The aging Shouda warrior looked back and forth between Alasie and the dilapidated shack she had called a house. "Agreed."

Alasie immediately began to scavenge any boards or fragments of boards that were scattered about the ground of Hazelton. These she stacked alongside the front door of the new house.

Ereben then considered the possible advantages of sharing his own selected home with Nootaikok. "Alasi," he called out, "could you ask Nootaikok to come and speak with me, the next time you see him?"

Hauling the newly built sled holding one Jadeite column required far more time and effort than Ereben had estimated. Even with all the adult males, the equines and Ja No all pushing or tugging, moving the one column to the nearest peak required nearly a week of struggling several hours each day. And each day, the grumbling about the need for erecting the column increased. Once it was as far up the slope as possible, Ereben explained that they would not move the other columns to their respective peaks until he and Nootaikok had figured out a method to lift them into the sockets that Brother Palmer and Sister Ariama had created at their summits. Prior to moving the first column from Blinkport, they had collectively rigged each of the columns with the harnesses required to move them.

Halfway back, in their journey to Hazelton from the western peak, rain began. At first it was a light sprinkle. But by the time they and the horses and mule had reached Hazelton, wind was ripping a heavy rainstorm horizontally. They all fled to their respective homes.

"At least the rain stopped everybody from complaining," Ereben quipped to Nootaikok, who offered no reaction or response. Water dripped onto Ereben's arm from a small leak in the roof of his shared house. He recalled repairing a leak in the roof of his home in Rippleton, and falling off, landing in the mud, and being saved from injury by Brindle Meadow. It was just before his final departure from his home, and his lengthy journey to this new, leaking roof.

By the middle of the night, the storm passed, leaving bright moonlight streaming through the windows and gaps in the walls. Ereben slipped on his boots, and stepped outside. Nootaikok's horse, Bones, was peacefully grazing nearby, along with several of the other horses. As he looked up at the moonlit mountain above the mine entrance, he thought he saw a shadow pass. He wondered if it had been the shadow of a dragon. He wasn't sure. He usually sensed the presence of a dragon, but sensed nothing now in the coolness of the night. He had understood from Bahsa that the five surviving dragons would be content to avoid humans forever. He returned to his leaky shack.

By morning, wind and rain had resumed, this time with lightning. This vicious storm persisted for two days, and caused flooding in some low areas. During that time, he saw and spoke only with Nootaikok.

Ereben awakened abruptly. The sky was bright outside, and not storming. He felt a sudden, deep connection to all of the island of Newhome—its land, its structures, and all of its living creatures. He could not explain this heightened awareness. He realized that he had slept fully dressed, so he stepped into his boots, and went outside.

Hamsa came running up the road from Blinkport. Catching his breath, he stood before Ereben. "I think two of the Jadeite columns have been washed into the sea!"

႙ႄ

When these trying events are over, and I look back on them in my old age, perhaps I will find that something happy came of it all, and that it had germinated itself unnoticed at the time.
                              Jasper of Nilwid: Personal Journal

Jasper sat alone in the Assembly. Events of the past two weeks had overwhelmed his ability to understand them or deal with them. The attacks on the roads by roaming bandits had become so common that there were food shortages everywhere in Sulalia. There were more frequent riots in Almirant. Attacks from Kehl Corban's demons had intensified.

And just the previous week, his son, Ethnan, riding alongside his closest friend, Atan, had been directly struck by a fireball from the sky. Of the 30 cavalry present, only one man survived to relate the disaster, shortly before he died from his injuries.

Jasper slowly walked out of the empty assembly. The halls were empty. He found his way to the series of stairways that ultimately opened to the highest parapet of the citadel. A bright sun of late-afternoon cast shadows to the east.

On gazing out over the wall, and over the green-glazed roof tiles of Almirant, he could plainly see that the famed city was in disorder. The usual lines of travelers and traders streaming in both directions north and south all seemed to be departing the city. Within the outer ring of Almirant's three, fortified walls, there was general mayhem. Within the middle ground between the middle and inner wall, no soldiers were visible. The great gate that opened between the outer and middle zones was closed, but partly broken.

He thought of his parents and his younger brother. All had died in the initial attack upon Nilwid so many years ago. He thought of his Albian wife, who had died in childbirth. She had died giving birth to Ethnan, who was now among the dead.

A great fireball dropped from the sky, and exploded over the sea. He shortly felt a brief, intense rumble of the fortress. That had seemed to momentarily quiet the shouts of fighting inside the outer wall. Jasper stepped to the northern wall of the parapet, but before he had looked over it, a shock of wind threw him to the paved floor, bruising his left hip and elbow. He stood again, and returned his gaze to the east. From his height, he could clearly see that the water in the sea was receding from the town, as though a great drain had been opened. Closer, he noticed that many of the green roof tiles of the city were missing.

The sea slowly began to return to the shore. Gradually, the shoreline vanished, as the sea continued to rush toward the city. Water poured through the gate in the outer wall, and continued to rise, eventually flowing over the top of the outer wall. The space between the inner and middle wall began to fill.

Jasper wondered if he would still have a city, once the water drained away. He was confident that the rise of the water was slowing, and would never threaten the inner citadel.

To the east, a miles-long wave slowly lifted from the sea, and seemed to move toward Almirant. As it neared, the wave grew taller. The closer it came, the more rapidly it gained in height. Jasper's last thought about the wave was that it reached dozens of yards above his head, as it crashed over the parapet.

༷

*Ternaria was all that we knew. Yet we knew so little
about its reality, its origin, or even our own origin.
Those of us who survived to reach a new home must
strive to create a record of our new reality and rebirth.*
                                                Wisfel: Who We Are

Wisfel sat cross-legged, listening to all the Faeries discuss their immediate needs. Although he had suggested the gathering, his only contribution was to ask the question, "What should we do now?" Albric sat beside him in the circle.

After a long pause, Margarida said, "We need to gather a supply of food."

"Shelter," her mate, Timo, said.

"Food first," Quiri said.

His mate, Laia, rolled her eyes. "We need both. We'll gather food, while the men start building our homes."

Others questioned what sort of homes they should build in this new land.

"If the men build a large barn first," Albric added, "then we can store food there, and all of us can live in there, while all the men join together to build each home, one after another."

The discussion droned on. Wisfel had not yet mentioned to anyone his discomfort at continuously seeing so many connections between so many things, Faeries, creatures, and the stone of the island itself. He saw all the large people—Valanders, Shouda, Orkahti, Beddu, Dwarf, Rock Gnomes, Sulalians, Albians, Icemen, Kasazi, as well as the mule and the horses. He was aware of their existence and their respective locations. The visible, green strands of connectedness had begun the moment that Hamsa had placed the third Jadeite column, forming a triangle of Jadeite enclosing their new Faerie land. It was all there, all of the time.

"What should we call this new land," one of them asked.

"Faeria," Albric stated definitively. All agreed. They would call it Faeria.

Once the meeting had ended, the group had accepted that they no longer understood how to live in mushrooms. They would build with wood twigs. While the women foraged for food, the men would begin by building a two story barn, with sufficient space on the ground level for everyone to sleep, and a loft for food. The roofs would be thatch.

As all the Faeries headed away for their designated chores, Wisfel remained seated on the ground.

"You don't look well," Albric said.

"It's the Jadeite. I see green strands of connections everywhere. My mind feels exhausted. I feel exhausted. Gedzik wrote about it."

"What will happen when the fourth column is placed in the center?"

Wisfel simply shook his head.

With ample food gathered, four of the Faerie women accompanied Wisfel to a raspberry patch that they had discovered while foraging. Wisfel explained the desired characteristics of raspberry spines that worked best for use as weapons. The five of them cut and trimmed as many as each of them could carry the distance back to the nearly completed barn. When they arrived, Wisfel noted that one Faerie woman was occupied in dusting spider web strands, while another was busily spinning dusted strands into thread. Yet another labored over the construction of a weaving loom.

The men could be heard shouting above them, working to complete the loft and roof. Through the unfinished doorway of the ground floor of the barn, Wisfel watched Jian and Jian pecking about for food. He had not seen them join together and attempt to fly since they had all fluttered down onto the deck of the Rashiq. The sentient birds appeared healthy.

"Wisfel," Margarida called out, "Albric asked me to tell you that he built a sleeping pallet for you back in that corner."

Wisfel nodded an acknowledgment, then walked to the far corner of the barn. There he found a well-constructed pallet attached to the outer wall in such a way that it could be folded upward, and hooked out the way. He noticed that a similar pallet had been attached further along the wall. Since he felt no particular need to have his own house, that eliminated one more pending task.

He sat on his pallet, pushed back the cowl that covered his head, and rubbed his head. The Blighted Faerie became aware that Hamsa was in the process of building a shop just north of the boundary of Faeria. It seemed to include a Faerie-size, covered walkway leading from the edge of Faeria into the human-size shop, similar to the legendary jewelers' shop in Shibam, that Hamsa, as a young man, had shared with his two older cousins, and in which he had crafted the special armor for Gedzik, first of the Blighted Faeries.

Laia approached, and sat beside him. "I found a honey hive this morning, but I'll wait for the men to go collect some. Maybe they can figure out how to train a drone."

"That sounds excellent," Wisfel replied, smiling. He felt that he was already vaguely aware of the honey discovery.

"You look tired, Wisfel."

"I feel a bit tired. A good night of rest should help."

Wisfel climbed up the ladder to look at the completed loft and roof of the barn. Although none of its windows had yet been fitted with shutters, the men had set about the task of building the nine, twig houses for the mated pairs of Faeries. One had already been built, though not finished, and a second was now under construction. Albric had told him that the men would leave the final trimming of each house to its inhabitants.

The Blighted Faerie seated himself on a pile of collected seed, providing a tranquil view of the birth of Faeria. His past night's sleep had not refreshed his mind or body. The ceaseless awareness of connectedness still tugged at him, though it seemed less intense at the elevation of the barn loft. *The high column of Jadeite has not yet been placed.*

Above Faeria, the clear, mid-morning sky suddenly darkened, showing turbulent swirls of dark clouds. He saw what appeared, high in the distance, to be a large flock of birds flying toward him. Above them, a large, deformed thing with wings descended. As they approached, Wisfel could clearly see that they were not birds, and the larger thing above them seemed to be an enormous, gnarled, tree-like being, flapping bat-like, membranous wings.

While the huge tree creature and most of the smaller beasts seemed to veer further westward, one of the small ones, twice the size of a human, landed in Faeria itself, and began destroying plants and trees. Horrified, Wisfel exerted all his conscious effort at elevating the green strands of connectedness from their stable positions near the ground, to attempt to drive away the intruder. As soon as the green strands touched the blackened creature, it exploded into droplets of liquid that scattered about the area. Where each drop landed, the plants that were struck melted into small pools.

Another of the smaller creatures seemed to turn about, and head again toward Faeria. Wisfel realized that the pile of seed upon which he had been seated was nearly gone. His body felt completely drained of energy.

A ball of fire descended from the sky, into the nearby sea, and exploded. Wisfel watched as a wall of water raised from the surface, and raced toward the coast of Faeria. He felt too drained to attempt to stop it from washing them all away.

At that moment, above Faeria's highest, central peak, Jianjian hovered in the air with the fourth and final Jadeite column. They gently lowered it into its socket. Wisfel closed his eyes, yet could still see. He could see every connection to everything and everywhere. He could see the destroyed Ternaria and the far Eastern Sea. He saw dragons flying in the North of the mainland. He saw Ereben Leaf marshaling his people for defense. He understood that the great creature had come from the land of the Dryads.

The sea sloshed against this new, tetrahedron of green connection strands, swept up its sides, but simply poured back to the coast, like a small wave striking the inverted hull of a boat, leaving the land of Faeria dry. The second approaching creature swallowed Jianjian, then seemed to grow a bit larger.

Wisfel collapsed onto the floor of the loft, overwhelmed by the intensity of the connections to everything, and exhausted from his exertion.

༄༅

Is there a distinction between the knower and the known? The two must join by some manner in order for the knower to comprehend the known. Thus the act of knowing irrevocably alters the known as well as the knower. The known may not have possessed what it gives to the knower. And the knower may receive what has not been given.

Meriwa: A Land of Belonging

Ereben knew immediately that the three Jadeite columns had been placed into the sockets on the three low peaks of Newhome. How that had been accomplished, and by whom, he had no idea. He turned, and looked toward the low peak at the northwest of the island. The column that all of them had dragged to as high as they could manage shone brightly, standing upright in the morning sun.

He faced Hamsa, who worried that two of the Jadeite columns had been washed into the sea, and said flatly, "All three Jadeite columns have been inserted into their proper locations on the three low peaks. I don't know how."

As Ereben watched, the sky suddenly darkened, with black clouds swirling westward across the Western Lands, toward Newhome. He saw strange creatures flying toward their island. When he pivoted, to return to his shack, to retrieve the Gnomish Sphere, he understood that it would likely not function within the triangle of Jadeite columns.

Minkar Jarad and Alasie had come out of their nearby shack, and stood before Ereben. Minkar pointed to the sky. "It is the Bane of the East—Kehl Corban—and his demons. We must alert everyone to the danger."

Ereben pointed to Alasie. "Can you do that?"

Nootaikok interrupted, "I will warn everyone."

"The horses are fleeing!" Brindle Meadow shouted.

Moap pranced from the area in which they had been grazing, and stood undaunted beside the group with Ereben. At that moment, Minkar pointed to the southeast. A huge fireball descended toward Newhome, but fell short, exploding into the sea.

A large, blood red demon flew toward them, and landed two yards away, flashing its huge mouth, rimmed with sharp teeth. As it surged toward them, Alasie slashed at its head with the steel claws of both her hands, then ripped off its head entirely. Both the head and the demon immediately melted into pools of slime. Alasie, promptly wiped her hands in the nearby, clean grass. "It burns my skin."

As another demon neared, Moap turned away, then mule-kicked the demon in the head, with both rear hooves. Brindle Meadow then used her layered steel mattock to behead it where it lay on the ground.

Just north of Ereben, a demon rushed toward Sawney Burn, but was instantly smashed to a puddle by Ja No's massive cudgel. Elsewhere around him all of his people seemed to be successfully defending against the demons. The Rock Gnomes smashed one with a rockfall near the entrance to the mine.

Ereben suddenly became aware of a fully completed Jadeite tetrahedron covering all of Faeria. He turned to look in that direction, and could clearly see the intense, powerful strands of connection emanating from the Faerie's land. His mind was feeling overwhelmed.

It was then that he realized the immense size of Kehl Corban—nearly a third the height of the tallest peak. It's gigantic, bat-like wings spread out from what appeared to be a massively deformed tree. Ereben felt that Kehl Corban was looking directly at him. He could sense the hateful character of Lord Corban in the creature. He could sense a fleeting conflict with Phaena Corban's love, as well as Phaena's pledged tree. There was also the capriciousness of a kelpie. Ereben understood the weighty sadness of unpredictable events that had deflected his hopes and expectations. He whispered to Kehl Corban, "I loved your mother."

Above the demon tree, a line of five dragons approached from the East. As they neared Kehl Corban, they flew into a wide circle around him. Kehl Corban seemed unable to move. Then the dragons slowly diminished the size of the circle. After a short while, the dragons were rotating their formation as a pentagon, with one purely magical dragon at each apex.

Kehl Corban appeared to struggle to free himself from the dragons' magic, but was unable to do so. Then the five dragons simultaneously halted, and hovered, turning their bodies to directly face the evil being. Gouts of dragon fire erupted from the mouths of all five dragons, directed at Kehl Corban from all sides.

Initially, nothing seemed to change. Then Kehl Corban began to slowly shrink in stature. His struggling appeared futile. The dragon fire from the five hovering dragons continued. When Kehl Corban reached the height of a normal tree, he burst into flame, then completely disintegrated into a shower of fine ash.

At the moment of Kehl Corban's destruction, all of the remaining demon creatures evaporated into the air.

Four of the dragons landed near the summit of the high peak, while one of them flew toward Blinkport. It shortly returned, grasping the final Jadeite column in the claws of all four extremities.

"That is Splendor," Bahsa Jarad whispered from behind Ereben.

As they all watched, Splendor rose to the highest peak, with the four other dragons circling above him, and precisely inserted the final Jadeite column into the socket that the Rock Gnomes had made in the stone. Ereben could clearly see that Splendor was now within the apex of the greatest Jadeite tetrahedron ever constructed. Splendor instantly vanished into nothingness. The four surviving dragons rose above the zone of magic, turned, and flew away to the northeast.

Ereben felt the burden of knowing the universe. All things connected to all things, and in so many unexpected dimensions. And he became aware that Jasper of Nilwid was dead. He knew that Wisfel was dead.

"Splendor knew that we were incapable of placing the Jadeite columns. He placed each one, even though he knew that he would perish," Bahsa said. "He said farewell to me in his thought."

Minkar placed a hand on his son's shoulder. "We have both lost dragons that we knew."

Ereben turned toward the shack he shared with Nootaikok. Walking seemed more difficult. Everything called out for his attention. His joints ached. His back ached. His fingers ached. And now his mind ached. Nootaikok grasped Ereben's arm, and assisted him into the shack.

Ereben seated himself on an old, wooden crate, and attempted to clear his mind, or at least organize its attention better. He glanced at the collection of books on magic, many translated for him from ancient Shadae, by Yassar. And there was the wooden case containing the Glaive of Brendan, properly called Ghelaif al Bryn Adin. Despite all the many distractions roaring through his mind, Ereben understood that the Glaive was merely a naive attempt at organizing all of magic, and that it held no meaningful insights. And he recognized that it could never be effectively used as a weapon. It was simply a curious artifact.

"Nootaikok, could you please carry all of these to Brother Palmer and Sister Ariama, and ask them to hide them within the rock of the mountain, and never reveal their location." He swept his hand over the entire, heavy pile of presumed knowledge of magic—things that were troublesome to collect, and troublesome to transport across the land and the sea.

Once Nootaikok left with the books and the Glaive, Ereben held his hands over his face, and struggled to think clearly. He realized that he had two choices. He could either depart from Newhome forever, to free himself from the intensity of the Jadeite tetrahedron, or he could remain here in Newhome, and wrestle with his burdensome, new awareness.

Ereben awakened the following morning, not feeling rested. He noticed that he was still fully clothed, with his dagger at his hip. He sat up, but was unable to clear the intrusive connections from his mind. He had decided that he would not leave Newhome. The journey had cost his body too much.

He knew what it is like to be a rock. He considered simply passing into the rock of the central mountain, and resting there, perhaps for just a short while. But his experience traveling within rock left no doubt that the passage of time was not really available to him there. He might go in for a short time, and emerge many years later. The temptation of resting his mind seemed reasonable.

He left his shack, while Nootaikok still slept, and walked toward the mine entrance, struggling to focus his attention on the task of securely placing one foot in front of the other. When he reached the sheer rock face beside the mine, he stopped and stared at its surface.

Ereben was startled by the voice of Nootaikok behind him.

"You have been standing at the rock all morning. Are you distressed?"

"It is the Jadeite, Nootaikok. It keeps my mind from ordinary things. I see green strands of connections between all things, both near and far away. Everything is connected to everything else. I was considering just passing into the rock for a rest."

"I have heard that you can do that. How long would you stay?"

"Until I feel rested." Ereben felt that the Iceman deserved candor. "Time does not seem to pass, when I'm inside rock."

"You might be gone a long time."

"I might be."

"Before you go, may I hold your dagger? Just for a minute. It carries some of my lineage within it. I have wanted to ask to hold it since we arrived in Newhome."

Ereben drew his dagger, the one he had made under the patient guidance of his grandfather, Chrysanthus—the dagger that had once contained a living Ice Leopard as well as Chrysanthus. It was his concrete symbol of being a Guardian of the Ruins—the last Guardian of the Ruins. He extended the Jadeite handle toward Nootaikok. The instant that the Iceman grasped the dagger, and Ereben released it, Nootaikok's eyes widened, and he immediately dropped it. At that same instant, Ereben felt release from the weight of connections to everything. He understood. It was his constant possession of the dagger that channeled the power of the Jadeite tetrahedron into his mind.

He smiled, placed his hand on Nootaikok's shoulder, and said, "You have just saved my mind."

After explaining his new understanding to the Iceman, he made a final decision about his personal future. Ereben bent down to the rocky ground, lifted up his dagger, then held it against the stone face. With some effort, he allowed the dagger to sink into the rock to a depth of his elbow, then released it, and withdrew his arm. "Now there are no Guardians of the Ruins."

〰

A path that leads us into the deepest chasm may also
be a path to the highest summit.

Meriwa: A Land of Belonging

Ereben Leaf stood in the market of central Hazelton, beside the Kasazi bread stall, and brushed crumbs from his ragged, gray beard with the back of his left hand. He supported himself with a simple staff in his right. Five years had slipped by, since he had given his dagger to the stone. His body felt as though it had aged far more than five years since then. But his mind seemed to glide from day to day with joy, and a new appreciation for all the treasures of life and friendships that had been hampered by his weighty burdens over the previous decades. He no longer pondered the imponderable. He was simply a maker of tools. Occasionally, he would harvest a small basket of munu, carry it back to his house, and blend a pungent, healing salve, which he provided at no cost to any who requested it.

Tocho, the ten year old son of Kwahu and Soyala, usually managed the bread stall. Today, Tocho's nine year old sister, Tawa, handled their weekly stall on her own, while Tocho shopped for the family at some of the other nearby stalls.

"How are your parents?" Ereben asked the girl. "I haven't seen them for a couple of weeks."

"The same. Papa does all the work, and Mama complains that she has to do all the work."

He chuckled. "I think all parents are like that."

"So are brothers." She glanced at Tocho, two stalls away.

"Tell your parents that I asked about them."

Ereben shuffled over to the adjacent stall, where the twelve year old Orkahti girl, Zaypo, offered goat milk. He could smell the rich aroma of the goat cheese that rested on the table near the milk.

"You get to have a piece of cheese, Ereben," the cheerful girl insisted. She held out a square of the white cheese on a small, wooden spatula.

"Thank you, Zaypo." He tossed it into his mouth. "It's wonderful," he said while still chewing it.

Mallo Burn, the five year old son of the Beddu, Ja No, and the Dwarf, Sawney Burn, entered Ereben's smithy. The fair-skin boy was of typical human stature for a five year old, though perhaps slightly plump.

"Ereben, Mama cut her toe, and needs some of that stinky stuff you make."

Ereben handed him a small, clay jar. "This is salve made of munu. It smells like a mushroom."

"Oh." He accepted the jar, and ran out.

Ereben grasped his staff, and walked outside. There he noticed many of the inhabitants of Newhome drifting southward as a group.

Bahsa Jarad and his spouse, Deena, both waved to him. Bahsa held his toddler daughter, Halla, in one arm. Deena held the hand of their three year old daughter, Maina, as they moved with the others.

"Will you come to the Faerie show, Ereben?" Bahsa asked.

"I forgot about it."

"He will be going," a voice behind Ereben stated definitively.

Ereben turned to see Minkar Jarad and his Iceman spouse, Alasie. Their three year old boy, Anthi, walked between them, excitement on his face. Ereben found it curious that the boy showed no resemblance to Alasie, although his skin was a lighter brown than that of his Shouda father.

"Hello, little brother," Bahsa shouted to Anthi. Anthi smiled and waved.

Behind Minkar, the brightly colored and trimmed houses of Hazelton seemed to Ereben the most impressive measure of how far their small community had embraced their new existence on Newhome. Unique locations had been given distinct names that everyone spoke of as if they had always borne those names: Mt. Splendor and Mt. Wisfel, among others.

Ereben followed those heading down the firmly packed trail southeastward, toward Hamsa's shop, which stood just beyond the boundary of Faeria. At one point, the trail swung directly eastward, where it intersected with the path toward Blinkport. Ereben looked out to the bay, where Captain Mahfud and his crew were returning the ship, Rashiq, from a fishing run. Tomorrow, there would be fresh fish to trade.

When Ereben, somewhat out of breath, reached the entrance to Hamsa's shop, he was followed by several more of the Icemen. Inside, the now crowded interior was brightly lit by its many, tall windows. To his far left, a special area included desks, a large writing board on the wall, and along that area's south wall, a small balcony with empty, Faerie-size desks. Three days a week, it served as Meriwa's academy, where both Faeries and people of any age were taught to read and to write. Hamsa had taken it upon himself to bind blank books, both large and tiny, for use by those who attended the academy. The Rock Gnomes, Brother Palmer and Sister Ariama, were the last to enter, but stood together on a chair, to see beyond the taller folks.

Hamsa played a loud series of thumps on his tambor. The crowd fell silent, shutters were closed on the windows, and a mirror directed bright light from one remaining, open window toward a tiny balcony area that opened into the interior from the south face of the shop. He then began a soft, rhythmic pattern on his tambor. The Iceman, Inuksuk, played a flute.

On the balcony, Faeries in brightly colored tunics and caps began to dance into view, in step with the music, sometimes in pairs, sometimes in one long line. As each dance ended, the audience, both adults and children, clapped their hands and chattered. The dances continued for half an hour. As the final dance ended, with music still sounding, the Faeries walked in a line, out of sight.

THE END

www.ingramcontent.com/pod-product-compliance
Lightning Source LLC
Chambersburg PA
CBHW030408030726
47497CB00002B/522